PRAISE F

"You won't regret taking a risk on Elle Kennedy."
— *Hypable*

"With all the heart, witty banter, and toe-curling romance that you'd expect from an Elle Kennedy novel, *The Play* is a fantastic addition to one of my all-time favorite series!"
— #1 *New York Times* bestselling author Sarah J. Maas

"An opposites-attract romance with plenty of laugh-out-loud humor, steamy love scenes and swoony, heartfelt romance...a phenomenal reading experience."
— *USA Today*, about *The Chase*

"Kennedy fans and newcomers will relish the well-crafted plot, witty dialogue, and engaging characters."
— *Publishers Weekly*, about *Hotter Than Ever*.

"A steamy, glitzy, and tender tale of college intrigue."
— *Kirkus Reviews,* about *The Chase*

"Another addictive read from Elle Kennedy! *The Play* is a steamy, swoon-worthy romance you won't want to put down!"
— #1 *New York Times* bestselling author Vi Keeland

"When I pick up an Elle Kennedy book, I know I'm not putting it down until I'm done."
— International bestselling author K.A. Tucker

OTHER TITLES BY ELLE KENNEDY

Out of Uniform Series:

Heart Breaker

Trouble Maker

Ladies Men

Sweet Talker

Hot & Bothered

Hot & Heavy

Off-Campus Series:

The Deal

The Mistake

The Score

The Goal

The Legacy

Briar U Series:

The Chase

The Risk

The Play

The Dare

AUTHOR'S NOTE

I am so excited to be re-releasing the *Out of Uniform* series! These new editions feature new titles and more discreet covers, but the characters and stories inside haven't changed.

For those of you who haven't read it before, this was one of my earlier series, and it also happens to be one of my favorites, probably because this is when I realized how much I love writing bromances. Seriously. The boy banter in these books still cracks me up to this day. You see more and more of it as the series progresses, and by the later books there are entire chapters of crazy conversations between my sexy, silly SEALs.

For new readers, you should know that a) you don't have to read the stories in order, though characters from previous books do show up in every installment. And b) four of the books are full-length novels (80,000+ words), while six are novellas (20-35,000 words).

I decided to release the novellas as two books featuring three stories each (*Hot & Bothered, Hot & Heavy*) making the total books in the series six rather than the original ten.

Heart Breaker (formerly titled *Feeling Hot*) is the first of the full-length novels.

**PLEASE NOTE: This book has NOT changed, except for minor editing, updating, and proofreading. There are grammatical differences and some deleted/added lines here and there, but for the most part, there is no new content. If you've previously purchased and read *Feeling Hot*, then you won't be getting more content, aside from a gorgeous new cover and title.

So, I hope you enjoy the cover, the better grammar, and the hot, dirty-talking SEALs who to this day hold such a big place in my heart!

— Elle Kennedy

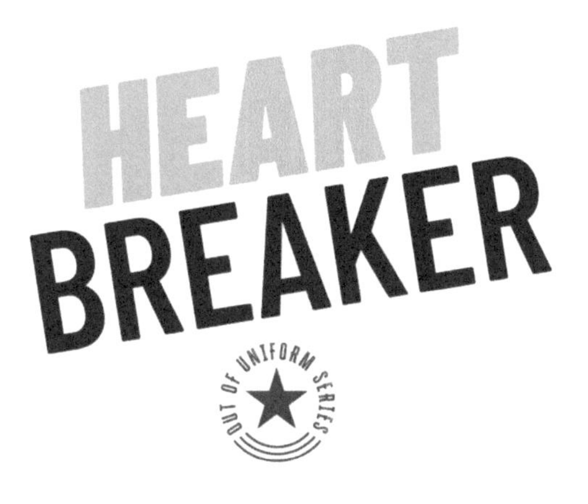

ELLE KENNEDY

Heart Breaker

CHAPTER **ONE**

"Yes...*yes*...Matt! Oh, that's good... Aidan, *yes*!"

Cash McCoy rearranged the monstrous bulge in his pants and tried to focus on the Chargers game blaring out of the flat screen. He'd cranked the volume full blast, but it still couldn't drown out the sounds of sex drifting from Matt O'Connor's bedroom. O'Connor and Rhodes had crazy stamina, and from the moans that kept slicing the air, it sounded like Matt's girlfriend Savannah was getting worked over real nice.

Sighing, Cash shifted on the couch again. He didn't feel an ounce of guilt over being out here in the living room, hard as a rock. Maybe if Savannah didn't broadcast her orgasms at top volume, he could actually concentrate on the damn football game. As it was, he was distracted as hell, and kinda wondering if he ought to knock on the door and ask to join in.

Nah. Probably inappropriate.

Despite his two deployments with the team, Cash was still considered the rookie. The other SEALs had known each other for years before he'd come on board, and even though he'd technically been living with Matt for a year now, they'd been out of the country for half that time and hadn't moved beyond the let's-have-a-beer-and-talk-sports stage. It'd probably take a while before his new roomie felt comfortable asking Cash to participate in any threeways, though how Matt could possibly share Savannah with anyone else boggled the mind. But apparently the sexy blonde was into it, and God knew O'Connor was up for anything.

"*Yes!*"

Cash stifled a groan—there was already too much groaning going on in this apartment.

Damn it. He was so fucking horny after listening to his roommate's sex show for the past two hours. He supposed he could retreat to his bedroom and jack off, but he'd rather have someone else's hand jacking his cock tonight.

Last time he'd gotten laid was...jeez, had it really been before the deployment to Afghanistan? While some guys managed to score a quick hookup overseas, Cash had a strict rule about not screwing around on the job, even if given a rare night off. His head was always on the mission, the objective. Sex didn't make a blip on his radar when he was out in the field.

But six months was too long to go without sex. He'd been hoping to remedy that bleak statistic when he got home, but his parents decided to spring a spontaneous visit on him the moment he was stateside, so he'd spent the past fourteen days doing the tourist bullshit with the folks. Which upped his celibacy statistic to six months and *two weeks*.

Fortunately, his parents had flown back to Phoenix last night. Cash had decided to indulge in a day of rest before satisfying his sexual appetite, but now, as Savannah let out another throaty moan, he was ready to gorge himself.

Shutting off the TV, he stood up, crossed the open-concept room and headed for the kitchen where he'd left his phone. He scrolled through his contacts list, shot a quick text to a few of his teammates, then leaned against the granite counter as he awaited a reply.

Matt's bedroom door swung open and Aidan Rhodes stumbled out, his brown hair tousled, cheeks flushed, and dark eyes hazy.

"What's up, McCoy?" Aidan called when he caught sight of him.

Cash grinned. "Nothing much. You look tired, Rhodes. The dynamic duo wear you out?"

Groaning, Aidan buttoned the blue shirt he wore over his black tee. "Yep. Those two are sex maniacs."

Cash's phone beeped, drawing his attention to the screen.

Can't tonight. Well, Dylan was out.

So was Seth, who texted back, *Too hungover to move.*

When Jackson chimed in with, *Next time*, Cash tucked the phone in the back pocket of his camo pants. Looked like he was flying solo tonight.

Unless... He glanced at Aidan. "Want to check out that new bar on 5th and Market with me?"

The dark-haired man shook his head. "Maybe another time. I've gotta be at the base early tomorrow morning. No downtime for me, remember?"

Right. He tended to forget that Aidan wasn't an active-duty soldier, probably because the guy was built like one. But Aidan worked on the base, doing some hush-hush intelligence stuff Cash wasn't privy to.

"Catch you later," Aidan said, giving a brisk nod as he let himself out of the apartment.

A moment later, Matt's door opened once more and Savannah Harte strolled out, wearing a silky red robe that molded to her tall, centerfold figure like plastic wrap. The woman was a damn knockout with all that pale hair cascading down her back and laughing gray eyes that always held a hint of seduction.

"Hey, Cash, heading out?" she asked as she waltzed past him. She buried her nose in the fridge and emerged with a can of soda in her hand.

"Yeah, I'm tired of being cooped up inside."

"We weren't being too loud, were we?"

"Couldn't hear a thing."

She smirked. "I know you're lying. You're doing that weird eyebrow twitch."

"I do not have a weird eyebrow twitch."

"Sure you do. Why do you think I always beat you at poker? You can't bluff for shit."

Matt's southern drawl wafted out of the bedroom. "Hey, darlin', grab me a beer while you're out there."

Cash lifted his brows. "You know, I'd never order you around like that." He shot her a wolfish grin. "I think it's time you dumped O'Connor and hooked up with me instead."

"I can hear you, you know," Matt yelled from the bedroom. "Stop hitting on my girlfriend, McCoy."

Laughing, Savannah ducked behind the fridge door and grabbed a bottle of beer. "I appreciate the offer," she said in a mock whisper. "I'll let you know when I tire of him, okay?"

"Deal."

With another laugh, she rounded the counter. She paused only to ruffle his hair before sauntering out of the room.

As he watched her go, he couldn't fight the little burst of envy that rippled through him. O'Connor had really lucked out with that one.

But just because he appreciated what the other man had didn't mean he was looking for that special someone just yet. At the moment, he was content with no-strings sex and the occasional—fine, frequent—threesome with Dylan.

Hell, he'd only turned twenty-six last month. He still had a shitload of sexual energy to release before he settled down. Besides, he sucked ass when it came to talking to women. He knew exactly what to say to entice them out of their panties, possessed all the right words during sex, but his out-of-the-bedroom conversational skills were lacking big-time.

Good thing tonight was all about the bedroom. Or the backseat of his car. Or wherever his chosen lady wanted to get naked. At this point, he wasn't gonna be picky.

Grinning to himself, he grabbed his keys and headed to the front hall, where he shoved his feet into a pair of scuffed black Timberlands. He snatched a brown leather jacket from the hook by the door and shrugged it on over his T-shirt. Soft moans floated through the apartment as he reached for the doorknob. Jesus. Matt and Savannah were starting up *again*?

Cash's cock started right up in response.

Christ.

He *really* needed to get laid tonight.

THIRTY MINUTES LATER, CASH WAS READY TO ADMIT defeat. The Gaslamp Tavern was a total bust. He should've expected that from a Monday night, but he'd hoped luck would be on his side. Unfortunately, almost everyone in the bar was coupled off, and the only girl who'd looked promising turned out to be a navy groupie he had no interest in taking to bed. The brunette had been interrogating him for the past five minutes, and he was ready to tear his fucking hair out.

"Do you have any tattoos?" she demanded as she sucked on the pink straw poking out of her even pinker daiquiri.

Cash scanned his brain for an exit strategy, but he couldn't come up with anything decent. Especially since he was the one to approach her in the first place. When he strode into the dimly lit bar and spotted her standing by the pool table, he'd definitely liked what he'd seen. A nice rack beneath a tight white tee, long legs encased in dark-blue denim. Great ass. Cute face. When their gazes met across the crowded room and he'd glimpsed the unmistakable interest in her eyes, he figured he had the hookup in the bag.

Which he did. Yup, this leggy brunette would go home with him in a nanosecond.

Problem was, he didn't want to take her home. Navy groupies were the worst. Starry-eyed and drooly, hoping to meet a real-life hero who'd sweep them off their feet—and straight to the altar. They didn't care what he looked like, what his personality was like. They just wanted to land a soldier.

He might be looking for casual sex tonight, but he wanted it with someone he could talk to, someone he connected with. Someone who wanted *him,* not just any random soldier who walked into the bar. Groupies doled out the sex freely, but once they got you in bed, they refused to go away. And that was when they thought he was just a *sailor*—when they found out he was a SEAL? Damned if they didn't go full stalker on him.

"Cash?"

Polly—or was it Patty?—stared at him expectantly. Gulping down the rest of his beer, he tried to remember what she'd asked him. Right, tattoos. "Got an eagle on my back," he said absently.

Damned if that didn't make her all breathless. "That's *so* hot. I'd love to see it."

Not gonna happen, babe.

Cash swept his gaze around the room, searching for a way out. He and Polly were standing by the two pool tables at the far edge of the room, but he had a good view of the main floor, which featured a handful of tables, booths lining the wall, and several high counters surrounded by tall-backed stools. Unfortunately, the two chicks Patty had been hanging out with earlier had disappeared, so he couldn't use the old your-friends-are-calling-you escape.

"I love how all you military boys have tattoos," Polly gushed. "I've always wanted one but I'm scared of needles."

His gaze strayed to the long counter against the opposite wall. He could always pretend he needed a fresh beer, then duck out of the bar before reaching the counter...but he feared his groupie would tag along and wait with him while he ordered.

"I know you probably hear this all the time, but you're, like, a real-life hero," Patty babbled on.

Ditto on the men's room—she totally seemed like the kind of girl who'd offer to keep him company while he waited out that monster line.

"Wanna know a secret? When I was a little girl, I always dreamed of marrying a navy man." Giggling, she sucked down the rest of her daiquiri.

Shit. Running out of options here. Time to resort to default mode—the phone fakeout.

Cash jerked a little, pretending to feel his phone going off. Luckily, the loud Katy Perry song blaring out of the Tavern's sound system masked the nonexistent vibrating of his phone.

He slid the phone out of his pocket and brought it to his ear, lifting one finger to signal Polly that he needed a minute. The one-sided conversation that ensued was one he'd perfected over the years.

"Mom? Hey, what's up? What? Well, that's not good. Hold on, I can't really hear you. Let me find someplace quiet to talk... what? No, don't do that. I'm on my way."

He punched the *end* button and pasted a regretful look on his face. "My mom's car broke down," he told Patty.

Disappointment filled her eyes. "Oh no. That's awful." An

edge crept into her voice. "Can't she call roadside assistance? Why do you have to be the one to help?"

Wow. Had she really just said that?

Okay, fine. So maybe he'd flat-out lied right now. But what if his mom's car really had broken down? Would Polly seriously still expect him to sleep with her? While his poor sweet mother waited on the side of the road, a sitting duck for roadside predators?

He shook his head. "Sorry, babe, this real-life hero needs to come to his mother's rescue. I'll see you around."

"Wait, don't you want my phone num—"

Cash was already heading far, far away from the pool table.

But he felt Patty's eyes burning a hole into his back like a laser, and every instinct in his body told him the chick would follow him, if only to slip her number into his hand. He picked up the pace, his gaze honing in on the door. Ten more steps and he'd be outta here.

The door swung open just as he reached it. He halted, politely waiting for two middle-aged women to stroll inside. They wore matching lemon-yellow tank tops with the words *Rita's Getting Married!* sewed on with blue sequins. And they were clearly sloshed, swaying and giggling as they burst into the bar. Two more women followed the duo. Then a third. A fourth.

Sweet baby Jesus. It was like a damn clown car. Female bodies kept popping through the door, all clad in those yellow shirts that had him inwardly cursing that wretched Rita.

He snuck a peek at the pool table and saw Polly eyeing him with the kind of determination you saw on the faces of covert operatives—set on accomplishing the task at all costs. She took a step forward.

Crap.

He tapped his foot in impatience as more women streamed into the bar. Shifting his gaze, he noticed a doorway to his right.

Another glance across the room revealed that his single-minded brunette had turned to retrieve the purse she'd left on the pool table.

Without hesitation, Cash ducked into the opening he'd spotted.

He found himself in a narrow passage that boasted yet another doorway. Making a beeline for it, he burst into a small room bathed in darkness and let out a breath heavy with relief.

Thank fuck. Now all he had to do was wait a few minutes, peek out to make sure the groupie wasn't looking, and get the hell out of—

"I know I'm not supposed to be in here!" someone yelled.

CHAPTER
TWO

Cash's heart stopped, then took off like a runaway train. As adrenaline surged through his veins, he spun around, searching for the owner of the panicked female voice that had just knocked ten years off his life.

"I need a few more minutes and then I'll be gone, okay?"

Squinting, he discerned a shadowy figure sitting on a cushioned loveseat on the other side of the room. "Jesus, you scared the hell out of me," he grumbled.

As his eyes adjusted to the darkness, he was better able to make out his surroundings. Small room, maybe twelve by twelve feet. A stack of dusty boxes against one wall. Metal racks.

He walked over to the little couch sandwiched between more boxes and an aluminum ladder. "What are you doing sitting alone in the dark?" he demanded, peering down at the woman.

"I'm sorry," she said sheepishly. "I know I shouldn't be lurking in here like a serial killer, but like I said, I'll be gone in a minute. There's no need to tell your manager or—"

"Relax, I don't work here." He expelled a sigh. "I'm hiding out too."

"Oh. Okay then." She awkwardly patted the cushion next to her. "You might as well sit down. Can't promise I'll be good company, but you're making me nervous looming over me like that."

After a beat of reluctance, he lowered his body onto the loveseat. Then he squinted to get a better look at his fellow hider—and realized she was beautiful.

Like absolutely fucking beautiful.

Didn't happen often, but he was stunned speechless as he let his gaze drink her in. Long waves of tousled, honey-colored hair. Big blue eyes. Delicate features and a lush mouth, pink and perfect.

Sweet Jesus.

This woman belonged on the cover of a magazine. Or maybe in a porno—one that starred the two of them and involved that sexy mouth of hers on every inch of his naked body.

His cock promptly turned to granite, voicing its approval of the dirty images that filled Cash's head. He clenched his teeth and breathed through his nose, trying to quell the rush of hunger that flooded his groin.

"Are you done staring at me?" she asked wryly.

Done? Christ, he hadn't even gotten started. His gaze traveled south, snagging on the full perky breasts outlined by a tight scoop-necked top, her shapely denim-covered legs, the red toenails peeking out of a pair of open-toed heels. His mental porno took a different direction, one that now featured his mouth on *her* naked body.

"You know what, Mr. Pervy Eyes? You're not making a good first impression," she announced.

She was right. He absolutely had a case of the Pervy Eyes. Cash wrenched his gaze off the beautiful stranger and distracted himself by glancing around the room.

"What is this place?" he asked when he noticed a pile of wooden clothes hangers cluttering the linoleum floor.

"It used to be a coatroom."

"How do you know that?"

"I used to work here, back when this bar was a French restaurant," she explained. "This was the coatroom."

"Those still exist?"

"Sure. But not here obviously, since this is no longer a coatroom."

"Stop saying coatroom."

"Stop asking questions that require the word *coatroom* in their answers."

Cash stared at her. Then he barked out a laugh. Okay, he liked this chick.

"So who are you hiding from?" she asked, crossing her ankles together in a nonchalant pose.

He stifled a groan. "A potential stalker."

"Oh, I know all about those."

He didn't doubt it. With those looks, she probably fended off the advances of hundreds of dudes on a daily basis.

"So you're also dodging someone who wants to get in your pants?" he prompted.

"Other than you, you mean?"

"Funny."

"I thought so." She paused, as if debating whether to confide in him. "I needed to get away from my friends for a few minutes. My best friend Tessa just landed a huge promotion at the advertising agency where she works, so a group of us went out to celebrate."

"And you're hiding out? Wow. You're a really shitty friend."

"Me? How about *Tessa*? She's the one holding this let's-gush-about-my-new-job get-together on the same day her best friend was fired."

"You got fired?"

"Yep, but that's the least of my problems. I also have a crazy ex to contend with." She exhaled loudly. "Let's just say I've been having a really bad month, okay?"

Cash could commiserate—his six-month sexual dry spell wasn't all sunshine and rainbows either. "Did you like your job?" he asked, deciding not to touch the *crazy ex* comment.

"No. I hated it, actually. I worked as a sales clerk at a jewelry store and my boss was a total creep. He kept offering to take me to Victoria's Secret to help me pick out lingerie. You know, in case I need a second opinion." She blew out another frustrated breath. "But that's not the point. The point is, I got fired. Again."

Cash couldn't help but laugh. "Happens to you a lot?"

"Sure does." She slanted her head. "What line of work are *you* in?"

He hesitated for a beat, then said, "Security."

Fine, he was lying again, but he'd already escaped one navy groupie tonight and he wasn't looking for a repeat performance. Then again, this woman was so beautiful he might be willing to make an exception.

"Huh. I figured you'd say military. You give off a military vibe. I mean, look at that big, buff body of yours—it ought to be illegal."

He didn't miss the slight note of derision when she said the word *military*. "Got something against military men?" he asked lightly.

"Nope. I respect the hell out of them," she answered. "I just don't want to date them."

He frowned, a part of him wanting to admit he'd lied about his job, just to see how she'd react. But she kept talking before he could get a word in.

"I bet you're good at security. Me, on the other hand? I suck at everything."

Cash smiled. "I don't believe that."

"It's true. That's why I always get fired. School was never my thing, so I didn't go to college. I have no interest in medicine like my mom, no distinguishable talents, no great passions. I like messing around with my camera and taking pictures, but that's just a hobby." Vulnerability flashed in her eyes. "Do you think there's a certain age when you should have everything figured out? Because I just turned twenty-five, and I still have no idea what I want to do with my life."

He shrugged. "I think everyone figures stuff out at their own pace. Eventually you'll find yourself on the right path."

"I guess." Her shoulders sagged. "Maybe I should get into porn. According to some creepy producer who approached me on the street, I have the 'look' for it."

"You really got asked to do porn?" Apparently he wasn't the only one who could totally picture this blue-eyed beauty in his own personal naked film.

"Yes, I really did," she said in a glum voice.

"Porn's an admirable profession," he said solemnly.

She pursed her lips in thought. "But my porn-star name sucks. You know how you're supposed to take the name of your first pet and pair it with the street you grew up on? Well, our dog's name was Boris and I grew up on Denton Street. Boris Denton. That sounds like a dictator."

"I'm not even going to ask why you'd name your dog Boris."

"That's my brother's doing." She gave him a curious look. "What would your porn name be?"

"I don't know. I never had any pets growing up." He shrugged again. "Besides, I've been told my real name sounds like a porn name anyway, so I guess I've already got one." He supplied his name before she could ask. "Cash McCoy."

She promptly shook her head. "That's not a porn-star name. That's cowboy all the way."

"Cowboy," he echoed dubiously.

"Hell yeah. Or maybe an actor." She clapped her hands together. "An actor who plays a cowboy. Can't you see it?" Her voice deepened to mimic the movie-man voice from the previews. "*One duel, one chance to avenge his pa's murder... Cash McCoy in...*High Noon Outlaw." She grinned at him. "Maybe that's what I should do—write the copy for movie trailers."

"I think you should stick to porn. *High Noon Outlaw* sounds like a shit movie."

As another peal of laughter left her Cupid's bow mouth, lust slammed into his groin again. Damn, her lips were so damn sexy. Pink, ripe and utterly kissable.

His mouth tingled, and he had to fight the urge to lean in and press his lips to hers. He was dying to know if she tasted as sweet as she looked. The kind of noises she'd make when their tongues touched.

"Why do you keep staring at my lips?"

Sheepish, he met her eyes, which were narrowed with distrust. "I can't help it. You have really nice lips."

"And let me guess, they'd look even nicer wrapped around your dick."

He choked out a laugh. "You said it, not me."

"But you were thinking it."

Sure was. And his cock seemed to enjoy the wicked thoughts running through his mind—the big boy was harder than a baseball bat, pushing against his zipper and begging for some attention.

"So it's true, huh? Men really do think about sex like every other minute."

"Afraid so," he confirmed.

Rolling her eyes, the blonde bombshell ran a hand through her hair, causing the scent of her shampoo to drift into his nose and wreak havoc on his senses. She smelled like cherries—man oh man, he loved cherries.

Make a move, McCoy.

His brain's order—or had that come from his dick?—called attention to the opportunity staring him square in the eye. Here he was, sitting in the dark with a beautiful woman and an erection—why the hell was he hesitating?

"You know, I just had a thought," he drawled.

"Is that a new occurrence for you? Is your brain tingling?"

Cash fought a grin and slid across the couch, stopping when only a mere foot separated them. "See, you just got fired, which means you're upset. And I'm not the kind of man who walks away when he encounters a damsel in distress."

"Uh-huh. Go on."

"It's in my nature to want to ease that distress. Lucky for you, I know exactly how I can make you feel better."

"I'm sure you do." Her lips twitched as if she were holding back laughter. "So, pray tell, what will make me feel better?"

"A kiss."

"Ah." She paused. "I think I'll pass."

"You sure about that?"

He slid even closer, so that his thigh pressed into hers. The moment contact was made, a jolt of heat seared through his pants and scorched his skin. The blonde's eyes widened at his nearness, but she didn't scoot away. In fact, he was certain he glimpsed a flicker of interest in those baby-blues. And he'd definitely heard the hitch in her breath.

Oh, and look at that, the tip of her tongue was sweeping over her bottom lip.

Cash chuckled. "You totally want to kiss me."

Even in the darkness, he saw the blush staining her cheeks. "I do not."

"Yes you do. You licked your lips."

"So?"

"So that's a clear sign of anticipation." His voice took on a note of pure male arrogance. "You're dying for me to put my mouth on you. And don't think I forgot about your big, buff body comment. You're into me—don't bother denying it."

He expected her to deny it. He expected her to hop off the couch in indignation and tell him where to shove it.

What he *didn't* expect?

Getting mauled.

Before he could blink, two warm hands cupped his chin and yanked his head down, and then that cute mouth collided with his in a hard, reckless kiss.

Oh yeah. *That's* what he was talkin' about.

His pulse accelerated as she devoured his mouth. *Devoured* it. Everything about the kiss drove him mad with arousal. The softness of her lips, the hungry swirl of her tongue, the nip of her teeth on his bottom lip. Every inch of his body throbbed, every muscle tight with sexual tension. Those long, desperate kisses summoned a low groan from his chest, making him want to flip her onto her back and grind his aching cock into the juncture of her thighs.

Shit, it had been way too long since he'd kissed a woman, and as satisfying as it was feeling that hot mouth pressed to his, it wasn't nearly enough.

He stroked the graceful curve of her neck, then dropped his hands to her breasts. When he squeezed, she moaned into his lips and wrapped her arms around his shoulders. Spurred on by her response, he continued to explore her body over her clothing, skimming his fingertips over her hips, her flat belly, firm thighs that clenched beneath his touch. His hands drifted back to her breasts, and he began to toy with her nipples through her shirt, his mouth flooding with saliva as he imagined sucking on those rigid buds.

"You know what, cowboy?" she murmured as she wrenched her mouth free. "I *do* feel better."

She sounded surprised, embarrassed even, but he didn't give her time to second-guess her decision to maul him. Instead, he dipped his head to kiss her again, slowly leaning into her until she lay flat on her back and his body covered hers.

Groaning, he deepened the kiss, then parted her legs with his knee and pressed himself against her.

"Oh," she squeaked. "You're...hard."

"Mm-hmm. That's what usually happens when I'm making out with a beautiful woman." He nuzzled her neck, then licked his way up to her ear, tracing the delicate lobe with his tongue. "What about you? Are you wet for me?"

She moaned.

He bit on her earlobe. "Is that a yes?"

"*Yes*. God, yes." Making an agitated sound, she shifted beneath him, wrapped her legs around his hips, and arched her back so that he was grinding into her warm mound.

Lust fogged Cash's brain. His dick ached, craving release. His balls drew up tight, tingling as his hips moved faster, needing the contact, the relief.

When she glided her hands down his back and squeezed his ass, he nearly lost it.

"Fuck," he mumbled. "I need more."

She responded with a breathy moan that made his groin tighten with need. As his pulse shrieked in his ears, he brought his hand to her waist and undid the button of her jeans. Screw it. So what if they were in a coatroom? So what if someone could walk in at any moment? So what if he didn't even know her name? He was no drama queen, but he feared he might actually die if he didn't fuck this woman. Like. Right. *Now.*

She made the sexiest noise he'd ever heard when his fingers dipped underneath the elastic of her lacy panties. He slid his hand inside, groaning at the first feel of her pussy. Holy hell. She was completely bare. And so wet.

Cash rubbed her with his palm, using the heel of his hand to apply pressure to her clit.

"Oh," she whimpered. "Don't stop."

Stop? Yeah, right. Not when the words *go, go, go* pounded in his head like some kind of tribal rhythm.

He pushed one finger into her wet heat, growling when her inner muscles clenched around it. Jesus, she was tight.

"I've never done this before," she said breathlessly.

Cash froze.

Holy hell.

Was she a *virgin*?

Guilt slammed into him. Followed by a tug of disgust—directed at himself.

He'd been so blinded by her angelic face and smoking-hot body that he'd completely ignored all the signs: her shyness, the nervous babbling, the sweet blush on her cheeks. She clearly wasn't some vixen seductress, and he was a real asshole for not picking up on that.

Soft laughter jarred him from his self-reproach. She must have sensed where his thoughts had drifted, because her eyes twinkled knowingly. "Relax. I'm not a virgin. I just meant that I've never fooled around with a stranger before."

He relaxed. "Oh. Okay, good. I was feeling like a total ass, thinking I was taking advantage of you."

She rocked her hips, reminding him of the fact that his finger was still inside her. "Nobody's taking advantage of anyone. You promised to make me feel better, remember?"

Chuckling, he brushed his lips over hers. "Right. I'll just get back to work then." To punctuate that, he slipped a second finger into her, drawing a delighted cry from her lips.

Their tongues tangled in a kiss as he pumped his fingers in and out of her tight pussy. His heart hammered out a frantic beat, each wild thud vibrating in his groin. Excitement built inside him, hot and hungry, making his skin burn. Damn it, he needed more.

With a growl, he lowered his other hand and fumbled with his zipper. The second his jeans came undone, his eager partner shoved her hand inside his boxer-briefs and gripped his erection.

A groan lodged in his chest. He thrust into her hand, literally seeing stars as she jerked his aching dick.

"Yeah, that's good," he whispered. "A bit faster, baby."

She quickened the pace, squeezing the engorged head on each upstroke, until he felt the telltale tingling sensation in his balls. Oh shit, he was close. Too close.

He distracted himself by focusing on her pleasure, feathering his thumb over her clit as his fingers worked that hot channel. Her arousal coated his fingers and drenched his palm, making him groan as he imagined his cock being bathed by all that sweet honey.

"Condom," he croaked. "We need a—"

"What the *hell* are you two doing?"

An outraged voice reverberated in the room, and then light flooded the small space.

Like a pair of teenagers who'd been busted by their parents, Cash and the blonde broke apart so fast he almost fell on his ass. Hands fumbled with buttons and zippers. Clothing was rearranged. After they made themselves presentable, they both shot to their feet, guilty gazes darting in the direction of the door.

A stocky man with a bushy mustache and furious eyes stood in the doorway, shaking his head in disgust.

"You two aren't supposed to be in here." He jabbed his finger in the air. "Both of you, out. Now. Don't make me call the cops."

As the man spun on his heel and stormed off, Cash offered a wry grin. "Well. That didn't go as planned." His gaze dropped to his crotch, which sported a big, unhappy bulge.

Discomfort flickered in the blonde's eyes, which were a brighter blue than he'd realized. In the light, they were the color of a clear sky, with flecks of silver around the pupils, framed by thick lashes.

Biting her bottom lip, she bent to retrieve the black leather purse on the floor. "I think the mustache man did us a favor. Sex in public is never a good idea."

"How about sex in private?" he suggested hopefully. "My car's parked down the street. We could–"

She cut him off. "I'm here with friends, remember? And I already feel like a jerk for disappearing this long. I should probably go back out there and put on my celebration face before Tessa un-friends me."

He swallowed his disappointment. The universe really didn't like him tonight.

"Trust me, you're dodging a bullet, cowboy," she added. "You don't want to get involved with me. My life is a total mess right now, and I'm not usually this fun and spontaneous. I'm a total space cadet. Seriously, I spend way too much time daydreaming. And let's face it, I'm weird. Nobody gets my sense of humor. I'm super forgetful–I have to leave notes all over my apartment just so I remember to do things, like eat, or breathe. Oh, and I babble a lot, in case you haven't noticed." She gave a firm nod. "So yeah, you're totally dodging a bullet."

Damned if that speech didn't make him like her even more.

"Maybe I'm not a dodging kind of guy," he said, raising his brows in challenge. "Maybe I'm the man who jumps in front of bullets."

"Well, then you're even weirder than I am." She took a step toward the door.

"Can I at least get your number?" he called after her.

She stopped. "Are you actually going to call? Because with those looks, I bet you collect a lot of numbers."

"I'll call," he promised. A grin lifted his lips. "I think we'd be doing each other a disservice if we didn't finish what we started."

She pursed her lips for a moment, indecision creasing her beautiful features. After a beat, she recited her number, and he resisted doing a little victory dance as he punched it into his phone.

Cash winced when he realized he didn't have a name for the new contact. "Oh, uh, what's your name?"

Awesome. He really was a manwhore, huh? Getting the girl's name *after* he nearly slept with her.

"It's Jen."

"Jen," he echoed sheepishly. "Nice to meet you, Jen."

"Pleasure was all mine, cowboy." That cute blush returned. "So, um, yeah, call me."

With that, she strolled out of the room, leaving him grinning like a goofy idiot.

Cash waited a few seconds before exiting the coatroom. Thankfully, the navy groupie didn't pop out of nowhere and ambush him as he left the bar.

A part of him still wished he and Jen had finished what they'd started, but at the same time he was happy they hadn't settled for a hurried lay in a public bar. He wanted more than a fully clothed quickie. He wanted her naked in his bed, while his mouth and hands and cock explored every inch of her X-rated body.

So, yeah, he'd left the house with a hard-on and would be going home with one, but he could survive one more day. First thing tomorrow, he'd call Jen and arrange for a repeat performance of tonight—one that wouldn't get interrupted.

Feeling rejuvenated, he strode down the sidewalk with a spring to his step. It was raining, but the cool droplets sliding down his face didn't dampen his mood. Neither did the water that splashed into his boots when one of them plopped into a puddle. Or the sudden downpour that soaked him to the bone by the time he reached his SUV. He couldn't remember the last time he'd had so much fun with a chick.

He slid into the driver's seat and started the engine. As he flicked on the windshield wipers, he was still grinning to himself.

But his good mood didn't last.

Nope, because just as he was pulling out of the parking spot, he realized the plopping sound he'd heard before? It wasn't just his boots sloshing through a puddle. It was his phone falling out of his pocket. The phone he'd just entered Jen's phone number into.

And when he found it floating in that puddle half a minute later and fished it out, the damn thing was completely fried.

And so was any chance of seeing Jen again.

CHAPTER THREE

"Not one word," Jennifer Scott announced as she and her brother entered her apartment.

Carson followed her to the living room, stood in front of her secondhand plaid-patterned couch, and opened his mouth.

"Not. One. Word," she growled.

Sensing she meant business, he lowered his six-foot frame on the sofa and sighed. But he didn't speak. Nope, he just sat there and watched her pace like a madwoman.

"I know you think I'm a screw-up, but this isn't my fault," she muttered as she made tracks in the frayed blue carpet. "Do you think I *enjoy* being stalked? I had no idea Brendan was a maniac, okay? He didn't exactly advertise that on our first date—'Hey, guess what, Jen, I'm actually a clingy nut job.'" She huffed out a miserable breath. "He seemed like a good guy, Carson. A normal investment banker who bought his mother a locket for her birthday—a heart-shaped locket! And he put both their pictures in it! It was the sweetest thing ever."

Carson opened his mouth again, but she whipped up her hand to silence him.

"Yeah, I know. He probably goes around the city to various jewelry stores and buys hundreds of lockets to lure unsuspecting salesgirls into going out with him. I guess I'm just a gullible idiot, right?"

"Jenny—"

"And please don't lecture me about losing my job at Arnold's. I know I can't claim to be the poster child for holding a job, but this time it wasn't my fault. Brendan showed up and caused a scene. I'm not sure I even blame Mr. Arnold for firing me. *I* wouldn't want a crazy person frequenting my place of business either."

"Jenny—"

"So fine, Carson, you're right. I'm a screw-up. I got involved with a lunatic and I'm unsuccessful in life. Just get it over with and have me committed or something."

Her rant died off, leaving her feeling not only exhausted but humiliated. She was so tired of being the family fuck-up. The one member of the Scott clan who couldn't hold it together.

Swallowing a lump of bitterness, she flopped down next to her brother and fought the sting of tears.

After a second, Carson's arm wrapped around her shoulders.

"I don't think any of this is your fault," he said gruffly. "All I was going to say, before you rudely told me to shut up, was *are you okay*?"

She blinked. "Really?"

"Really. Look, I know I rag on you a lot, but that's because I'm your big brother. That's the kind of shit we do." He grasped her chin with one callused hand and forced eye contact. "I don't think you're an idiot for getting involved with Brendan. Hell, I hung out with the guy for an entire afternoon when he came over to Mom and Dad's for brunch, and I didn't get a psycho vibe from him either. Does that make *me* an idiot?"

"Yes," she said glumly. "You're a SEAL. Your instincts are supposed to be spot-on."

"You've got great instincts too. Brendan was just a good actor. He had us all fooled." Carson shrugged. "As for the job thing, you wouldn't have to worry about getting fired all the time if you took Mom up on her offer. She'll pay your way through nursing school. All you've gotta do is say yes."

Jen's jaw tensed. "I don't want to be a nurse."

"Why not? It's a great gig. Solid pay, benefits, job security."

"Bedpans, blood, ornery patients..."

She trailed off, knowing that no matter what she said, Carson wouldn't get it. No one in her family understood why she hadn't gone into nursing like her mother, or enlisted in the navy like her dad and brother. Well, blood made her squeamish and violence made her nervous. End of story.

Unfortunately, her parents were incapable of accepting she might not be good at—or passionate about—the same things they were.

Unlike Carson, who was good at frickin' everything. A decorated soldier, a husband, her parents' Golden Boy. Even his man-slut past didn't reduce him in their parents' eyes. Their dad laughed it off as "boys will be boys," while their mom simply chuckled in that "oh, you" manner whenever anyone—well, *Jen*—reminded her that Carson's life used to be a revolving door of women.

Now that Carson was married to Holly, his star shone even brighter. Jen loved her sister-in-law to death, but come on, would it kill Holly to be a little less perfect? The chick wasn't only a talented chef, but she was smart as hell, cute as a button, and probably the funniest person on the planet.

And then there was Jen. Little Jenny, who had no ambition, no serious boyfriend, and no self-control when it came to shoe stores. She was twenty-five years old, yet everyone in her family treated her like an inept five-year-old who couldn't make smart decisions.

That's why she'd been so thrilled when she'd met Brendan. He had a successful career, money in the bank, a practical head on his shoulders. She knew he'd impressed the hell out of her parents when she'd introduced him, and for the four months they'd been together, Jen had been pretty damn happy.

Until she discovered Brendan had a case of the crazies.

"My unemployment status isn't my main concern right now," she said tersely. "How am I going to tell Mom and Dad about Brendan?"

"I can tell them if you want," Carson offered. "But that's not important right now either. We need to take measures to make sure this asshole doesn't come after you again."

"I just filed a restraining order," she reminded him, gesturing to the manila envelope she'd tossed on the glass coffee table. "He won't risk violating it."

"This guy is nuts. Of course he'd risk it." Carson paused. "When is his work transfer thing happening?"

"Three weeks."

And thank God for that. Brendan's transfer to his firm's Oakland office had been the reason she'd broken up with him. On the surface, anyway. His clingy behavior was what really triggered her inner alarm system. But when he'd told her about his impending move, he'd provided her with the perfect exit strategy.

Brendan, however, had wanted them to keep seeing each other long-distance. When she'd refused, he'd gone batshit crazy on her, proceeding to give all those movie stalkers a run for their money.

"Are we sure he wasn't lying?" Carson asked sharply.

"He wasn't. I helped him pack up his apartment. Oh, and we ran into one of his colleagues when we went out for dinner last month, and the two of them were talking about the transfer."

"So in three weeks, Psycho McGee will be gone."

"Glory hallelujah."

"Did you join a Baptist church when I was overseas? Forget it, don't answer that. Knowing you, you probably did. Anyway, we need to make sure he stays away from you until then."

"My super had the locks changed this morning, and I won't leave the apartment unless I'm with somebody."

"Not good enough."

A warning bell chimed in her head. "What does that mean?"

Without answering, Carson gave her shoulder one last squeeze before getting to his feet. "I gotta go. I wanted to stop by the restaurant to surprise Holly for lunch."

As he strode toward the door, Jen shot off the couch and hurried after him. "What did you mean by *not good enough*, Carson? What are you planning and why do I get the feeling it's going to annoy the shit out of me?"

Shooting her a saccharine smile, Carson reached out to ruffle her hair, a gesture that never failed to aggravate her. "Don't you worry your pretty little head, Jenny. I'll make sure nothing happens to you." He reached for the doorknob. "Lock up behind me."

Stifling a sigh, she watched her brother go, then flicked the deadbolt and locked the chain. She couldn't shake the feeling that Carson was about to add a little more misery to her already miserable life. He'd always been incredibly overprotective of her, just like their dad. But what else could she expect? When you were related to a retired admiral and an active-duty SEAL, macho posturing was a fact of life.

Her shoulders felt heavier than stone as she went to the kitchen and poured herself a glass of water. She kind of wished it was a shot of whiskey, but she wasn't much of a drinker, and besides, no amount of alcohol could improve her mood.

When had everything become such a mess? She'd lost her job, her love life had turned into *Fatal Attraction*, her brother had snapped into alpha-male caveman mode, her parents would probably lecture her for falling for a psycho.

And to make matters worse, her sexy stranger hadn't called, even though it had been two days since she'd given him her number.

You're better off. This isn't the time for a new relationship.

Yeah, that was probably true. Adding a new complication to the mix would undoubtedly lead to disaster, but even knowing that, she couldn't help but feel a spark of disappointment.

She'd really enjoyed the encounter with Cash McCoy at the Tavern. The conversation, the laughter, the hot make-out and groping session. After being on edge for the past month, looking over her shoulder and expecting Brendan to pop out of the shadows, it had been nice to let loose and flirt with a hot guy.

And kiss a hot guy.

And almost have sex with a hot guy.

Just the memory of those piercing blue eyes and chiseled male-model features made her pulse speed up. Hands down, Cash McCoy was the sexiest man she'd ever met. She shivered, remembering the feel of his hard chest against her breasts. The thick ridge of arousal pressing into her thigh. The firmness of his lips and greedy thrust of his tongue.

Jen gulped down the rest of her water, suddenly parched. She didn't normally fool around with complete strangers, but Cash had unleashed some kind of primal urge inside her. The urge to fuck him senseless.

If they hadn't been interrupted, she knew without a doubt that senseless fucking would've been on the agenda.

And she would've loved every second of it.

"You're such a little slut," she mumbled to herself, then couldn't help but laugh.

Ha. Hardly. Truth was, she was the furthest thing from slutty. She wasn't a virgin, but she hadn't sown any wild oats either. Which sucked, because sowing some oats sounded unbelievably appealing to her.

Unfortunately, she'd yet to meet a man who was interested in helping her explore her sexuality. Her past boyfriends had treated her with kid gloves, like she was a fragile object that would break if they got too rough. They'd seen her as a pretty little thing they needed to protect. But she didn't want a protector. She wanted hungry kisses and husky demands, a man so desperate to get her naked and screw her brains out that he didn't bother with the when or where or how—he wanted her *now* and he'd damn well take her.

She'd experienced that with Cash in the brief moments they'd spent together.

Fighting a rush of frustration, she slammed her glass in the sink, then marched out of her tiny kitchen, crossed the tiny living room, and entered her tiny bedroom. Running motif of her place? Tiny. It was all she could afford on her wages, but this one-bedroom apartment sure beat living under her parents' roof. Their constant lectures and relentless nagging were detrimental to her sanity.

She froze in the middle of her bedroom as a terrifying thought struck her. Now that she'd lost her job at Arnold's, she might actually have no choice but to move back home. She had enough money saved to pay a few more months of rent, but after that?

"Don't think about it," she mumbled, banishing the scary notion.

Squaring her shoulders, she approached the wooden desk beneath the small window that offered a stunning view of the brick wall belonging to the building next door. Her camera bag sat on the desk, and as she slung the strap over her shoulder, the familiar weight of the bag and the Nikon digital SLR it housed brought a sense of tranquility.

Her camera was the one thing guaranteed to soothe her soul. Whenever she peered through the lens, she felt so confident, so utterly in control. Everything else seemed to melt away —the problems, the stress, the bullshit bogging her down. Taking pictures had always been her means for escape. And right now, she needed to escape. Big time.

However, she'd promised Carson she wouldn't venture out of the apartment unless it was absolutely necessary, which meant she'd have to make do with taking pictures from the balcony.

As she left the bedroom, Jen tried convincing herself that everything would be fine. She'd find a new job. She'd be rid of Brendan once he left San Diego—and until then, the restraining order would keep him in line. And if Cash didn't call, then no biggie.

She would be just fine.

Still, that didn't stop her mind from drifting back to the blue-eyed charmer who'd almost rocked her world two nights ago. She wondered what he was doing right now. Probably working, though she wasn't sure what "security" entailed. He'd been pretty vague about it. Was he a security guard? A bouncer? Sitting in an office right now, designing security software or something?

Or maybe he had the day off and was at home at this very moment. Bored, restless—and not thinking about calling her. Evidently Cash hadn't felt the same combustible chemistry.

Too bad. Considering she'd be housebound for a while, it would've been nice to pass the time with her dark-haired hottie.

"You're missing out, McCoy," she murmured as she stepped out on the small balcony that overlooked the quiet street below.

Yep, he was totally missing out. With the way her life was going right now, she would've jumped at the chance for some hot, sweaty, forget-about-your-problems sex. He wouldn't even have to buy her dinner—that's how much of a sure thing she was.

But oh well. He clearly didn't plan on calling her.

Apparently he had better things to do.

"That's it, babe, suck my cock. Ah, just like that."

Cash pushed his dick deeper into the brunette's mouth. Her teeth scraped the underside of his shaft, sending a zip of heat to his balls. Sweet baby Jesus, he'd needed this. A hot mouth surrounding him, wet tongue lapping him up, soft fingers teasing his sac.

Vanessa bobbed her head as she got into the blowjob, sucking with such fervor Cash found his ass bumping into the arm of the couch. He hadn't wasted any time once he'd walked into Dylan Wade's living room and found Vanessa on her knees, servicing his buddy. He couldn't even be mad that the impatient jerks had gotten started without him—these two were even bigger sex maniacs than he was.

Vanessa was awesome, though. Gorgeous, confident. She was Dylan's latest friends-with-benefits, but she'd taken a liking to Cash too when the three of them hung out last week. So when Dylan called tonight inviting Cash to "chill" with them, it was a no-brainer. Clothes had come off, positions had switched, and now Cash was on the receiving end of that wicked tongue while Dylan screwed Vanessa from behind.

By some miracle, he hadn't come the second she took him in

her mouth. After six months with no sex, he'd figured he'd explode like a Fourth of July firecracker if a woman so much as looked at his dick.

The sounds of sex bounced off the walls. Dylan's roommate Seth had gone out for the evening, but even if he walked in right this very moment, Cash knew Vanessa wouldn't balk. She had an adventurous spirit, and, according to her, "more was *always* merrier."

"Fuck, you're so tight," Dylan muttered, gripping Vanessa's ass as he fucked her with slow, steady strokes. "So sweet. I love this hot, tight pussy. Feel good?"

She lifted her mouth from Cash's dick. "*So* good," she told Dylan. Her tone got sassy. "Now quit talking and get me off."

Dylan laughed in approval. "Yes, ma'am." His hips thrust forward, the deep plunge pushing her face into Cash's crotch.

Cash cradled the back of Vanessa's head to steady her, groaning as her eager mouth sucked him so deep his balls tickled her chin. The tingling in his groin told him he was close, and he squeezed his eyes shut, trying to ward off impending release. He didn't want to come yet, not until he was buried inside that tight channel Dylan kept waxing poetic about.

"Slower, babe," Cash choked out. He tangled his fingers in her long, silky hair and stilled her enthusiastic bobbing. "I want this to last."

She slowed down, tickling the head of his cock with her tongue. While her lazy mouth tended to his dick, one hand teased his balls, rolling them between her fingers, fondling, squeezing. She kept her other hand on the hardwood floor to brace herself.

Dylan's bare chest gleamed with sweat as he drove into the place Cash was dying to be. "You want to come, don't you, honey?" he teased. He slowed the pace and rolled his hips.

"*Yes*," she burst out, the sound sending tremors up Cash's shaft.

Dylan reached one arm around and brought his hand between her legs. Cash knew the moment his buddy's fingers found her clit, because she reared her ass like a filly in heat and moaned against Cash's erection.

Didn't take long until she started to orgasm, and before he could make a preemptive withdrawal, Dylan had already tugged Vanessa's mouth off Cash's dick.

"Easy there," Dylan drawled. "No biting, V. Cash plans on using that cock of his again after tonight."

She laughed breathlessly at that, still trembling. As she recovered from her climax, Cash sank to his knees, positioned her so she was draped over his chest, and slid his hand between her legs. He took over for his friend, rubbing her pussy and huskily urging her to another orgasm while Dylan pumped into her.

A groan sliced through the air as Dylan began to come, followed by Vanessa's delighted cry as she came again. Cash rode out the orgasm with the duo, stroking her swollen clit, kissing her neck, watching as Dylan rested his forehead between Vanessa's shoulder blades and shuddered with release.

The pair finally went still, Dylan's green eyes glazed as he pulled out. Vanessa sagged into Cash's chest. Her tongue darted out to briefly taste one of his nipples and then she lifted her head, brown eyes hazy with desire.

"I've wanted you in me since the moment I met you," she said in a breathy voice.

She didn't have to ask him twice.

He donned a condom, then took her hand and led her to the couch. A second later, he covered her body with his and plunged into her with one fluid stroke.

And then his phone rang.

He froze.

So did Dylan, who stood in the middle of the room, ditching his condom.

"You gonna get that?" Vanessa asked, looking annoyed that he'd stopped midthrust.

When a second ringtone didn't join the first, both men relaxed.

Cash bent down to plant a kiss on her lips. "Nah. If we had to report in, both our phones would've gone off."

"You're good to go, McCoy. Resume the fucking," Dylan drawled.

Ignoring the smartass remark, Cash brushed his lips over Vanessa's and rocked his hips as he eased back into a nice, languid rhythm. Watching her eyes grow misty with pleasure, he admired just how pretty she was. High cheekbones, pouty lips, smooth olive-toned skin. She wasn't as beautiful as Jen, but—

Uncool, bro.

Shit, what was he doing, thinking about another woman right now?

And why had his dick hardened to a whole new level the moment Jen's face floated into his mind?

"Faster. I need it faster."

Swallowing, he forced himself to focus on the woman beneath him, who was bumping her pelvis against his groin, trying to deepen the contact. He withdrew completely, slammed back in to the hilt, and gave the lady what she wanted. Hard, fast strokes guaranteed to drive them both over the edge.

It didn't take long before he was coming in a hot rush. He shortened his strokes and dug his fingers into her hips as the orgasm burned through his body like wildfire. When Vanessa let out a throaty cry and clenched her inner muscles around him, the fire burned hotter, making his balls ache with exquisite agony.

Fuck.

He'd needed that.

Once the pleasure finally ebbed, Cash caught his breath and gently pulled out. The haze of satisfaction fogging Vanessa's eyes brought a jolt of matching satisfaction to his gut. He might not have given her his full attention by the end, but at least he'd gotten her off again. He still felt shitty, though, for tastelessly thinking about Jen. Vanessa didn't deserve that.

Fortunately, Dylan was considering her feelings for the both of them. As Cash removed the condom and staggered to his feet, Dylan quickly took his place, launching himself at Vanessa, making her laugh as he nuzzled her neck and whispered something in her ear.

Cash stalked naked across the living room to the spot on the floor where he'd ditched his pants.

It really sucked, losing Jen's number. He'd had to buy a new phone the other day because the puddle killed his other one, but he'd hoped maybe his contacts had been updated on the cloud or some shit before it died. No such luck, though. The number was gone. Which was a real fucking shame. He couldn't remember the last time he'd had that much fun with a woman. He'd been dying to see her ever since they'd parted ways at the Gaslamp Tavern, but he had no idea how to track her down.

You can't. Deal with it.

Resignation fluttered through him and settled in his gut. Yeah, he needed to put Jen out of his mind. The chances of seeing her again were pretty much nonexistent, and as much as that sucked, he needed to face the facts.

With a weary exhale, he fished his new phone from one of the many pockets of his cargo pants. A moan caught his attention, and his gaze drifted to Dylan and Vanessa, who were still tangled together on the couch. Gripping the back of Dylan's blond head, Vanessa held him in place as he kissed her breasts. Dylan's mouth latched onto one dusky nipple, and he made a little growling sound of approval as he suckled her.

Despite his frustrated mood, Cash's body responded to the scene in front of him.

"Ready for round two or are you abandoning us?" Vanessa teased when she caught him looking.

Cash winked. "Round two. Let me just check my messages."

He glanced at his phone, cursing when he noticed the missed call on the screen. Carson Scott.

Shit, why was the lieutenant calling him? Did they have plans he'd forgotten about?

He was just punching in the code for his voice mail when the phone vibrated in his hand. Text message coming in. From... Carson Scott.

Frowning, Cash opened the message. Wariness crept up his spine as he skimmed the terse note.

NEED TO TALK. IMPORTANT. MY PLACE—NOW.

Well, okay then. That didn't sound good. And all caps? Definitely important.

He shot back a quick text saying he was on his way, then cast a rueful look in the direction of the couch, where Vanessa now lay on her back, legs spread wide. Kneeling on the floor, Dylan had his head buried between her thighs.

So much for round two.

"Actually, I gotta go," Cash announced.

Dylan lifted his head long enough to mumble, "See you later," then resumed feasting.

Lucky bastard.

Stifling a sigh, Cash got dressed and headed out the door.

CHAPTER
FOUR

"Hey, man, thanks for coming over." Carson gestured for him to enter the apartment.

As Cash stepped inside, he experienced a sense of disorientation. He'd been to Carson's place a dozen times, for poker games and whatnot, but something felt off tonight. It took him a moment to realize it was the smell. Or lack thereof. Every time he'd been here, Carson's wife had been cooking up a storm, thrilled to use her husband's teammates as guinea pigs for whatever recipe she happened to be experimenting with.

"Where's Holly?" he asked, shooting his commanding officer a quizzical look.

Carson's jaw tensed. "She's crashing at her sister's tonight."

He didn't elaborate, and Cash didn't push. But damn, he hoped there wasn't trouble in paradise. Carson and Holly were the most rock-solid couple he'd ever met, and so well suited for one another it was almost disgusting. They'd been together five years, married for two, and every time Cash saw them, he experienced a raw pang of envy. They were so at ease with each other, on the same wavelength in every conceivable way, something Cash had never experienced with a woman.

The girls he'd dated accused him of being too blunt, too detached, too selfish. It grated, because he truly didn't see himself as any of those things. Sure, maybe he didn't always know the right thing to say, maybe he didn't understand all those mind games chicks liked to play, but that didn't make him a shitty person, did it?

Pushing aside his troubling thoughts, he followed Carson into the living room and settled on the couch, while Carson disappeared into the kitchen to grab them some beers. He returned a minute later, handed Cash a bottle, and sank into the leather recliner opposite the couch.

"So listen, I need a favor," Carson began, his blue eyes crinkling with discomfort.

Cash furrowed his brows. "Sounds ominous."

"Not really. It's just... My sister drives me crazy sometimes. You won't believe the trouble she winds up in."

"Your sister? The favor has to do with her?"

"Yeah. She's got this psycho ex-boyfriend." Carson's mouth flattened. "Well, more like a stalker."

"Your sister has a stalker."

"I know, right? Sounds really fucking dumb when you say it out loud. But it's not a joke. This guy is a total creep. She broke up with him about a month ago, but he refuses to leave her alone. I went to the police station with her this morning to file a restraining order."

Shit. That sounded bad.

"What'd he do?" Cash narrowed his eyes. "Did he get physical?"

Carson's cheeks hollowed, as if he were grinding his teeth together. "Son of a bitch manhandled her outside a club. She managed to get in a cab and hightail it home, but the next day,

Psycho McGee shows up at her store with flowers. She says *thanks but no thanks, asshole*, but he doesn't stop there. Starts sending her creepy texts and emails, along the lines of *if I can't have you, no one else will*."

"Fuck."

"She changed her number and blocked him on social media. You know, hoping if she keeps ignoring him he'll give up. But then last night she comes home from work and finds rose petals all over her fucking bed. He figured out where she hides the spare key and let himself in—and before you ask, yes, she had the locks changed. Anyway, Psycho McGee left another note with the rose petals. Some real sicko shit." Carson shook his head. "I'm worried a restraining order isn't going to stop the guy, that he'll come after her again, except this time he really won't take no for an answer."

"So what do you need from me?" Cash asked slowly.

"I want you to keep an eye on her."

He blinked. "What?"

"His office is transferring him to Oakland, so he'll be leaving town soon, but until then, I don't want my sister to be alone. She'll come stay with you for a few weeks—"

"Wait, what?"

Carson shot him an impatient look. "Should I slow down and talk in words you understand?"

"Yes," he grumbled. "What do you mean, your sister's coming to stay with me?"

"I can't leave her all alone in her apartment, not while this guy is still around. I'd let her stay with Holly and me, but—" Carson paused, looking vaguely embarrassed, "—but it's not a good time, okay? And I can't stay at Jenny's and leave Holly here by herself."

"Don't you have parents?"

He knew he sounded like a whiny brat, but come on, he

wasn't in the mood to babysit Carson's sister. He didn't go back on duty for a few more weeks, and he'd been looking forward to the downtime.

"She won't go for it," Carson said with a sigh. "My parents give her a lot of shit, and there's no way she'll agree to stay with them. Besides, I'd like her to be around someone who can protect her in case Psycho McGee shows up and gets violent."

Great, this just got better and better. Babysitter *and* bodyguard.

"I already spoke to Matt and he agreed to give up his room for the next few weeks. He'll stay at Savannah's."

Cash stifled a groan. Looked like the lieutenant had it all planned out. Would've been nice if *Cash* had had a say in the matter before Carson decided to rearrange his life.

He quickly scanned his brain for another option, one that didn't involve spending the rest of his leave babysitting.

"She can stay with Seth and Dylan," he suggested. "They have a spare room."

"And send my baby sister into the lion's den?" Carson looked horrified. "No way. I know the kind of shit that goes on there. Not that I'm knocking the lifestyle—I was all about the fun and games before I met Holly. But those guys give a whole new meaning to the word *player*." He paused. "Well, so do you, but I figured you're probably not as bad as the tagteamers."

Uh... Cash decided not to mention what he'd been doing before he'd been so rudely interrupted.

Instead, he tossed out another suggestion. "Jackson's got an empty room too..."

"Yeah, and the second he gets my sister in it, he'll turn up the Texan charm and have her out of her clothes in five seconds flat." The lieutenant shrugged. "You're the lesser of four evils, man. And I know you're planning on going to Officer Candidate School first chance you get, so..."

So you'd be a fool to deflower my sweet virgin sister and risk a bad recommendation from me, was Carson's unspoken warning.

Fuck. He really wasn't getting out of this, was he?

"It'll only be for three weeks," Carson said, picking up on his hesitation. "You don't have to entertain her or prepare home-cooked meals or any of that shit. Just tag along if she needs to go somewhere and make sure she's safe. That's all."

That's all? He wanted to point out that having a houseguest pretty much guaranteed he wouldn't be getting laid for the next month, but he suspected Carson valued his sister's safety over Cash's sex life.

And wow, didn't *that* make him a total jackass. Was he really bitching about the lack of sex he'd get when some poor girl was being terrorized by a stalker?

As everything shifted into perspective, he let out a resigned breath, knowing he couldn't refuse the request. Carson never asked him for anything, and the man had taken Cash under his wing once he'd joined the team. Invites to dinner, poker night, the mini-golf tourney Carson and his buddies held every month. Carson had done a helluva lot to welcome him into the fold.

"Okay," he agreed. "I'll keep an eye on your sister."

Relief flooded the other man's face. "Thanks, Cash. I'll drop her off tomorrow morning."

He took a swig of beer, then set the bottle on the coffee table and eyed the flatscreen. "Wanna catch the NFL highlights?"

Carson reached for the remote. "Sure." But rather than switch on the TV, he turned with a deadly look. "One more thing I forgot to mention."

"Yeah?"

"Keep your hands off my sister."

Cash frowned. "I wasn't planning on—"

"I'm serious. You touch her, and I'll drown you. Your building's got a pool in the back, so I won't have to go far."

He had to laugh. "You'll drown me? That's the most creative death you can come up with?"

"I'm in the navy. I do my best work in the water." Those blue eyes glittered with menace. "And don't think I'm kidding, McCoy. Touch my little sister and you're a dead man. She's off-limits."

The temperature in the room had dipped below the freezing mark, and from the look on the lieutenant's face, Cash didn't doubt the dude meant business.

With a pleasant smile, Carson clicked a button on the remote. "What'll it be? ESPN or SportsCenter?"

Sitting in the passenger seat of Carson's Range Rover, Jen resisted the urge to reach over the center console and strangle her brother to death. She was beyond furious, but he'd been pretending not to notice the steam rolling out of her ears as they'd driven in complete silence.

Up ahead, a low-rise apartment building came into view. Seven stories or so, it boasted a sleek gray exterior, balconies with wrought-iron railings, and colorful flowerbeds lining the lush lawn out front. It was much nicer than her building, but that didn't make this situation any less annoying.

With an overly pleasant smile, Carson pulled over by the curb and killed the engine. "We're here."

She shot him a stony glare.

"Come on, Jenny, stop with the silent treatment already. You know this is a good idea."

Right, because being blackmailed into staying with a complete stranger was a *splendid* idea. She couldn't believe she was letting Carson call the shots like this, but the alternative he'd posed was even worse: he'd threatened to tell their parents that her life was in danger. Which wasn't only an exaggeration but also a surefire way to get her locked up in the family panic room for the next month. If the admiral believed his little girl was even in the slightest bit of danger, he'd throw her over his shoulder in a fireman's carry and march her all the way back to the family homestead in Del Mar.

Jen loved her parents—she really, truly did—but the two of them drove her absolutely crazy. No way could she survive living under their roof again.

So Carson's "solution," as much as it aggravated her, was clearly the better option.

Didn't mean she had to be happy about it, though.

"How do you know Brendan didn't follow us here?" she asked in a last-ditch effort to derail her brother's plan. "Maybe he's been watching my apartment, tailed us, and ruined your cunning scheme to keep me hidden. In that case, I might as well go back to my place."

Carson smirked. "Do you honestly think I didn't keep an eye out for a tail? Trust me, we weren't followed."

"Fine." She pursed her lips. "But what if Brendan *does* show up, and this rookie you're sticking me with drops the ball? What if he gets, um, rookie freeze-up syndrome or something?"

"Rookie freeze-up syndrome? I like it. Remind me to accuse one of the guys of having that."

"I'm serious, Carson."

"So am I. And trust me," he said again, "Cash has mad skills. He won't let anything happen to you."

Jen froze as the name registered in her head. When he'd tried selling her on this plan, Carson had kept referring to her new roomie as "one of my rookies."

But his rookie's name was *Cash*?

No, she must have heard wrong.

And even if she'd heard right, that didn't mean it was the same Cash she'd met at the Tavern. Her Cash worked in security, or at least that's what he'd told her. Unless he'd lied... But why would he? If he was a SEAL, why not just tell her?

Yeah, had to be a different guy. Maybe the name Cash was more common than she'd realized. People were naming their kids all sorts of weird things these days. Maybe Cash topped one of those Most Popular Baby Names lists, along with Apple and Potato and every other stupid name making the rounds.

Jen put on her most nonchalant tone. "Cash? That's the guy you're dumping me off on?"

"Yeah. Cash McCoy."

McCoy.

Oh no.

It *was* him.

Annoyance rippled through her when she realized Cash *had* lied about what he did for a living. But the irritation couldn't mask the rush of heat that flooded her belly as she grasped what this meant.

She was going to be playing house with her sexy cowboy for the next three weeks.

"How come I've never met him?" she asked suspiciously. "And if he's such a good guy, why wasn't he at your birthday party?"

"Because his parents were in town and they had tickets to a show. He came over the next night for beers."

"Oh."

Jen suddenly felt queasy. Did Cash know she was going to be his new houseguest? She hadn't told him her last name, and knowing Carson, he'd referred to her as Jenny-Pie or some other juvenile name when he'd told Cash about her. Chances were, the guy was in for the surprise of his life.

As panic jolted through her, Jen got ready to blurt out a protest, but Carson was done talking. He threw open the driver's door and slid out of the SUV, rounding the vehicle to get her bags out of the trunk.

She stayed rooted in her seat, her heart lurching. She couldn't spend the next few weeks with Cash McCoy. Maybe if he'd called, things would be different. But looking into his sexy blue eyes and drooling over his spectacular body, all the while knowing he wasn't interested? That would *suck*.

And the icing on the cake? He was military. She had a firm rule about military men: *don't date one.*

Who says you have to date him?

True. She could always just fuck his brains out.

Except he clearly wasn't interested in doing *that*, seeing as how he hadn't called.

A sharp rap on the window jarred her from her thoughts.

She turned to see Carson's exasperated face peering into the half-open window. "Out of the car, Jenny."

She opened her mouth, nearly confessing that she already knew Cash. But she stopped herself at the last second. She couldn't tell her brother about the night at the Tavern. Not only did it make her look kinda slutty, but it suddenly occurred to her that if she *did* tell Carson she knew Cash, he might scrap this whole houseguest plan and act on his threat of involving their parents.

Another knock sounded on the window.

"I'm getting annoyed," he announced.

Sighing, Jen got out of the car. "I doubt you're as annoyed as I am."

Her brother's gaze softened. "I'm just trying to look out for you. Maybe I'm overreacting, seeing a threat where I shouldn't, but I won't take chances with your safety. Until Brendan is gone, I refuse to leave you unprotected."

An arrow of guilt pierced her chest. Carson sounded so genuinely concerned that she felt like an ass for the way she'd bitched at him all morning. "I know. I'm sorry I'm being such a brat."

"'S'all good. I'm used to your brattiness."

He reached out and tugged on the end of her ponytail, the way he'd always done when they were kids, and Jen couldn't help but smile. As infuriating as Carson could be, he was still her big brother and she loved him something fierce.

Besides, as much as she didn't want to admit it, he was right. She *didn't* feel safe. She'd been on edge ever since Brendan started playing these sick games with her, and although she wasn't convinced her ex would actually cross the line from creepy to violent, she'd definitely breathe easier once he left town.

"Come on, let's go in," Carson said.

Her anxiety returned once they entered the building. She wondered how Cash would react when he saw her. If he even remembered her. A guy as good looking as him probably hooked up with ten girls a night. What if she'd just been another one of his faceless conquests?

Lugging her bags, Carson crossed the small, clean lobby toward the stairwell door. "Cash and Matt are on the second floor," he told her. "But Matt'll be staying with his girlfriend while you're here."

When they reached the second-floor landing, Carson led her to a door at the very end of the hall.

"Oh, and Ryan and Annabelle live upstairs," he went on. "So if you want to do any girlie things, just call Annabelle. You met her, right?"

Jen nodded. Although she'd yet to meet her brother's newer teammates, she knew most of the older ones well, along with their wives and girlfriends. Out of all the women, Annabelle

Holmes was her favorite. They'd gone out for dinner a few times, and she'd hung out with the sarcastic brunette at Carson's thirty-fourth birthday party last month, so it was a relief knowing that Annabelle would be nearby.

"By the way, I told Mom and Dad your apartment is being fumigated," Carson added. "So if they call, tell them you were overrun with ants."

"Ants? *That's* what you came up with?"

He shrugged. "First thing that popped into my head."

They reached the door, which Carson opened without bothering to knock first. "McCoy," he called. "Come say hi to Jenny."

She cringed. Of course, he just *had* to refer to her by the name she hadn't used since grade school.

Carson dropped her two suitcases on the hardwood floor with a thump, while Jen examined her surroundings. The apartment looked like a typical bachelor pad—no surprise there. It featured an open-concept layout, with a spacious living room boasting a leather couch, two big armchairs, a TV mounted on the wall, and an entertainment system that screamed *man cave*. A small kitchen with stainless-steel appliances and an eat-in counter took up the other side of the room, next to a dining area with a big glass table and a shelf lined with an assortment of beer glasses. Her gaze flicked to the corridor in the back, which she assumed led to the bedrooms.

When footsteps thudded from the vicinity of that corridor, her pulse kicked up a notch, then took off in a mad sprint at Cash's appearance.

Oh boy. He was as gorgeous as she remembered. Actually, even more gorgeous, because instead of a leather jacket, today he wore a black T-shirt that clung to his massive chest and revealed his bulging biceps. Jeez, he had great arms. Tanned, sinewy, roped with muscle. The kind of arms you wanted pinning you down while those trim hips pumped into you.

The rest of him was equally appealing. Long legs encased in camo pants, strong jaw dusted with stubble, black-brown hair cut in a short military style. Her nipples tightened involuntarily, her core clenching at the sight of all that manly goodness. Lord, the guy was sexy as hell.

And shocked as hell, judging by the way those piercing blue eyes widened when he spotted her.

Recognition splashed across his face, and his voice came out in a startled rasp. "Oh. Hi."

She met his gaze, her mouth drier than a desert. "Hi."

Carson swung his head from her to Cash. "Do you two know each other?"

After a moment of hesitation, during which Jen transmitted a silent warning with her eyes, Cash visibly swallowed and turned to her brother. "No. I was just...I, ah..." He stuck out a hand in her direction. "It's nice to meet you, Jenny."

"Jen," she corrected, moving forward to shake his hand.

The second their palms touched, heat seared into her like a bolt of lightning, spreading through her body and warming every inch of her skin. Their gazes locked again, and the fire inside her burned hotter, making her dizzy and breathless. Holy mother of God. She craved this man on a basic, carnal level she hadn't known existed.

Sucking in a breath, she jerked her hand back. Touching him was too big a temptation. It only intensified the crazy urge to strip him naked.

"So we're all cool with this, right?" Carson spoke, oblivious to the tension hanging in the room. "Jenny will stay here until Psycho McGee leaves town?"

Cash's gaze rested on her before turning to Carson. "Yeah, it's cool. Matt's room is all ready."

"Good." Carson focused on her. "Jenny?"

She sighed. "It's fine. But only until Brendan is gone."

Carson nodded in agreement, then picked up her suitcases. "I'll put these in Matt's room."

The second her brother disappeared, Jen cast a slightly embarrassed look in Cash's direction. "I had no idea you were the one I was coming to stay with."

"I figured," he said wryly.

An awkward silence settled between them, bringing a jolt of annoyance. She hadn't expected him to greet her with a passionate kiss or anything, but did he have to look so unhappy? As he fidgeted with his hands, his chiseled features creasing with discomfort, her self-esteem took a couple more hits. Couldn't he at least pretend to be pleased to see her?

"Jen—" he started, only to be interrupted by Carson, who sauntered back into the living room as if he had no care in the world.

Well, of course he didn't. *He* wasn't the one who had to spend the next three weeks with someone who wanted nothing to do with him. Oh no, Carson just got to drop her off, leave her in the clutches of the man she'd almost fucked, and be on his merry way.

"You're all set," Carson said. "I guess I'll head out now."

Panic flitted through her. "Now?"

"Don't worry. McCoy will take good care of you." He frowned as he turned to his teammate. "Remember what I said—she doesn't leave the house unless someone is with her. You, preferably, but any of the other guys are acceptable alternatives. Annabelle and Holly, too, since they've taken self-defense classes. But not Savannah—I don't want her corrupting my little sister."

Jen waved her hand around. "Hello? I'm right here, you know. Quit talking about me like I'm a five-year-old."

As usual, Carson ignored her. "And make sure she stays away from her usual haunts. Psycho McGee might be lurking around, waiting for her to show up."

"Got it," Cash said with a nod.

"Good. Okay, I'm out." Her brother didn't rumple her hair again, probably because he could see the murder in her eyes, but he did lean in and plant a loud smack of a kiss on her cheek. "Don't give Cash any trouble."

He strode toward the door, then paused to shoot Cash a sharp look over his shoulder. "And remember what I said, McCoy. There's a pool right downstairs."

Once Carson was gone, another silence fell over the room.

Jen studied Cash's face, wishing she could make sense of that indescribable expression. He obviously wasn't happy to see her, but she refused to spend the next three weeks tiptoeing around without clearing the air between them.

Her brows puckered into a deep frown as the silence dragged on. Finally, unable to stand it, she crossed her arms and said, "So why didn't you call?"

CHAPTER
FIVE

Cash couldn't fucking believe Jen was actually here. In his apartment. Standing right in front of him. Three steps and she'd be close enough to kiss. Twenty steps and they could be in his bed. Naked.

She's Carson's sister.

Despite the warning bells in his head, he couldn't tear his gaze off her. Those tight-fitting jeans of hers were damn sexy, but the rest of her outfit was cute and girlie. Bright yellow T-shirt. A pair of flip-flops with yellow daisies on the toes. Her blonde hair was tied in a low ponytail, and she wore no makeup except for shiny, pink lip gloss.

Cash gulped. Fuck, he wanted to kiss the gloss right off her lips. To slide his hand underneath the hem of her shirt and stroke her smooth, tanned flesh. Squeeze her firm ass. Undo her ponytail and tangle his fingers through all that golden hair.

Christ, there were so many things he wanted to do to this girl, he didn't even know which one to focus on.

But...he'd promised her brother he wouldn't touch her.

Jen's eyes darkened with displeasure. "You're just going to avoid the question?"

He blinked out of his trance. "What?"

"Why didn't you call? Not that I cried about it or anything, but I'm curious, especially since you gave me that whole speech about finishing what we started."

"I lost your number," he admitted.

She looked dubious.

"Well, technically, my phone fell in a puddle and I had to get a new one." He shook his head in aggravation. "Trust me, I wasn't too happy about that."

Her expression relaxed. "So you really planned on calling?"

"I told you I would," he said gruffly.

"Okay. Next question—why did you lie about your job?"

Discomfort curled around his spine. "Some women go a little nuts when they find out I'm a SEAL. Like the chick I was hiding from that night. So I don't always advertise what I do." He shrugged. "Sometimes I like knowing that the woman I'm with actually wants me for *me*, you know?"

She gave a slow nod. "I don't like being lied to, but I get it. I've watched girls throw themselves at my brother for years all because he's a SEAL."

They both went quiet again.

Cash raked a hand through his hair, wanting to kick something. Fuck. The universe really did hate him. Here he was, standing in front of the woman he'd been fantasizing about for days, and he wasn't allowed to touch her.

"Why do you look so pissed off?"

Her weary voice drew him from his thoughts. "I'm not pissed, I'm frustrated."

"Why?"

He bit back a groan. "Because I really want to kiss you right now."

Her eyes widened. "Oh." She swallowed. "I probably wouldn't mind if you did."

He chuckled. "Probably?"

"Fine. I wouldn't mind at all."

Their gazes locked. The air between them sizzled.

The groan he'd been holding slipped out as he remembered how good her lips had felt pressed against his own. How sweet she'd tasted.

Jen took a timid step forward.

He took a speedy step back.

"But I can't," he said flatly. "We can't get involved, Jen."

She frowned. "May I ask why?"

"Because I promised your brother I wouldn't."

Her jaw fell open. "Are you joking?"

"Dead serious. Carson made it crystal clear that I'm to keep my hands off you."

She laughed in disbelief. "And I don't get a say in it?"

Annoyance and anger had stained her cheeks red, and her eyes glittered like bright blue diamonds. She looked really fucking hot when she was pissed off. Then again, it was probably impossible for her to not look hot. Hell, she turned him on by breathing.

Fuckin' universe.

Clenching his fists at his sides, Cash cursed under his breath. "I know, okay? This sucks. Three days ago, I wanted nothing more than to tear your clothes off and—well, and, you know. But three days ago, you were Jen, the amazing girl I met at the Tavern."

She huffed out a breath. "I'm still Jen."

"Yeah—Jen, Carson's sister," he said unhappily. "Which means you're off-limits now."

She arched one eyebrow. "You're seriously going to blow me off because you're scared of my brother?"

"Yes. And I ain't too manly to admit it—your brother scares the shit outta me."

"Wow." She shook her head in amazement. "You're breaking up with me and we weren't even dating."

"I thought you said you don't date military men, anyway."

"Date them? No. But I'm not averse to sleeping with them." She smiled faintly. "Come on, cowboy, you know you want to."

Hell. He was in hell. No, scratch that—he was in the Garden of Eden, and Jen was dangling the forbidden apple under his nose.

He licked his suddenly dry lips. "I can't. I promised Carson I'd behave. In case you haven't noticed, he's ridiculously protective when it comes to you."

"He's *over*protective. And just because he's my brother doesn't mean he can dictate who I spend time with." She went quiet for a beat. "So Carson gets to dictate your life too now?"

"It's guy code," he muttered. "You don't mess around with your friend's sister, especially when that friend tells you not to. And especially when that friend isn't just a friend, but also your lieutenant. I made him a promise."

"You kind of already broke it. We almost had sex in a coatroom, remember?"

His dick twitched at the memory. He briefly closed his eyes, then opened them to pin her with a firm stare. "I promised Carson to behave," he repeated. "And I'm a man of my word."

She smirked. "You really think we can live together and be able to keep our hands off each other?"

No.

He dismissed that deviant burst of cynicism and gathered up some willpower. He was a grown man—surely he could respect his friend's wishes and keep his goddamn pants zipped. Jen might be appealing as hell, but he'd met her only three days ago. His friendship with Carson trumped three measly days.

Steeling himself against her mocking eyes, Cash smirked

right back at her. "I've got great discipline, sweetheart. I think I can keep my hormones under control."

"Really." She slanted her head. "What if I told you I like to walk around naked?"

The image caused saliva to fill his mouth. Gulping, he crossed his arms over his chest. "Then I'd politely ask you to put on some clothes."

"What if I sleepwalk in the middle of the night—naked—and wind up in your bed?"

"Then I'd carry you to *your* bed, tuck you in, and go back to my room."

"What if I want to sit in the living room and watch porn? Naked," she added.

"I'd read a book in my room until you're done, then come out and watch football."

She looked frazzled. "You sound very confident in your ability to resist my charms."

"Discipline," he reiterated.

"Is that a challenge?"

Aw, hell. This entire discussion was treading on dangerous territory.

He shrugged. "I won't deny I'm attracted to you, but I won't act on the attraction. That doesn't mean we can't be friends, though."

Friends? Christ, he was grasping at straws here. His dick was so hard it had started to tent in his pants, and Jen's gaze, of course, immediately dropped to his crotch.

"Friends," she echoed, her eyes twinkling.

He willed his semi to subside. "Why don't I show you to your room?" he suggested, desperate for a distraction. "You can unpack, and then maybe we'll grab some lunch or something." AKA, get the hell out of the apartment before he jumped her bones.

Her mouth tightened in a resigned line. "Fine. I'll unpack. But I don't want lunch. I'm kind of pissed off and the only thing that'll improve my mood right now is Choctastic Verryberry Swirl."

He gave her a blank stare.

"It's an ice cream flavor. There's a place a few blocks from here that sells it."

"You want to go out for ice cream."

"Yes." Those delicate eyebrows lifted in another challenge. "That's what friends do, no? Go out for ice cream, have a friendly conversation, walk down the sidewalk while keeping a respectable friend distance between each other."

"Yeah, I guess that's what friends do," he said lightly. "Come on, your new room awaits."

They were two steps to the hallway when his phone rang. Sliding it out of his pocket, he saw Dylan's name flashing on the screen.

He was about to ignore the call, but Jen stopped him. "Answer it. I think I can manage unpacking by myself."

Frustration gathered in his chest as she flounced off. He brought the phone to his ear and said, "Hey, man. Now's really not a good time."

"Why? Are you washing your hair?"

"Yes, that's exactly what I'm doing."

Dylan laughed. "Seriously, why do you sound so weird?"

"I'm about to take my new houseguest out for some Choctastic Verryberry Swirl."

"I don't know what that means. Is that a code?" Dylan paused. "Are you being held hostage and this is your way of signaling me? Blink twice for yes."

"How's that going to work? You can't see me, asshole." Cash shook his head, unable to contain his amusement. Life was never boring with Dylan Wade around. "And I'm not being held hostage. I really am going out for ice cream with my new roomie."

"O'Connor moved out?"

"Short-term. He's giving up his room so Carson's sister has a place to stay."

"The LT's sister is staying with you?" Dylan sounded mystified. "Why?"

"Long story." He shot a quick look at the empty hallway, then lowered his voice. "This is bad, man. Like really, really bad."

"Oh, I get it—total cockblock, huh? You can't exactly bring chicks home and parade them in front of the LT's sister." Dylan made a sympathetic noise. "And speaking of chicks, did you ever track down that girl? The one you met at the bar?"

A hysterical laugh bubbled in his throat. "It's her."

"It's who?"

"Carson's sister. *She's* the girl from the bar."

A beat of silence. Then his friend began to laugh. "Seriously?"

"Seriously," Cash said glumly.

"That's awesome. See, I told you everything would work itself out."

"This isn't awesome. It's a total fucking disaster."

"Didn't you tell me how badly you wanted to hook up with her?" Dylan reminded him. "And now she's crashing at your place? Dude. Forget about the ice cream and bang her instead."

"I can't."

"Okay, I have to ask this again—are you being held hostage? This whole conversation is confusing me."

"I can't sleep with her. Carson said she's off-limits." He sighed. "The threat of drowning may have been involved too."

A soft whistle filled the line. "The LT threatened to drown you?"

"Yup." Cash chewed on the inside of his cheek. "But he was just messing with me, right? He probably wouldn't care if I hooked up with his sister, right?"

"No, he really will kill you," Dylan said matter-of-factly. "Trust me. One time he caught me flirting with Holly and threatened to clock me if I ever did it again. But you know me, I totally did it again. It took two weeks for the swelling in my eye to go down."

"Wait, you got that shiner from Carson? You told us some loser sucker-punched you at a bar."

"I lied." Dylan's normally lazy voice turned serious. "If Carson said hands off, then listen to him. You know what they say about playing with fire..."

"Yeah, yeah, you get burned."

"No, you get drowned." With a hearty laugh, Dylan hung up.

CHAPTER SIX

Un-freaking-believable.

Jen snuck a sidelong look at Cash as he parked his SUV at the curb in front of the ice cream parlor. The entire ride over, he'd been making idle conversation and acting like they were nothing but a pair of buddies going out for ice cream.

It was disconcerting to realize he hadn't been kidding about keeping things platonic between them. Not that she was some sex-crazed nympho who couldn't keep her pants on, but come on. Their chemistry at the Tavern had nearly set the place on fire. And she hadn't missed the tent situation under his pants earlier. An entire Boy Scout troop could've camped under there.

At least he wasn't denying the chemistry between them. His admission that he wanted her had been a definite ego boost... until he announced that he wouldn't be acting on that attraction.

Because of her *brother*.

And you're surprised because...?

True. Why *was* she surprised? Carson had been doing the whole macho big-brother bullshit her entire life. He'd scared away more potential boyfriends than she could count. He'd ruined her first kiss by bursting onto the porch, pulling Ben Sampson off her mid-liplock, and ordering Ben to keep his tongue in his own mouth. And who could forget prom night, when Carson guaranteed she wouldn't lose her virginity by informing her date of all the ways he could kill a man thanks to his military training.

And then, when she'd finally lost her virginity to Kyle Parker, Carson was the one who sent Kyle running afterward by giving him a speech about condoms and threatening to drown him if he knocked her up.

To *drown* him. Who threatened to drown people, for Pete's sake?

And now her brother had gotten to Cash, the only guy who'd ever managed to arouse her by merely breathing.

Sure, Cash's military status squashed any notion of something long-lasting between them, but that didn't mean they couldn't indulge in a little fling as long as they were living together. She got the feeling that sleeping with Cash would be a whole new experience, an introduction to the kind of sex she'd always craved. Wild, passionate, uninhibited.

But Carson had officially thrown yet another wrench in her love life.

"So you weren't kidding the other day when you mentioned a crazy ex," Cash remarked.

"I never kid about stalkers," she said glumly.

A bell dinged as they walked through the door of the ice cream parlor. Jen made a beeline for the counter and ordered without glancing at the menu posted on the wall. "Two scoops of Choctastic Verryberry Swirl in a waffle cone, please," she told the pimply-faced kid who greeted her. "And a to-go gallon of the same flavor."

Cash whistled. "As your friend, I should warn you that all that ice cream can't be good for your figure."

She bestowed him a sweet smile. "As the woman you refuse to sleep with, I should tell you that my figure is none of your concern."

The kid behind the counter coughed and averted his eyes. "Um. What can I get you?" he asked Cash in a squeaky pubescent voice.

"Double scoop of rocky road. Waffle cone."

After they paid for their cones and stepped outside, Jen headed for the wooden bench out front, but Cash took her arm and led her back to the SUV. "We'll sit in the car," he announced.

"We can't eat ice cream in your air-conditioned car. You're supposed to eat ice cream outside, where it's hot and sunny and the *cold* ice cream hits the spot."

Unfazed, he dragged her to the passenger door. "Considering your knowledge of obscure ice cream flavors, you probably come to this place a lot. Which means Psycho McGee probably knows that. Which means he might be lurking in the bushes. Ergo, get in the fucking car."

Lord, his hand felt like a steel band around her forearm. This man was *strong*.

More than a little annoyed at being manhandled, Jen reluctantly got in the SUV, frowning when Cash slammed her door and rounded the vehicle. He slid in next to her without a word and focused on his waffle cone.

Her gaze followed the movements of his tongue. Gosh, look at him go. Lick. Swirl. Flick. Her thighs clenched together as she imagined that tongue working between her legs with the same focused precision.

Plop.

She squeaked when something cold landed between her

breasts. Great. Her ice cream was melting.

A second later, Cash shoved a paper napkin in her direction.

Shrugging away his hand, she curved her lips in an impish smile. "I got it."

She dipped her finger into her cleavage, swiped at the ice cream, and brought her finger to her mouth.

Cash made a hissing sound as she licked her finger clean.

"So, out of curiosity, how many female friends do you have?" she asked.

His expression turned stony. "None. How many stalkers do you have?"

"Just the one," she said cheerfully. She licked the side of her cone before another drop of melting ice cream slid off.

From the corner of her eye, she saw that the tables had turned. Cash was now watching her, his vivid blue eyes glued to her mouth. Deciding to milk it for all she was worth, she licked her ice cream until she heard that sexy little hissing sound again.

She met his eyes. "Everything okay?"

"Yes," he said stiffly. "So...uh...how'd you hook up with Psycho McGee anyway?"

"He came into my store to buy his mother a locket." She lapped at the top of the cone, then rubbed her lips over the cold cream. "Gosh, this is so good. Wanna taste?"

Licking her lips, she stuck out her cone.

Cash stared at it as if it carried the Ebola virus. "No thanks."

"Suit yourself," she said, shrugging as she went back to diligent licking.

The temperature in the SUV spiked. The sound of crunching filled the air as Cash polished off his cone with impressive speed. The second he swallowed the last bite, he wiped his hands and mouth with a napkin and abruptly started the engine.

"That was fun," he said in an overly cheerful voice. "We should do this again sometime."

She rolled her eyes as he practically burned rubber pulling away from the curb. So he didn't enjoy a little harmless teasing. Too bad, because he deserved it. It bugged her how he could so easily give in to her brother's demands. That he was actually willing to shove her in the friend zone all because his commanding officer told him to.

As frustration boiled in her belly, Jen focused on her cone, wishing she weren't so damn attracted to the man sitting beside her. But he was just so...hot. And he smelled terrific—the scent of his woodsy aftershave kept wafting into her nose and giving her a head rush.

"Four months," Cash finally said, bringing the conversation back to Brendan. "When did you realize he was nuts?"

"Just in the last month or so. There were little red flags at the beginning, but they got bigger and more noticeable toward the end. Like, when he started texting me every hour." She shook her head, the arousal in her body fizzling as memories of Brendan crept in. "And if I didn't respond, he'd call and demand to know where I was and what I was doing."

"Sounds fun."

"Yeah, real fun. Clingy and possessive are deal-breakers for me when it comes to relationships."

"No kidding."

"Once he showed me that side of himself, I knew I had to end it, so when he told me he was being transferred, it gave me the perfect opportunity to break it off. He tried convincing me to have a long-distance relationship, but I held my ground and told him it was over."

"And he didn't take it too well," Cash filled in.

"Nope. He caused a huge scene at the restaurant, cursing and yelling, which was embarrassing as hell, by the way. I figured he'd cool down in a few days and get over it, but he didn't. He started sending me long, desperate emails, and lots of texts and DMs begging me for another chance. He had flowers delivered to my apartment every day for a week. Finally I called him and told him to stop, making it clear that it was *over*." She paused. "He didn't like that one bit."

Cash's jaw went stiff. "Carson said he attacked you."

"He grabbed me," she admitted. "I was at a club with my friend Tessa and he followed us there. When we were leaving, Tessa was on the sidewalk hailing a cab, and Brendan just appeared out of nowhere. He grabbed my arm and begged for another chance, and when I told him to leave me alone, he shook my shoulders and started yelling." Jen had to grin. "I kicked him in the balls and dove into the cab."

"Good girl." Cash's eyes glimmered with approval.

She popped the last piece of waffle cone into her mouth and chewed slowly. "The next day, Brendan showed up at the jewelry store with flowers and apologized. I told him for the hundredth time that it was really over, and he seemed to accept it. But he kept up with the emails and texts, which only got angrier and creepier. Then he started leaving handwritten notes in my mailbox." Her chest tightened with anger. "But the last straw was breaking into my apartment. Did Carson tell you about the rose petals?"

Cash nodded.

"How freaking creepy is that?"

She still remembered the fear shuddering through her veins when she'd walked through the door and found the trail of crimson petals. Rather than follow it to her bedroom, she'd raced into the kitchen and grabbed a butcher knife. Then she'd called the cops and her brother, and waited out in the hall until help arrived.

Fortunately, the apartment had been empty, save for the

roses and the note Brendan had left on her pillow. She ended up spending the night with Carson and her sister-in-law, and the next morning Carson drove her to the station to file the restraining order.

"I can't believe I didn't see what a psycho he was," she grumbled. "I must be the biggest idiot on the planet."

"You're not an idiot. Guys like that know how to manipulate people. They wear this perfect mask to lure you in, and once they have you, they drop the mask and let their inner crazy shine."

His reassurance bolstered her spirits, as did the lack of pity on his face. She hated being pitied, which happened a lot in her family. Each time she failed at a job or admitted she hadn't found her life's direction yet, her parents stared at her with those big pitying eyes and made her feel like an even bigger failure.

They reached Cash's building a few minutes later and hopped out of the car. Jen glanced up at the cloudless blue sky and let the sun's rays heat her face, enjoying the balmy breeze that lifted her ponytail and tickled the nape of her neck. The one good thing about getting fired was that she didn't have to spend the afternoon indoors, stuck behind a jewelry counter. But if she wanted to keep her apartment—and her independence—she'd have to start combing the job ads and find work ASAP.

"Let's sit by the pool," she suggested. "I'm not ready to go in yet."

"Sure, but we should probably take this upstairs first." He held up the gallon of ice cream that had been sitting in the backseat.

After a quick trip up to the apartment, they emerged onto the manicured grass in the back. A rectangular pool sat in the center of the sprawling lawn, surrounded by a concrete deck offering white lounge chairs and tables topped with red-and-blue umbrellas. Despite the great weather, the pool was devoid of swimmers. They had the area to themselves as they approached the deck.

"You look relieved to not be going inside," she remarked.

His eyes became veiled. "I like the outdoors. And it's a nice day."

She fought laughter. "Know what I think? I think you're worried that if we're inside, in close quarters, your trusty discipline might fail you."

He mumbled something unintelligible.

She kicked off her flip-flops and rolled up the bottom of her jeans, then sat by the ladder next to the deep end and shoved her bare feet in the water. Cash did the same, leaving his sneakers on the grass as he joined her.

"Why don't you have any platonic female friends?" she asked, tilting her head toward him.

"I've always been more of a guy's guy." He shrugged in a seriously adorable way. "Talking to women isn't my strong suit."

She grinned. "So you can hit on women, but you can't talk to them?"

Adorable shrug number two. "Everything leading up to sex is easy. During sex is a piece of cake too. Everything after sex? It's like walking through a minefield. I mean, why can't I just tell you that a certain outfit looks bad? Or that *Grey's Anatomy* sucks? Why do I have to recite a whole bunch of little white lies and play all those games?"

"I hate games," she agreed. "Say what you mean, mean what you say. That's how I roll."

"Good to know, bro."

Jen laughed. "Look at you, you're doing just fine talking to me. Honest, cute, joking." She raised her eyebrows. "Or is it easy for you because this is all leading up to sex?"

He scowled. "We're not going to have sex."

"Right, because you took an oath. Hey, did Carson make you sign the oath in blood?" When his scowl deepened, she simply laughed again. "Fine, I'll stop. Let's keep doing the friend thing." She paused in thought. "So what's up with the name Cash?"

"What do you mean?"

"I mean, what made your parents decide to name you after money?"

"Can we change the subject?"

She furrowed her brows. "Wait, you mean there's actually a story behind your name? I was just passive-aggressively making fun of you."

"Gee, thanks."

Her curiosity was piqued. "I want to hear the story."

"No."

"Please?"

"Don't bat your eyelashes at me like that. That move might work on other guys, but—oh, Jesus, are you crying? Damn it. Fine, I'll tell you. Just stop crying."

She blinked rapidly to clear the moisture in her eyes and offered a broad smile. "Great, can't wait to hear it."

Cash looked betrayed. "Those were fake tears?"

"I can cry on command," she confessed. "Used to work wonders when I was a kid, but once my family caught on, the trick ended up backfiring. Like when I was fourteen, I took gymnastics—yet another pointless activity I absolutely sucked at—and I broke my arm falling off the uneven bars during a meet. My parents saw the tears and thought I was faking. It took thirty minutes, while I was in excruciating pain, mind you, to convince them I was actually injured."

Cash threw his head back and laughed. "I don't even feel bad for you. It's not cool, manipulating people like that."

"Duh. That's why I don't do it anymore."

"You just did," he shot back.

"Because you were being difficult," she said defensively. "I want to know about your name."

"Fine, but no passive-aggressive commentary."

"Deal."

He leaned on his elbows and tipped his head up to the sky. The pose was casual, but hot as hell. His biceps bulged in the most delectable way. The tilt of his head revealed the strong tendons of his throat and the stubble shadowing his square jaw. Why hadn't she noticed he had a tiny cleft in his chin? Gosh, she wanted to lick that spot with her tongue. And then lick the masculine curve of his jaw. And that hard chest and mouthwatering six-pack. And—okay, she pretty much wanted to lick every inch of Cash McCoy's body.

Dragging her mind out of the gutter, she mimicked his pose and fell back on her elbows. "I'm waiting..."

He shifted his gaze toward her. "Short version? My parents found out they won the lottery five minutes before my mom was about to have an abortion."

Jen's jaw dropped. "Are you serious?"

"Yup." A self-deprecating smile lifted his mouth. "Fetus-me was gonna be aborted, even though my parents constantly assure me that they loved me and were devastated that they couldn't keep me."

"Why couldn't they?"

"Mom was sixteen, Dad was two years older. They both came from bad homes, ran away together, and were living in a rundown trailer outside of Phoenix when my mom got pregnant. They had about ten dollars in the bank. Dad just lost his job flipping burgers at some fast food place, and Mom dropped out of high school to help pay the bills."

"Sounds tough," Jen said sympathetically.

"They were in no position to have a kid. Even carrying the baby and giving it up for adoption would've been hard. They had no money to pay for food, let alone medical bills. So yeah, they made a hard choice."

She studied his chiseled profile, but he didn't look upset about the decision his parents had made.

"Anyway, once my dad turned eighteen, he started buying lottery tickets. He figured their situation couldn't get any worse than it already was, so he shelled out two bucks a week, and every week they didn't win a damn thing." Cash grinned. "So they're sitting there in the waiting room of the clinic and the TV's on. The news is replaying the winning numbers from the night before, and Dad realizes he forgot to check his ticket. So he pulls it out and what do you know—he's won the jackpot."

She stared at him in amazement. "You're joking."

"Dead serious. They won ten million dollars."

"Ten million! Holy shit."

"Mom decided it was a sign from God telling them to keep me. She says he knew they needed cash and so he graciously gave them some. That's why they named me Cash."

"Wow. I can't believe that's a true story. It sounds like the plot of one of those feel-good movies."

He rolled his eyes. "Your turn. Why'd your parents name you Jennifer?"

"It's my mom's middle name."

"That's it? That's the story?"

"Gee, Cash, I'm sorry the origins of my name aren't to your liking."

A familiar voice interrupted before he could respond. "Jen!"

Squinting, Jen looked up and spotted Annabelle Holmes waving at her from a third-floor balcony.

"Stay there. We're coming down," Annabelle called before disappearing from view.

Cash looked surprised for a moment. "You know Annabelle?" He quickly answered his own question. "Wait, of course you do. You probably know her better than I do, huh? Evans, too."

"Yeah, Annabelle's awesome. But I don't know Ryan as well as some of the others. I'm probably closest with John Garrett and Will Charleston since they're my brother's BFFs. Do you know them? Neither of them is active duty anymore, but I'm sure you've at least heard of them."

"Will was one of my instructors during BUD/S training," he answered. "And Garrett hosts poker night every now and then, but we're not close."

"You're missing out. He's hot."

Cash snorted. "How am I missing out?"

She pictured John Garrett's soulful brown eyes and ripped body, and a little shiver danced up her spine. "Because he's... well, hot," she said again. "I had the biggest crush on him when I was a teenager. He was eight years older and completely unattainable. Treated me like a pesky little sister, and then, by the time I was old enough to catch his eye, he'd turned into a manwhore and had enough threesomes with my brother that hooking up with him would've felt like hooking up with Carson."

She suddenly noticed that Cash's expression had hardened, almost as if he was...jealous? Because she'd admitted to having a crush on someone else when she was younger?

Before she could ask, the back doors of the building swung open and Annabelle emerged, looking gorgeous and relaxed in a print sundress and sandals. Ryan Evans tailed his girlfriend, his tall, muscular frame clad in bright blue surf shorts and a black wife-beater.

"Hey," Annabelle said happily as Jen stood to greet her. The two of them hugged, while Ryan reached out to tap fists with

Cash. "Carson said you were moving in today. He ordered us to make you feel welcome."

Jen frowned. "He specifically called you to tell you that?"

Annabelle snickered. "He called everyone."

"Conferenced us all in this morning," Ryan piped up.

"He held a *conference* call?" Jen said in disbelief.

"Everyone was on the line," Annabelle confirmed with a grin. "Even Garrett and Will."

Ryan laughed. "It was like a high school reunion over the phone."

Wow. Her brother was *really* taking this Brendan thing seriously. Sweet as it was, she couldn't fight the urge to strangle him.

"Anyway, we wanted to have you over for dinner this week," Annabelle said. She glanced at Cash. "You too, Cash."

"We'll be there," he answered. "Thanks for the invite."

"You're welcome. Now, shoo, both of you," Annabelle said, dismissing the men with the wave of a hand. "I want to talk to Jen alone."

Ryan rolled his eyes. "Where exactly do you want us to go?"

She waved her hand again. "I don't know. Over there. Out of earshot."

Jen hid a grin as the two guys lumbered off toward the shallow end of the pool.

"Yeah, I'm thinking of dumping her," they heard Ryan say loudly. "She's incredibly bossy."

Annabelle ignored her boyfriend's taunt and flopped down on one of the lounge chairs. "Sit. I need to ask you something."

Intrigued, Jen sat on the neighboring chair and met Annabelle's concerned brown eyes. "What's going on?"

"That's what I wanted to ask you. Are you seriously in danger from this Brendan guy?"

Jen sighed. "I don't think so. His creep levels are high, but I think the messages will stop once he leaves town. He's being transferred to Oakland at the end of the month."

"Yeah, Carson mentioned that." Annabelle's expression turned shrewd. "Are you just saying this so nobody will worry? Because if you believe this guy might actually go *American Psycho* on you, you need to say something."

"I'm not just saying it. Brendan is weird and clingy, and yes, he did get aggressive one time, but I don't think he's capable of anything extreme. He's got a good position at his investment firm and there's no way he'd risk throwing away his career. Success is important to him."

Annabelle relaxed. "Okay. But if you feel like you're in real danger, don't brush it off. Tell Cash, or Carson, or Ryan. Don't think that a restraining order means you're protected."

"I promise I'll tell someone if I feel like I'm in danger."

"Good." Annabelle ran a hand through her dark hair. "Now I'm going to be extra nosy and ask you something else."

"Um...okay?"

"What's going on with Holly and your brother?"

"What are you talking about?" Jen asked in confusion.

"The arguments... Holly staying with her sister...?"

"What?"

The other woman instantly backpedaled. "Nothing. Forget I said anything."

"Wait a minute, you can't just say something like that and ask me to forget it. What do you mean Holly is staying with her sister?"

And why the hell didn't Jen know about it? She'd seen her brother several times this week and not once had he mentioned that he and his wife might be having problems. Granted, he hadn't offered to let her stay at *his* place, but she'd figured that was because Carson and Holly's apartment only had one bedroom. Sleeping on a couch for a month wasn't Jen's idea of a good time. She'd assumed her brother had dumped her on Cash out of a sense of decency, so she'd have a real bedroom and some actual privacy.

But had he done it for another reason? Made her stay with Cash so she wouldn't find out about the rocky state of his relationship?

"What do you know?" she demanded.

"Not much. Holly won't talk about it, and whenever I ask, she says everything is fine. But I know she's lying. I caught her crying after the wedding we planned last weekend, but she chalked it up to nostalgia and said it reminded her of her and Carson's wedding."

"You said they were fighting?"

"Ry and Matt heard them arguing last week when they showed up early for poker night. And I overheard Holly fighting with Carson over the phone when I went by the restaurant to have lunch with her a couple of days ago. That's when she told me she'd stayed with her sister the other night. She admitted they've both been really busy and on edge lately, and she claims they needed some breathing room." Annabelle shook her head. "Why on earth would they need breathing room when he's been gone for the past six months?"

Jen absorbed the information, wondering if she ought to be worried. It was true, her brother and sister-in-law did lead busy lives. Holly spent five days a week working at a five-star restaurant, as well as co-owned an event planning and catering company with Annabelle. The business ate up a lot of their weekends, and several weeknights now that the venture had gained more recognition. Carson, meanwhile, was a SEAL, which not only meant lengthy deployments every other year, but that he was forever on call, ready to get on a chopper at a minute's notice and often gone for weeks or months at a time with no way to contact his wife.

The long absences had the power to destroy a relationship—which was precisely why Jen shied away from military men. Growing up, her father had been a complete stranger to her; he was the strict, taciturn man who made an appearance whenever his tour of duty ended. Her mother had shouldered the burden of raising Jen and Carson alone, while working as a full-time nurse.

Watching her mom struggle and seeing her parents attempt to reconnect each time her dad came home had cemented Jen's decision to avoid that kind of relationship. She wanted a partner in every sense of the word, a man who'd be there day in and day out, not one who'd hand all the responsibilities to her while he went off to fight for his country.

It troubled her to hear that Carson and Holly were having problems. Those two had a strong, loving marriage, but even the strongest and most loving marriages could buckle under the pressure.

"I didn't know anything about it," Jen admitted. "But then again, nobody in my family tells me anything."

"Well, if you get a chance, talk to Holly, okay? She won't confide in me or Shelby or anyone else. Savannah thinks we should have a girls' night next week and pry the truth out of her."

"Count me in."

"I'll text you the details when I know them. But if you talk to her before then, see what you can find out."

"I will."

When male laughter met her ears, Jen's gaze drifted over to Cash and Ryan, who were chortling about something at the other end of the pool. It suddenly occurred to her just how much they resembled each other. They both had dark brown hair, blue eyes, the same muscular body type. They could easily pass for brothers, yet while she found Ryan attractive, the sight of him didn't elicit the same rush of desire she felt when looking at Cash.

Annabelle followed her gaze and smiled coyly. "How do you like Cash?"

She didn't bother coming up with an offhand reply; she got the feeling her sexual longing was written all over her face. "What do you think?" she answered in a wry voice.

"He's yummy, right? This one time, I suggested we invite him to have a threesome, but Ryan said no way." Annabelle's voice lowered to an amused whisper. "I think he's scared that Cash might have more stamina than him or something. Ever since Ry turned thirty, he's all paranoid about his manhood. Personally, I think a threesome would only benefit him. You know, force him to up his game."

Jen hoped the other woman couldn't see the blush on her cheeks. But jeez. Was she the only person on the planet who'd never indulged in a threesome? Envy burned in her belly. Seemed like pretty much everyone she knew got to experience the kind of sex she'd always dreamed about. Hot, kinky, exciting.

She cast another look at Cash, annoyance creeping up her spine. He was laughing at something Ryan had said, looking sexy as all get out with his T-shirt clinging to his washboard abs and perfectly defined pecs. Bastard, depriving her of all that sexiness.

She turned back to find Annabelle grinning at her. "Ha! You *do* want him. And bad, from the look of it. It sucks about Carson's ruling, doesn't it?"

Jen narrowed her eyes. "What do you mean?"

"Carson mentioned in the conference call that Cash has been ordered to keep his hands off you." Along with sympathy, barely restrained humor danced in Annabelle's expression.

Jen was outraged. "Oh my God. He actually told everyone that?"

"Yep."

"I'm going to kill him one day."

"Not sure I'd blame you. The way he talks about you, you're all of twelve years old. I don't think he realizes you're practically the same age as his wife."

True. Holly was only three years older than her, now that she thought about it.

Annabelle waved a hand again. "My advice? You want Cash, go for it. Life's too short to not go after what you want."

"Good advice, except that Cash has decided we're just friends. He keeps bragging about his formidable discipline."

The brunette snorted. "He's been undressing you with his eyes for the past twenty minutes. One little push and you'll have that boy in your bed."

Jen shifted her head. Sure enough, Cash's hot, hungry gaze was glued to her, even as he continued to chuckle and shoot the shit with Ryan.

Did she have the guts to follow Annabelle's advice, though? To go for it?

Why not?

Yeah, why not? Things would be different if Cash wasn't interested, but she knew he was. And she'd be a fool to pass up the chance to sleep with the guy. She'd yet to meet a man she could explore her sexuality with, and she knew without a doubt that Cash McCoy would be up for anything.

So what if Carson had laid down the law? Annabelle was right. One little push and Cash's resolve would collapse like a house of straw.

"What kind of push?" Jen asked.

Annabelle stared at her.

"What?" she said defensively. "You brought it up. You can't go all judgmental on me now."

"I'm not being judgmental. I'm just shocked. Have you

looked in the mirror? You're gorgeous. Are you telling me you don't know how to seduce a man?"

She gulped down a lump of insecurity. "I don't have much experience in seduction."

"Carson will be glad to hear that," Annabelle said dryly. "But seriously, how can you not have men wrapped around your little finger?"

She shrugged awkwardly. "I guess I do. Kind of, anyway. I get hit on a lot, but..." She blushed. "I've only slept with three guys and they were the ones who did the seducing."

And they'd all disappointed her colossally in the bedroom. She didn't have anything against slow, tender lovemaking, but sometimes a girl just needed...well, to be *fucked*, damn it.

"Trust me, it'll be a piece of cake," Annabelle said confidently. "Just utilize the three S's—skimpy clothing, subtle touches and sexual innuendo."

She had to laugh. "That's it?"

"That's it. Cash won't be able to resist you."

"What about bros before hoes?"

"Yeah, the bro loyalty might slow you down, I'm not gonna lie. But you just have to keep cranking up the heat until he's feeling so hot all he'll be able to think is, *Carson who?*"

Jen pursed her lips in thought. Okay. That didn't sound too difficult.

She glanced over and found Cash's eyes focused on her. She didn't miss the brief flicker of desire before his expression went shuttered. As he broke the eye contact, she felt a smile tugging on the corners of her mouth. So...Cash McCoy was convinced he could keep his hands off her?

Fine, well, let him try.

She was officially putting his discipline to the test. And once she was through with him, his hands were going to be *all* over her.

CHAPTER SEVEN

What kind of self-respecting woman ate pizza in her underwear? Any meal, for that matter. There was a reason restaurants had a dress code—food was meant to be eaten while *clothed*. Come to think of it, that should be a law, Cash decided. He made a mental note to write his local congressman about it.

As he inwardly stewed, he kept his gaze focused on *The Office* rerun playing on the TV, refusing to let Jen see how much she affected him. They sat on opposite ends of the couch, with the pizza box on the cushions between them, yet she was still too damn close for comfort. From the corner of his eye, he saw her graceful throat working as she chewed and swallowed her slice. When she reached for the beer bottle on the coffee table, his peripheral vision honed in on the side of one full breast.

Jesus. This girl would be the death of him. When she'd strolled into the living room in a black sports bra and tiny green boy shorts, his eyes nearly popped out of their sockets. He'd casually suggested that she might be more comfortable if she had more clothes on, but she'd laughed and told him this was what she always wore around the house. Her relaxing outfit, she'd called it. Then she'd released her hair from her ponytail and all those tousled, honey-blond waves cascaded over her shoulders and halfway down her back, making her look like a golden goddess.

He'd been trying valiantly not to ogle her—or touch her—all evening, but it was only eight o'clock and he was running out of willpower. If he retreated to his bedroom claiming he planned on turning in, she'd see right through him—and know that his so-called discipline was failing him big-time. Which meant he had to stick it out. Watch TV, make small talk during commercials, maybe have another beer or two.

He could totally do this. As long as he avoided eye contact and kept the conversation neutral he'd get through this night, no problem.

And what about the other twenty or so nights?

Cash promptly silenced his inner Negative Nancy. He just had to take a page out of the Alcoholics Anonymous book. One day at a time. The next three weeks would fly by as long as he kept his cool.

"I can't eat another bite," Jen said with a satisfied groan. She grabbed a napkin from the table and demurely wiped the corners of her mouth like she was the queen of England.

Though he highly doubted the queen of England wore her fucking underwear to dinner.

"Thanks for treating," she added. "I'll get dinner tomorrow."

"Sure," he agreed, wincing at the hoarse note in his voice.

He concentrated on the television again and pretended to care about the antics of Steve Carell and the rest of the cast, but when another commercial break came on, he had no choice but to glance over at Jen and wait for the next round of neutral small talk.

When he glimpsed the thoughtful light in those big blue

eyes, he started to get a bad feeling. Gulping, he picked up his beer and took a long swig.

"So what's your favorite sexual position?"

Cash choked mid-sip.

Coughing, he put the bottle on the table and gawked at her. "Excuse me?"

"Your favorite sexual position," she repeated.

He gritted his teeth. "I'm not telling you that. It's inappropriate subject matter for two people who won't be having sex."

"Friends talk about stuff like that. Me and Tessa do it all the time."

He gave a stubborn shake of the head. "No way."

"Come on," she cajoled. "Let me guess, it's doggy-style, right? You totally seem like the doggy-style kinda guy."

His jaw started to hurt, he was grinding his teeth so hard. "I know what you're doing, *Jenny*, and it ain't gonna work."

Her expression epitomized innocence. "I'm just trying to get to know you. As a friend."

"You want to get to know me? Ask me what my favorite color is, or my favorite movie." He answered before she could say a word. "Black. *Die Hard*. There, sharing time is over."

"My favorite position is missionary," she said, ignoring him. "Very vanilla of me, I guess, but I think there's a deeper intimacy there. Oh, and when the guy's on top, it's easier for me to come because his pelvis rubs against my clit—"

"Jesus!" Cash interrupted.

Too late. Her words had sent an onslaught of images into his head and now all he could picture was Jen's perfect body writhing beneath him as his stupid pelvis stroked her clit with every thrust of his cock. His very hard cock. Like the hard cock pushing against his shorts at the moment.

Breathing sharply through his nose, he ordered the erection to retreat. When it didn't, he had to wait for Jen to lean forward to set her beer on the table before he made a subtle rearrangement down below. From the smirk she shot him, he knew she'd noticed what he'd done.

"You really won't tell me your favorite position?" she prompted.

"Nope."

"Okay. I'll just keep guessing then." She lifted her knees and sat cross-legged on the couch, her hair falling over one shoulder. "I'm thinking missionary-ish, except you're on your knees and the chick's ankles are up on your shoulders so you can drive deeper—"

"Girl on top," he burst out.

"Huh. Really?"

Cash clenched his jaw. "Yes."

"Why?"

Because there was nothing hotter than watching a pair of sexy tits swaying as their owner rode him like a cowgirl...

He bit back the response, shoved away the new swarm of dirty images, and glared at her. "Just because." Then he picked up his bottle and drained the whole damn thing.

"Have you ever been in a threesome? I haven't," she said matter-of-factly.

Cash briefly closed his eyes. Would it be rude if he excused himself and spent the rest of the night jacking off in the shower?

Probably.

"Well, have you?" the relentless blonde pushed when he didn't respond.

He sighed. "Yes."

Was that disappointment in her eyes? He studied her closer. Oh hell, it *was*. And he couldn't explain the rush of unhappiness that flooded his gut at the thought of this woman being disappointed in him.

But wait... There was a spark of jealousy there too.

Oh brother. She wasn't disappointed in *him,* but over the fact that she'd never experienced a ménage.

Jen tipped her head to the side. "You, another guy and a girl, or two girls and you?" Her eyes widened. "Oooh, or maybe you and two guys? *That* would be hot."

"Me, guy, girl." His voice was as stiff as his cock.

"What's it like?" she asked curiously.

God help him.

"I'm not talking about this anymore," he muttered.

"Pretty amazing, I bet," she mused, tucking a strand of hair behind her ear. "I've always wondered what being with two men would feel like. Two sets of hands on my body, two mouths and tongues and—"

Cash shot to his feet. "I feel like another beer. You?"

He heard her chuckling as he sprinted to the kitchen, where he threw open the fridge door and shoved his head into the cold space, hoping the chill would ease the hot throbbing in his body. The woman was tormenting him. On purpose. And judging from the laughter that continued to trickle behind him, she was enjoying every second of it.

He grabbed two longnecks from the bottom shelf and shut the refrigerator.

Damn it. He had to gain the upper hand here. Find a way to get Jen to back off. Because if he didn't, he was in real danger of succumbing to temptation and fucking this girl until neither of them could walk properly for days.

"Here," he said, thrusting a fresh beer in her direction.

"Thanks."

He sat down and twisted off the cap.

"Anyway, back to the subject of threesomes," Jen said. "Who's your go-to threeway buddy? Carson had Garrett before they both got married, and I hear all sorts of rumors about Ryan and Matt. So who's your wingman?"

Christ, this chick was tenacious. Did she think if she kept talking about sex she'd get him so turned on he wouldn't be able to control himself around her?

A thought suddenly occurred to him. Why couldn't he play the same game? Except instead of turning her on, he'd turn her *off*. If she didn't want to jump his bones anymore, then he'd finally be able to breathe easy.

"Dylan Wade," Cash said, lifting his beer to his lips.

Interest flickered in her eyes.

Honest-to-God interest.

"Dylan Wade. That's your threesome buddy?"

"Yep."

"Is he hot?"

"Women seem to think so." He shot her a pointed look. "The one we hooked up with yesterday wasn't complaining."

Jen's eyebrows soared. "Yesterday? You had a threesome *yesterday*?"

Relief trickled through him. Good. Perfect. Now she would view him as some huge manwhore, back off, and nobody would get drowned courtesy of Carson Scott.

"Was it good?"

For the love of...

He whirled his gaze to her, bewildered by the equal parts curiosity and arousal shining in her eyes. "It doesn't piss you off that I was with another woman yesterday?"

"Why should it? We didn't vow our undying love to each other before we parted ways at the bar. A man has needs, right?"

He ignored the throbbing down below. Yeah, a man had needs, all right.

"Anyway, was the threesome good? Did she like it?"

Cash let out a strangled groan. "Yes, she liked it. She loved it. So did Dylan. So did I—" Except for that one moment when he'd been fantasizing about Jen, but he kept that tidbit to himself. "We all had a great time, orgasms all around, and then I bid them adieu and left." Sarcasm dripped from his words.

There was a beat of silence.

"How long are you going to hold out on me?" Jen asked with a sigh.

He scowled at her. "Forever."

"Forever's a long time."

"Yup."

Rolling her eyes, she stood up. "Fine. Then if you'll excuse me, I'm going to retreat to my bedroom. This discussion has gotten me hot, so I need to take care of business since you're clearly not going to be any help."

Huh?

Cash quickly pasted on an indifferent look and acted like the announcement hadn't sent a bolt of desire straight to his groin. "Have fun," he said lightly.

Her lips twitched in humor as she edged away from the sofa. "I will. And just to give you fair warning, I can be loud when I'm coming. Don't be alarmed if you hear screams."

With that, she flounced off, her bare feet slapping against the hardwood floor. A few seconds later, he heard Matt's door creak open and shut. And then...silence.

Cash staggered to his feet, busying himself with gathering the beer bottles, empty pizza box, and used napkins cluttering the coffee table.

She wasn't *really* getting herself off. She was just trying to lure him in by planting a new slew of sinful images in his head.

At least that's what he told himself before the first strains of the masturbation symphony filled the air.

Soft moans. A husky groan. He thought he heard an "Oh God" in there.

Ignore it, he told his hurting dick. *It's a trick, buddy.*

He folded up the cardboard pizza box and shoved it in the recycling bin under the sink.

"Oh!"

Cash bit the inside of his cheek and poured Jen's half-empty beer down the drain.

"Oh...oh...*ohhhhh!*"

By the time the tenth moan or so sliced through the apartment, Cash knew he was being played.

Shoulders rigid, he shut off the faucet and marched toward Matt's room. He didn't knock. Just threw the door open, crossed his arms, and glared at Jen.

She lay in the center of the bed with her head resting on the cedar headboard. In her hands was a copy of *Twilight*.

"Oh, hey, Cash," she said when she spotted him. With a broad smile, she held up the book. "Have you ever read this? Team Edward, right?"

He growled in sheer frustration and spun on his heel.

"Ah, Team Jacob," he heard her murmur.

Gritting his teeth, he strode into his bedroom, shut the door behind him, and raked both hands over his scalp.

Jesus.

It was going to be a long three weeks.

CHAPTER EIGHT

Two days later, Cash breathed a sigh of relief as he slid into the passenger side of Ryan's olive-green Jeep. It was Saturday morning. Jen was upstairs having breakfast with Annabelle, and Cash was officially allowed to relax for the next couple of hours. In fact, he couldn't wait to put some much-needed distance between him and the evil temptress named Jennifer Scott.

The damn woman had been testing his limits for the past forty-eight hours. Parading around the apartment in next to nothing. Brushing up against him in the kitchen. Talking about sex nonstop. Christ, she'd even managed to make updating her resume look hot—leaning close to her laptop in a way that emphasized the sexy curve of her spine, biting her plush bottom lip as she studied the screen.

He'd been sporting an unceasing boner for two days now. Couldn't even remember what it was like to not be hard as a rock. His daily workout hadn't helped take the edge off. Neither had his daily—fine, twice daily—jack-off session in the shower. If anything, he was even more hard up, especially since Jen had taken to taunting him whenever he stepped out of the bathroom, innocently inquiring whether he'd enjoyed himself.

Any day now, he might actually kill her.

Or fuck her.

Discipline.

"Screw discipline," he mumbled to himself.

"What was that?" Ryan asked as he steered across the Coronado Bay Bridge.

"Nothing," Cash said. "Just thinking out loud."

Ryan gave him a strange look. "Okay. Anyway, Jane wanted to know if you got her email."

"The one about Becker-approved baby gifts for Sadie?"

"That's the one," Ryan said dryly. "And before you ask, yes, I wholeheartedly agree—Beck was abducted by aliens and replaced with a crazy pod version of himself."

"*Thank* you. I didn't want to be the one to say it, since I don't know him as well as you guys do. I thought maybe he's always like this and I just started picking up on it now."

"He's not always like this. Personally, I think Jane should divorce him."

Cash snickered. Nobody could deny Lieutenant Commander Becker was overprotective when it came to his daughter. Not to mention obsessed. Cash had spent the entire trip back from Kabul listening to his CO drone on and on about Miss Sadie; what an advanced child she was, how she smiled at Beck more times than she smiled at Beck's wife, Jane, how she preferred mashed carrots to applesauce. Cash knew a scary amount about that baby, far more than he wanted to, actually.

Since Miss Sadie was turning the big 1 next weekend, the presence of everyone on the team had been requested for the kid's party. Cash had been worrying about what kind of present to buy, but fortunately the CO had come up with a list of suggestions—all of which had been thoroughly researched and undoubtedly tested for safety purposes. He'd even compiled a second list entitled "DON'T BUY." Like Cash would ever give a one-year-old lead paint.

"*Lead paint* was actually on the DON'T BUY list," Ryan said in disbelief. "Why would any of us buy that?"

He laughed. "I was just remembering that one. Hey, do you want to chip in and get the Baby Animal Planet books? I checked online and the box set is like a hundred bucks. I refuse to spend more than fifty dollars on a baby, so if you want to go halfsies..."

"Done," Ryan said. He pulled into a parking space on the street running parallel to the beach. "I'll tell Annabelle she can fend for herself."

They hopped out of the Jeep and headed for the concrete steps leading down to the sand. They'd both worn swim trunks and cross-trainers, and the second their sneakers hit the sand, Cash peeled off his ratty Cardinals T-shirt and tucked the edge under the waistband of his shorts. Normally they trained closer to the base, but Dylan had insisted they go to the northern end of the island today, claiming a little eye candy made him more productive.

When Cash spotted Dylan and Seth doing push-ups on a stretch where the sand was more compact, it was clear that the guys were the ones providing the eye candy; ten yards away, four bikini-clad tourists were stretched out on fluffy beach towels, tongues hanging out as they ogled the two SEALs, whose bare backs glistened with sweat.

Those hungry eyes shifted to Cash and Ryan, both of whom winked at the ladies as they walked past.

"So things are going good with Jen?" Ryan asked, shrugging out of his T-shirt.

Trying to stay nonchalant, he slid his Aviators onto the bridge of his nose. "What do you mean?"

"Any problems from that stalker guy?"

"Oh. No. He sent her an email yesterday but she deleted it."

"Why doesn't she remove his address from her contact list?"

"She did, but he keeps creating those free accounts and she doesn't know what to look for anymore. The spam folder usually catches them, but sometimes they wind up in her inbox."

"This guy doesn't give up, huh?" Ryan popped on his own shades, then rolled up his shirt and draped it around his neck.

As they strode toward the guys, Cash tried to maintain the casual front, but inside he was annoyed as hell. It bugged him that Jen wasn't as troubled by the email as he was. Yeah, it'd been more whiny than threatening, but he still didn't like it. Brendan's obsession with Jen didn't seem to be waning, only increasing. And the more Cash got to know her, the more determined he was to keep her safe.

When she wasn't trying to seduce him with skimpy outfits and sexual innuendo, she was actually pretty incredible. Smart, funny, entertaining. She'd even cooked him dinner last night—and then, once they'd decided that her burnt lasagna might give them food poisoning, she'd bought him dinner, which had been nice. Not that he was the kind of man who liked mooching off women, but once in a while it felt nice not to be the one pulling out his wallet.

The thought of Psycho McGee coming after Jen made his gut burn. A part of him almost wished Brendan would make a move, just so Cash could have the pleasure of kicking the creep's ass.

They reached Dylan and Seth, who hopped to their feet to exchange some heys and knuckle taps with the new arrivals. Jackson had yet to show, but that was no surprise. The Texan lived by his own clock and took his sweet-ass time in everything. Except on the field. There, Jackson epitomized efficiency. As the team medic, he got the job done with lightning speed and had saved all their asses countless times.

"FYI," Dylan told them as he wiped his sweaty forehead with the back of his hand, "I bought the CO's kid those educational building blocks that were on the list, so don't double purchase."

"What the fuck are educational building blocks?" Ryan asked.

"Wooden blocks with words on them."

Ryan looked mystified. "What kind of words?"

Dylan shrugged. "You know, like *mom, dad, dog, bunny*." He rolled his eyes. "That way Miss Sadie can increase her vocabulary while she's playing."

"Pod person," Ryan muttered under his breath.

Cash's laugh died in his throat when he noticed Seth eyeing him. "What?" he demanded.

"I hear you have a hot new roomie," Seth mocked.

"Yeah. It's your mom," he answered sweetly. "I can't wait to fuck her."

Ryan grinned.

Dylan chuckled.

"Screw you," Seth retorted. But he didn't seem put off by the jab.

Seth was used to the mom jokes. Hell, he had to expect it, seeing as his mother, Missy, was a bona fide Las Vegas showgirl. Seth, the lucky bastard, had pretty much been raised in a dressing room filled to the gills with half-dressed women. The dude lost his virginity at the age of twelve, for fuck's sake.

"How hot is the LT's sister, exactly?" Seth inquired, running his hand over the dark stubble coating his jaw.

Cash didn't think he'd ever seen the guy clean-shaven, but he'd witnessed firsthand just how much the chicks liked Seth's scruffy badass-ness. Seth was definitely the bad boy of the crew, a total asshole when he wanted to be, but he was also lethal as hell and someone you wanted watching your six on a mission.

"Hot," Cash replied, albeit grudgingly.

"Very hot," Ryan confirmed before fixing a frown on Seth. "But Carson's got this thing about keeping his teammates away from his sister, so don't get any bright ideas, Masterson."

"Me?" Seth donned an innocent face. "I think you should be dishing out that advice to McCoy. According to Dylan, he's already very acquainted with—"

"Sorry I'm late," Jackson's voice came from behind.

Saved by the Texan.

Cash glared at Seth as Ryan turned to greet Jackson, who'd shown up in sweatpants and a white T-shirt with the words "Don't Mess with Texas" blazing across the front.

"Not a word," Cash muttered.

Seth's gray eyes gleamed, lips twitching. "Fine. But I want details later."

Jackson strode up and slapped Cash's shoulder. "I heard you're shackin' up with the LT's little sister."

He suppressed a groan. Why did everyone feel the need to give him heat about this? "Yes. I am. Now how about we quit gossiping like a bunch of preteens and get a move on?"

Fortunately, nobody argued, and a few minutes later, the only heat Cash got was the sun's rays beating down on his head and shoulders. He zoned out as his sneakers slapped the wet sand, drawing in the scent of salt and sweat on each inhale.

They ran their usual four miles. The only sounds breaching the comfortable silence were the thud of sneakers on sand and the squawking of gulls overhead. Sweat rose on Cash's bare chest, dripping down his forehead and sliding between his pecs. Fuck, it was hot out. Only nine thirty in the morning, but he'd bet the temperature was somewhere in the eighties already, and climbing steadily. But it beat the desert climate of Phoenix, where the summers could be unbearable. Plus, Coronado had the ocean factor going for it. Nothing he loved more than the salty spray of the Pacific misting his face as his feet whipped across the sand.

When they neared the beach's northernmost point, they turned around and slowed their pace, making their way back to the main stretch. Ryan and Jackson paired off, jogging up ahead, while Cash found himself flanked by Dylan and Seth, both of whom were grinning like a pair of idiots.

"How's the hands-off plan going?" Dylan asked with barely restrained amusement.

"Terribly," Cash admitted. "The woman is determined to seduce me."

Seth hooted. "Poor baby. A hot chick wants to screw you. Whatever will you do?"

He clenched his jaw. "Not her. I promised Carson I'd behave."

"What Carson doesn't know won't hurt him," Dylan said in a singsong voice.

Cash snorted. "Right, because it's so easy to keep secrets in this group. I can recite all the women every single one of you has slept with. If I fuck his sister, Carson will find out."

"Not from us," Dylan said.

Now Seth snorted. "No, you're right," he told Cash. "If Dylan knows, everyone will know."

"Bull. I know how to keep my mouth shut."

"Not after a few shots of Jägermeister, you don't."

Dylan shrugged. "Good point." He glanced at Cash. "How about I become your sponsor? You know, like AA-type shit. I'll help keep you in line."

"So you'll strap on the chastity belt for him?" Seth cracked.

"Whenever you're tempted to unzip your pants, just call me and I'll talk you out of it. I'll even check in with you every few hours and give you gruesome facts about what it's like to drown, as an incentive not to piss off the LT."

Cash had to laugh. "You're a good friend."

"You know it."

They caught up with Ryan and Jackson at the water's edge, where they kicked off their sneakers and waded into the water. Cash welcomed the initial rush of cool relief as he submerged himself, but it wasn't long before he was sweating again. The two-mile swim was one he could do in his sleep with one arm tied behind his back, but damn, it was sweltering hot today.

A throb had built in his temples by the time they staggered back to shore, but he felt more relaxed than he had in days. He loved hanging out with his boys. The camaraderie they'd formed during BUD/S training had only grown stronger over the years, which was funny considering how different they all were. Dylan, the California boy with his preppy clothes and natural charisma. Tough guy, chain-smoking, chip-on-his-shoulder Seth. Jackson, with his sweet-talkin' ways and good ol' boy charm.

Ryan and the others were great too, but those friendships didn't come close to rivaling the tight-knit bond he'd formed with his three fellow rookies.

"Don't forget," Dylan said before they parted ways in the parking lot ten minutes later. "Your sponsor is only a phone call away."

Grabbing a towel from the back of Ryan's Jeep, Cash dried his dripping wet chest and said, "That's actually kinda reassuring."

Dylan grinned. "She's really gotten under your skin, huh?"

He let out a heavy breath. "You don't know the half of it."

Jen was curled up in a recliner clicking through job ads on her laptop when Cash lumbered into the apartment. Her heart skipped a beat at the sight of all that hotness. The sweaty T-shirt pasted to his chest emphasized every hard ridge and ripple of his broad torso, and since he hadn't shaved before leaving this morning, dark stubble covered his strong jaw, lending him a feral air.

When she noticed the flush on his cheeks and the weary set of his mouth, she narrowed her eyes. "You okay?" she asked, closing her laptop and setting it on the coffee table.

"I think I overdid it," he muttered. "I might have heatstroke."

She grinned. "The big, tough Navy SEAL let the sun get to him?"

He ignored her and strode toward the corridor. "I'm taking a shower."

After he disappeared, Jen leaned back in the chair and stared up at the ceiling. Her grin faded, muscles knotting with frustration. She wasn't ready to admit defeat yet, but it was becoming glaringly obvious that Cash possessed a disgusting amount of willpower. She'd brought her A-game to the table the past couple of days, yet the infuriating man continued to resist her advances.

She wasn't sure whether to be insulted or impressed.

Either way, enough was enough. She wanted Cash McCoy so badly she couldn't think straight. Everything about him turned her on.

That old saying about wanting what you can't have had become her life's theme song. She craved Cash on a whole new level now. The more he resisted, the more attracted to him she was. Sad, really.

"You hungry?" Cash asked when he reappeared ten minutes later.

"Not really. I'm still full from breakfast."

"Good, because I'm too beat to deal with food right now." With his hair damp from the shower, he crossed the room and collapsed on the couch, stretching out on his back. A groan slipped out as he closed his eyes. "My head is killing me."

A spark of worry lit her belly. "Maybe you do have heat-stroke." She hopped off the chair and approached the couch.

Cash's eyes flew open when she touched his cheeks. "What are you doing?" he said hoarsely.

She frowned. "Your skin's hot to the touch. Did you replenish your fluids?"

His eyelids fluttered closed again. "Chugged half a bottle of water when we finished up," he mumbled.

"How strenuous of a workout?"

"Ran four miles. Swam a couple miles. Push-ups, crunches, some other stuff."

Jen shot him an incredulous look, even though he couldn't see it. "You did all that, in the sun, in ninety-two-degree weather, and you only drank half a bottle of water?"

"I was distracted."

She grumbled in frustration and flew toward the kitchen, where she grabbed two waters from the fridge. Returning to the couch, she uncapped one bottle and thrust it at Cash. "Drink," she ordered.

He slid up, took the bottle, and drained it. "Can I take a nap now?" he asked, weary.

"Only if you don't complain when I wake you up to drink this second bottle."

"I won't complain," he said obediently.

"How's your head?"

"Throbbing."

Jen shoved her hands underneath his wide shoulders. "Scoot up."

His gaze darkened with suspicion. "Why?"

"I can help."

After a moment of visible reluctance, he raised himself up. Jen wedged her body on the couch and pulled Cash's damp head into her lap. That he didn't protest at the close contact told her his headache must be worse than he was letting on.

"Close your eyes," she murmured.

He did, and his features relaxed as she lowered her thumbs to his temples. Drawing her brows together in concentration, she massaged his temples in a circular motion, keeping the pressure steady.

Cash groaned huskily. "Where'd you learn to do that?"

"I got a lot of headaches when I was younger. My mom's a nurse, so she knows all sorts of tricks to get rid of the pain. She gives the best temple massages. She taught me how to do them."

Jen used her fingertips to stroke the area between his eyebrows and hairline, slowly rubbing his hot skin.

He groaned again. "She taught you well. That feels fantastic."

She made small circles between his brows, gently pressing down, then massaged from his temples to the strong line of his jawbone. With his eyes closed, she was able to admire every inch of his gorgeous face. The sharp jut of his cheekbones. His surprisingly long eyelashes. The tiny scar nicking the corner of his jaw.

She knew he'd fallen asleep when his breathing steadied and his bottom lip dropped out in a sexy pout. She kept massaging. Watched the rise and fall of his spectacular chest. His skin felt cooler to the touch, but she only allowed him a twenty-minute catnap before waking him up.

"Drink," she said after she'd coaxed his eyes open.

His answering moan was seriously endearing, but he didn't resist when she brought the bottle to his lips. He drank greedily, then lolled his head to the side and snuggled into her thigh.

Jen couldn't fight the rush of heat that sizzled through her. She wore only a tank top and a pair of cotton boxers, and the way Cash's whiskers scraped her bare thigh brought goose bumps to her skin. And his head kept rubbing over her pelvis as he tried to get comfortable again, which made it impossible *not* to get turned on.

As she ran her fingers through his hair in soothing strokes, excitement pricked her flesh, making every inch of her burn. Her nipples beaded, pushed into the lacy material of her bra. Her pussy ached, throbbing in tune to the persistent beating of her heart. Lord, she wanted this man.

Frustration seized her insides. Damn her brother for ordering Cash to keep his hands off her.

Her fingers froze in Cash's hair as a thought dawned on her. Carson might have tied Cash's hands, but he hadn't tied *hers*.

A devilish smile tickled her lips. Nope, her hands were certainly not tied.

Without giving herself the chance to chicken out, she shuffled and slid down the couch so that she and Cash lay side to side.

His eyes popped open, narrowing when he realized their faces were inches apart.

"What are you doing?" he croaked.

"Taking advantage of the loophole."

Then she lowered her hand to his groin and cupped him over his shorts.

Cash jerked as if he'd been shot.

"Hear me out," she said in a throaty voice that couldn't possibly belong to her.

His features grew taut, but she knew it had nothing to do

with his headache and everything to do with that darn restraint of his.

"Carson told you to keep your hands off me, but he didn't say anything about *me* keeping my hands off *you*." To punctuate, she dragged her palm up and down his hard-on.

His expression creased with torment. "Jen—"

"Let me touch you. I'm going crazy here, Cash. I don't think I've ever wanted anyone this much."

Surprise filtered into his gaze. "I want you too," he said roughly.

"Good." She gripped both his wrists and forced his arms over his head. "Just keep your hands up there, cowboy. That way if my annoying brother asks whether you touched me, you can honestly answer that no, you didn't."

When his mouth opened to voice another objection, she shut him up the only way she knew how—she kissed him.

And boy, his lips were as addictive as she remembered. She brushed her mouth over his in a fleeting caress, then peppered little kisses on the corners of his mouth, his cheeks, his jaw. When she returned to his lips and teased the seam with the tip of her tongue, he made a low noise and granted her access. She licked her way into his mouth, planting her palms on his chest as she deepened the kiss. When their tongues met, Cash thrust his hips, pushing his erection into her thigh.

Jen's lungs burned from lack of oxygen as the kiss grew hotter, more desperate. Cash tried to lower one hand to touch her, but she shoved it back up and locked his wrists with her fingers.

"No touching," she said breathlessly.

She glided her other hand down his rock-hard chest, past his rippled abs, and under the waistband of his shorts.

Cash moaned.

"How's your head?" she asked.

"Still hurts," he said in a strangled voice.

"Don't worry, I'll make it better."

With a wicked smile, she moved to the foot of the couch and slowly worked his shorts off his hips. Her mouth watered when his dick sprang up to greet her. Lord, the man was hung like a bull. Thick, long, hard. His balls were drawn tight, and the engorged head of his cock bobbed against his navel, leaving a streak of moisture on his abs.

Jen was suddenly hit with a pang of self-consciousness. She might have started this, but truth was, she didn't have much experience in the oral sex department. Giving it *or* getting it. She'd gone down on her boyfriends, Brendan included, but it had always been rushed because they'd been in too much of a hurry to get inside her.

She swallowed the saliva pooling in her mouth and collected her composure, then peered up at Cash, who was watching her with a heavy-lidded look.

"My technique probably isn't what you're used to," she confessed. "Tell me if I do it wrong."

His lips quirked. "Sweetheart, I'm pretty sure I can come from the *thought* of being in your mouth. Trust me, I'll like whatever you do."

Warmth traveled down her chest and settled between her legs. When she dropped her gaze and saw a bead of moisture glistening at the tip of his erection, she decided to quit hesitating before Cash regained his senses and put a stop to this. So what if she didn't have experience? She'd just have to do some exploring and figure out how to drive this man wild.

She started by dipping her head and tentatively licking that tempting little drop of moisture.

Cash hissed out a breath.

"You okay?" she teased.

"Uh-huh."

Emboldened by his reaction to that one teeny lick, she rested her hands on his thighs, teasing the coarse hair and feeling his muscles clench beneath her fingertips. Then she licked him from root to tip, savoring the clean, salty taste of him. His ragged breathing spurred her on. She swept her tongue up the length of him, rubbing her lips over the head before licking the fluid seeping from the little slit.

"You done teasing?" he grumbled.

"Not by a long shot," she said before flicking her tongue against the underside of his cock.

He mumbled a savage curse.

Why hadn't anyone ever told her how empowering it could be reducing a man to a panting, cursing mess?

Fighting a smile, she skated her tongue up and down his shaft, then wrapped her lips around the head and sucked.

His hips shot up, trying to push his entire length into her mouth. With a slow exhale, she gave him what he wanted, her cheeks hollowing as she brought him deeper, testing how much she could take. Breathing through her nose, she relaxed her throat as he fed his cock to her inch by delicious inch. Though he kept his arms above his head, Cash controlled the encounter with his hips, driving in and out of her mouth with leisurely but steady strokes.

"That's it, baby." His voice was a cross between a whisper and a groan. "Suck me nice and slow."

Realizing she'd completely neglected the tight sac bumping against her chin, Jen lowered her hand and cupped his balls, eliciting a hoarse cry from him. His hips retreated and that thick cock slid out of her mouth with a wet pop.

"Lick my balls," he rasped. "Do that teasing thing again."

Her heart thudded. She licked, sucked one in her mouth, then the other, then replaced her tongue with her hand and squeezed him hard.

Cash released a wild groan.

His response to her exploration turned her on beyond belief. An ache formed between her legs. Her breathing went shallow. Every inch of her body tingled.

God, she was going to explode.

But not until she made him explode first.

Wrapping her fingers around him, she brought his cock back to her mouth, sucking hard. His groans grew more desperate, his body pistoning harder. She swirled her tongue over his head at each upstroke, quickening her pace.

"Fuck. Yeah, like that. Jerk me faster. And suck harder."

Jen gave him what he wanted, pumping his shaft as she sucked him into oblivion.

"Oh, Jesus. Yeah, that's it...that's *it...fuck*."

Then he moaned, disregarded the no-touching rule, and shoved his hands in her hair as his dick throbbed and spasmed in her mouth.

Hot pulses of liquid shot to the back of her throat and she eagerly swallowed each drop, loving the taste of him, loving the way he gripped her hair, the way he rocked his hips with complete abandon.

When he finally grew still, Jen lifted her head, unable to control the cocky smile that tugged on her lips. Cash's eyes were closed, his frantic pulse ticking in the hollow of his throat.

"Feel better?" she asked, amused.

To her irritation, his eyes snapped open to reveal not the glaze of post-orgasmic bliss she'd expected, but a look of utter betrayal.

"I can't believe you took advantage of my heatstroke and seduced me."

She lifted one eyebrow in defiance. "Really? You're going to play the wounded virgin here?"

He didn't seem to hear her. "Oh man. If Carson finds out

his little sister gave me a blowjob..." Cash made a swift move to yank his shorts up.

Rolling her eyes, Jen intercepted his hand before he could cover himself up. "He won't find out. Not unless we tell him. And we're not going to tell him, are we, cowboy?"

"Never," he confirmed miserably.

"Good." She flashed a cheeky smile. "Just like we're not going to tell him how you fucked his little sister on the couch."

"I'm not going—" The words died when she hopped off the couch and whipped her tank top over her head.

A groan left his mouth, heavy with frustration and thick with lust.

"Oh yeah. This is happening, cowboy." Grinning, Jen wiggled out of her shorts. She climbed on top of him wearing nothing but a skimpy black bra and matching bikini panties. "Sorry to be the bearer of bad news, but your days of being a prude are officially over."

CHAPTER
NINE

A prude? Here he was, trying to be honorable, trying to be a good friend, and the damn woman accused him of being a *prude*. Would a prude have come in her mouth the way he'd just done?

Cash was still kicking himself for that. But once she'd put her hands on him, he'd caved like a house of cards. He couldn't remember ever coming that hard. His balls still tingled from the bone-melting climax, and now, with Jen straddling his lap, his dick hardened again, eager for another go.

You've already dug your grave, man.

Truth. Carson wouldn't make a distinction between sex and a blowjob. Both would be equally unforgivable in the dude's eyes.

So why was he still hesitating? He had a sexy woman in his lap, for fuck's sake. A sexy woman who happened to be in her underwear. A sexy woman whose lips were swollen and moist from sucking him off. And her brother would kill Cash regardless, so why bother putting up a fight? Might as well take what he'd been dying to get his hands on for nearly a week now.

Meeting her challenge, he sat up straighter and leaned back on the arm of the couch. "Lose the bra," he ordered.

After the way she'd gone to town on his dick, he half expected an enthusiastic striptease, but what he got was a whole lot of hesitation. Jen's straight white teeth sank into her bottom lip, her obvious distress digging a groove in her forehead.

He furrowed his brows. "What's wrong?"

She opened her mouth and a shaky breath flew out. "I lied to you, Cash," she said, looking miserable. "I talk a big game, but the truth is, I don't have much experience with sex. That stuff about my favorite position being missionary? It's the *only* position I've ever tried. I haven't even..." Embarrassment stained her cheeks pink. "I've never had an orgasm during sex. I can get myself off, but the guys I've slept with never made me come."

"Never?" he echoed in surprise.

"Never." Her cheeks turned redder. "At first I tried telling them what I needed, how to touch me the way I like, but I think they felt insulted. Eventually I started faking it so I wouldn't hurt their feelings."

She looked so upset that Cash experienced a burst of unexpected tenderness. He drew her into his arms and kissed the top of her head, breathing in her sweet scent. Fuck, he should've seen through all her bold flirting and seduction attempts, but she'd gotten him so twisted up in knots of lust that he hadn't paid attention.

Whatever reluctance he'd been feeling about this encounter dissipated like a cloud of smoke. No way would he leave this girl wanting. Her inexperience had definitely shone through during that blowjob, but she'd sent him careening over the edge with her exploratory licks and uncertain pumps. She deserved to experience the same kind of mind-blowing pleasure.

"Cash? Do you want to stop?"

"No," he said gruffly. "I don't want to stop."

"It doesn't bother you that I'm not...you know, an accomplished sexpert? You don't wish I'm a porn star or something?"

He chuckled. "I don't want to fuck a porn star, Jen. I want to fuck *you*." When her eyes widened, he suppressed a curse and wished he'd kept his mouth shut. His blunt nature had gotten him into trouble with women in the past. "Ah, sorry. I should probably watch my language."

"No, don't."

He arched a brow.

"I like it. It's a huge turn-on." Her lips quirked in a smile. "I don't know why you think you can't talk to women. You do a pretty good job of it."

He traced the curve of her jaw with a lazy finger. "Dirty talk doesn't count as real talking."

"Sure it does."

"Whatever you say." His fingers moved to her collarbone, drawing circles over her silky skin. "Now why don't we stop talking so I can get started on the making you feel good part. So...lose the bra."

Her breath hitched. Then, without a word, she flicked the front clasp of her bra. The lacy cups popped open, revealing a pair of perky breasts tipped by pale pink nipples.

Oh yeah. Cash licked his suddenly dry lips, then cupped those spectacular tits with his palms and swept his thumbs over her nipples, watching them harden beneath his touch.

He studied Jen to gauge her response. Her face was awash with pleasure, her pulse hammering in her throat.

Happy with what he saw, he leaned forward and kissed the swell of each breast, then closed his lips over one nipple. He sucked gently, flicking his tongue over the velvety soft bud.

Jen's moan rippled through her body and vibrated against his mouth. He peered up, a satisfied noise rumbling out of his chest when he glimpsed the sheer rapture on her face.

"You like this?" he murmured before turning his attention to her other nipple.

"Uh-huh."

He alternated between fleeting licks and deep pulls. Kissing and sucking until Jen started making sexy whimpering sounds and grinding her lower body against his in an agitated rhythm. The heat of her pussy scorched his thighs, sent a bolt of lust to his thickening cock.

"I need to touch you," he said, rubbing his cheek on the underside of her breast.

She choked out a laugh. "You are touching me."

"It's not enough. I need to touch every fucking inch of you."

With a growl, he flipped her on her back and latched his mouth to hers, kissing her roughly.

His hands took on a life of their own, exploring the soft body sprawled beneath him. He skimmed his fingertips over her stomach. Stroked the baby-fine skin of her inner thighs. Squeezed her luscious ass. And while his hands played and roamed, he used his mouth to tend to the places his fingers were too impatient to reach, like the graceful arch of her neck, which he nuzzled and kissed. The spot right beneath her ear, which he nipped at with his teeth. The sweet crease between her breasts, which he lapped his tongue over.

Jen shifted restlessly beneath him, her arms coming around his shoulders, her short fingernails gouging into his skin. "I want to come," she said desperately. "Make me come."

His pulse roared in his ears, his cock so stiff he was actually in pain. Breathing hard, he moved off the couch and got on his knees, digging his fingers into her thighs. "Spread for me, baby."

She spread, and he almost came from the sight of her. Her pussy was as perfect as the rest of her, pink and smooth and glistening with excitement. His mouth went parched. His heart thumped a wild beat in his chest.

He needed to taste her. Now.

With a groan, he parted her legs farther apart and buried his head in her tempting paradise, licking his way down to her wet opening. The sweet, tangy taste of her coated his tongue and he lapped her up like a cat, every muscle in his body coiled tight. He nibbled on her slick folds, tickling her slit with the tip of his tongue, kissing and sampling but making a pointed effort to avoid the swollen bud begging for his attention.

"Stop teasing," she begged.

"No," he muttered.

His tongue danced down to her core again, jabbing inside with sharp strokes. Jen's hips bucked, a wild cry leaving her mouth.

Fighting a smile, he continued to fuck her with his tongue. His fingers circled both her ankles so he could lift her legs up to his shoulders and bring her pussy closer to his face. Her anxious moans egged him on, heightened his own arousal and summoned a growl of satisfaction.

"Oh, God. Cash. Please. *Please.*"

The begging nearly did him in, but he willed away the impending release and distracted himself by plunging his tongue into her again. When her pleas turned into nonsensical muttering and tortured whimpers, he finally gave her what she wanted.

The second his mouth suctioned around her clit, she orgasmed in a loud, hot rush, thrashing on the sofa and grabbing his head to keep his mouth glued to her.

Cash rode out the release with her, licking and sucking until her body went as limp as a rag doll.

Chuckling, he lifted his head and studied Jen's face, pleased with what he saw. Flushed cheeks, glazed eyes—a woman who'd just been thoroughly satisfied.

His erection demanded that same satisfaction. Staggering to

his feet, Cash peeled his T-shirt off and tossed it on the hardwood floor.

When Jen started to sit up, he fixed her with a stern look and said, "Don't move."

He darted into the hall to grab a condom from a drawer in the bathroom and hightailed it back to the living room like a man possessed. Jen was still sprawled on the couch, her eyes dazed, her tits red and splotchy from his mouth. His fingers had even left red marks on her thighs, which would've made him feel guilty if not for the way she spread those thighs the second he approached.

She eyed him with unabashed passion. "Get in me. Now."

"Aren't you bossy." He taunted her by gripping his condom-covered dick and giving it a lazy stroke, ignoring the deep ache of anticipation in his balls. "Maybe I don't want to do that yet. Maybe I want to stand here and look at you for a while."

Her eyes widened as he stroked himself, but she must have seen the need burning on his face, heard his labored breathing, because she gave a soft laugh and taunted him right back. "Liar. You're *dying* to be inside me."

No point in denying it. "Busted," he agreed. And then he launched himself at her and slid his cock into her with one smooth glide.

She gasped.

He cursed.

Jesus, she was *tight*, her inner muscles clamping around his dick as if to trap him there. And he didn't mind one damn bit.

Sweat beaded on his skin as he began to move. Slow, languid, trying to prolong the sensations. The sofa dipped under their weight. The air in the living room grew hot, a thick sexual fog that made it difficult to breathe.

Cash placed a palm flat on either side of her, his biceps flexing and straining as he tried to control the pace. A sheen of sweat broke out on his forehead. Christ. He wanted to go faster. He wanted to fuck the living daylights out of her, to hear the sound of flesh slapping flesh, to feel the couch cushions bounce as he drove them both over the edge.

"Stop," Jen ordered.

He froze. Started to pull out, but she dug her fingers into his ass to keep him in place.

"Stop reining it in," she clarified with a frazzled look. "I won't break, cowboy. So stop with the slow and gentle routine and do what I know you want to do to me."

He hissed out a breath. "What I want to do is fuck you like a goddamn animal."

"Good. Now *do* it."

The last thread of restraint snapped inside him like a rubber band.

No finesse, no controlled movements. All he heard was their ragged breathing, the rhythmic squeaking of the couch springs, the deafening roar of his pulse. He fucked her hard. Deep, steady strokes that soon became shallow and erratic. It didn't take long before Jen's body arched beneath his, before she was moaning again, begging for more. Cash angled his hips in order to stimulate her clit with each stroke, and when her pussy spasmed around him and she started to come, he let himself go. A zing of pleasure set fire to his balls and unleashed an orgasm that shot up his shaft, sizzled his spine, and made him forget his name.

His mind fragmented. Heart stopped. Surroundings faded. The only thing that registered was the agonizing pleasure seizing his body.

When he finally regained his senses, he became aware of something ringing.

"Phone," he mumbled.

His reaction time was slower than usual, but he managed to

stagger off the couch in search of his cell, glancing at Jen over his shoulder. "Sorry, but it could be the—"

"Base," she finished. "Don't worry, I know the drill."

It took him a moment to remember that both her father and brother were military.

Her brother. Oh shit.

Cash quickly pushed all thoughts of Carson from his mind as he headed for the kitchen counter and grabbed his phone. He'd deal with the threat of drowning later.

Fortunately, the call wasn't from his CO. He almost didn't pick up when he saw Dylan's number on the screen, but changed his mind at the last second, answering before the call kicked over to voice mail.

"What's up?" he asked in lieu of greeting.

"Just doing my sponsor-ly duty and checking in to see how you're holding up," Dylan said. "Or should I say, how you're holding *out*."

Cash's gaze moved to the couch, where Jen was pulling her panties up her legs. Her bare breasts swayed as she bent down to search for her bra.

"Let's just say you're the worst sponsor ever," he muttered.

A hoot sounded in his ear. "You caved? *Already*? We saw each other two hours ago."

It'd only been two hours since he'd left the guys? Shit. Apparently he had even less self-control than he'd thought.

His friend's laughter continued to fill the line.

"Is there anything else you wanted?" Cash asked through clenched teeth.

"Yeah, to remind you we're having beers on Monday. You know, when my guys beat the shit out of your guys."

"You mean when *my* guys clean up the field with yours?"

"You wish, bro. So we're still on for the Monday-nighter?"

"Definitely."

"Cool. See you then."

Cash hung up and saw Jen's quizzical expression. She'd put her tank top and shorts back on, and was in the process of tying her hair into a ponytail. "What was that about?" she asked.

"Football rivalry," he explained. "Arizona's playing San Fran on Monday, so Dylan's coming over to watch my team kick his team's ass."

"Dylan? As in your go-to ménage buddy?"

He scowled at her. "Don't get any ideas."

"Me? You're the one who's naked."

Shit. She was right. Ignoring her mocking look, he crossed the room and gathered up his clothes. As he bent over to pick up his shorts from the floor, he heard Jen gasp.

"Holy hell," she breathed. "That's hot."

Cash had to grin. "Didn't realize my bare ass was gasp-worthy."

"It's not. Well, it is. But I was looking at your tattoo."

He tugged his shorts up to his hips, jumping when he felt Jen's warm hand on him. There was nothing sexual about the touch—she was tracing the tattoo on his upper back, which spanned from shoulder to shoulder—yet his dick jerked at the contact.

Get yourself together, he ordered the big guy.

Her finger danced over the bumps of his spine. "What's the date underneath the eagle?" she asked curiously.

"The day I got my SEAL trident."

"Nice." Her fingertips continued to travel over his skin. "Is it weird that this tattoo really, really turns me on?"

Smothering a groan, he ducked out of her grasp. He quickly pulled his T-shirt over his head before turning around to face her. "Jen," he began.

Her expression grew cloudy. Perching her hands on her hips, she searched his face, then frowned as if she didn't like what she saw. "Don't you dare tell me what happened just now was a mistake. You know you enjoyed it as much as I did."

He couldn't deny it even if he tried, but that didn't change the fact that he'd totally screwed up. He'd promised Carson he wouldn't touch Jen, and horn dog that he was, he'd caved the second she'd placed her dainty hand on his dick.

"It can't happen again," he said in a firm voice.

"Like hell it can't."

Frustration jammed in his throat. "I'm not good at relationships. And I'm not looking for one right now."

"I don't want a relationship either. I already told you, I don't date military guys. So relax, okay? All I want from you is more of what we did on the couch right now. Sex, cowboy. Just sex."

"Sex," he echoed warily.

"Look, I've had three lovers and the sex sucked with all of them." Aggravation creased her forehead. "I don't want someone who'll hold my hand and shower me with sweet words or kisses. I want someone who'll fuck my brains out."

Cash blinked in surprise.

"I just dated a psycho. Do you honestly think I'm in the mood to open myself up to another guy right now? This won't be a relationship. I'm not handing you my heart and pleading with you not to break it. I'm asking you to rock my world for the next few weeks."

He choked out a laugh. "Is that all?"

"No." She arched one brow. "I also want you to teach me how to rock *your* world. I want us to do all the things I've always wanted to try, and pretty much see how many times we can make each other come in three weeks."

Cash swallowed. Hard.

"Three weeks," she said flippantly. "It'll just be a little fling, Cash. We'll have sex, hang out, and then I'll move out and we say goodbye."

He hesitated. If his lower body was in charge of making the decision, it would be a no-brainer. *Fling. Sex. Make each other come.* That's all his dick needed to hear.

But his brain told him this was a bad idea. Not to mention ridiculously unrealistic. A fling with an end date? Every fling he'd ever experienced, the chick ended up pushing for a relationship no matter what the initial agreement had been.

And even if Jen didn't end up wanting more, he didn't feel right about using her this way. Well, they'd be using each other, he amended, but still...it didn't sit right with him.

Truth was, he *liked* her. He liked her a lot. He'd never had a girl worry about him before, the way Jen had when he'd come home suffering from a pounding headache. She'd given him a *temple* massage, for chrissake. A woman like Jen deserved to be worshipped, not fucked for three weeks and then discarded.

"I can see that sexy brain of yours working," she said in irritation. "Don't overthink this, Cash. Three weeks of sex, nothing more, nothing less. If it makes you feel better, we'll even agree to remain friends afterwards."

He cracked a smile.

"Come on," she coaxed. "You know you want to say yes."

And then, evil seductress that she was, she stepped closer and pressed her index finger to his chest, drawing little figure-eights between his pecs.

Cash groaned. "Carson's going to kill me."

"He'll never have to know."

"Fuck."

She smirked. "Is that a yes?"

"No." He cleared his throat, but it still felt like someone had jammed a handful of gravel in there. "I mean, maybe."

"Maybe?" Humor tinged her voice.

"Yes," he said with a sigh.

"Yes?"

Smothering a curse, he yanked her into his arms. He kissed her, then pried his mouth away and repeated himself. "Yes."

"So 'fess up, why are you *really* single?" Jen asked later that evening.

She and Cash were lying on the couch again, naked beneath a fleece blanket that he'd haphazardly wrapped around them. She still couldn't believe he'd agreed to have a fling with her. She'd figured it would take a lot more convincing, but it appeared that all you needed to do was give a man a BJ and he caved.

And thank God he had, because sex with Cash was everything she'd known it would be. A little rough, a tad demanding, a lot awesome. And nobody could accuse the man of being a selfish lover. He didn't come until he made sure she got off, and he seemed to really, *really* enjoy getting her off. Earlier, he'd had his head buried between her legs for a good forty minutes, bringing her to the brink only to retreat and start the slow, teasing torment all over again. The resulting orgasm had been more powerful than any she'd ever experienced.

Which raised the question she'd just voiced—why on earth was this guy still single?

"Cash?" she prompted when he didn't respond.

His hand absently toyed with a strand of her hair. "I'm not looking for a relationship."

"Why not?"

She felt his pecs ripple beneath her cheek as he shrugged. "I don't think I make a very good boyfriend."

"Right, because you can't talk to women. Which is total bullshit, by the way. You talk to me just fine."

His voice sounded troubled as he said, "Yeah, I guess I do.

But that's not how it normally goes down. Usually, I screw up by saying the wrong thing, or not saying anything at all. I got tired of hearing chicks complain about how I don't talk to them." He paused in thought. "Being single is probably a good thing. For now, anyway. There's still a lot of stuff I want to do with my life, stuff I couldn't do if I settled down."

"Is this about your parents? Because they had you so young, you don't want to make the same mistake?"

"Yeah, maybe. My folks didn't get to do all the things they wanted to do in life."

She lifted her head from his bare chest and shot him a mocking look. "With ten million dollars in the bank, they couldn't do what they wanted?"

Cash smiled faintly. "Big spenders they ain't. They're very practical. They used the lotto money for the basics—putting food on the table, a roof over our heads, and clothing on our backs. Dad always wanted to be a mechanic, so he bought a garage and started his own business. After that, they set aside some money for my college fund and invested the rest. They both grew up poor, so spending money on pointless luxuries isn't in their DNA. Neither is hiring a nanny for their kid. They were hands-on parents, so, thanks to me, neither of them got to enjoy their teens or twenties. The moment I left for college, they started making up for lost time. They've been traveling a lot. Dad joined a football league. Mom got her GED and enrolled in college."

The pride in his voice brought a rush of warmth to Jen's heart. She was a total sucker for men who adored their parents.

She propped herself on her elbow. "So what are all the things *you* want to do?"

"Well, when I was a kid I wanted to either play professional football or enlist in the navy."

"And you chose the navy."

"Actually, no. I chose football. I went to Notre Dame on a full athletic scholarship."

"You did?"

He nodded. "I was the starting quarterback for the Fighting Irish during junior year, and then senior year came along and I injured my shoulder, right before the draft."

"Oh. That's terrible."

"Yeah, it was. I was out for eleven months, and then I threw myself back into training. My shoulder healed perfectly, but it was clear I wouldn't be able to play at the same level anymore. Pro football is damn competitive, and by the time I got back in shape, a whole new crop of talented players was graduating and my chances of being drafted weren't that great anymore. So I enlisted."

"Okay, then you're still living one of the dreams. What else would a relationship hold you back from?"

His features creased. "I don't know what other things I want to do yet, but I'd like to have the freedom to do them. Traveling, for one. I doubt a serious girlfriend would appreciate me dropping everything and leaving town if I suddenly decided to do it." He paused. "I don't want to be tied down yet."

"Relationships don't have to tie you down," Jen pointed out.

Before she could blink, Cash flipped her on her back, his strong body hovering over her. "This conversation is getting too serious. Let's do something to lighten it up."

"Interesting. Like what?"

He swept his tongue over his bottom lip and pushed the blanket away to expose her naked body. "Well, I'm hungry."

"We just had all that leftover pizza."

"Not that kind of hungry." A predatory gleam entered his eyes. "I think I'll nibble on you for a bit."

Lord. Clearly the S in SEAL stood for *stamina*. Not that she was complaining. In fact, she wasn't complaining at all as Cash buried his face in her neck and kissed her feverish skin. A moan slipped out when he sucked hard enough to leave a hickey, and little pinpricks of pleasure danced along her flesh.

His rough hands teased her breasts as he dragged his hot mouth along the curve of her neck. His intoxicating scent surrounded her, spice and aftershave and pure man. The heavy weight of his cock on her belly made her shiver and arch her hips.

"Your body is perfect," he murmured as his hands and mouth continued to explore. He cupped her breasts. "So full." His fingers skimmed down to her waist. "And then this round, tight ass." He reached underneath her to squeeze. "These sexy legs." His callused palms traveled down her thighs, her knees, her calves, before returning north and parting her legs.

Jen gasped when he pushed one long finger inside her.

"And then this sweet, wet paradise," he rasped.

His finger slid out and he gently stroked her clit in light circular motions that made her squirm. How did he know exactly how to touch her? She'd never had a man so attuned to her body and its responses, and she couldn't control her shock when his skilled ministrations brought the first ripples of orgasm to the surface. Three past lovers and not a single one had brought her to climax with his touch. One day with Cash McCoy, and she'd come so many times she'd lost count.

The man just might be her new hero.

"You're close, aren't you?"

She met his eyes, floored by the naked passion glittering there. From the moment she'd met him in that coatroom, she'd known he'd be like this, capable of making her go up in flames with one heated look, one sinful touch.

"Well, we can't have that," Cash said after she nodded in response.

A disappointed groan lodged in her chest when he moved his hand away.

His husky laugh made her shiver. "You've gotta learn some patience, sweetheart." He flung out his arm and grabbed the condom sitting on the coffee table. "Besides, I want you to come while you're riding me."

A thrill shot through her. The thought of straddling his big, powerful body and having this big, powerful man at her mercy was hot as hell.

Heart pounding, she sat up and waited for Cash to sheathe himself. When he got on his back and beckoned her, she climbed up with no hesitation, encircled his thick shaft with one hand and brought it to her core.

Their eyes stayed locked together as she lowered herself on his cock. When she was fully seated, they let out simultaneous moans.

Shockwaves of pleasure seized her, but she stayed motionless, keeping him trapped inside her as she bent down to kiss him. His mouth was pure heaven, his lips firm, his tongue demanding. They shared long, drugging kisses, each one hotter than the last. And still she didn't move. She felt Cash's heartbeat thudding against her breasts. His breathing grew ragged, coming out in sharp bursts that she swallowed with her lips as she continued to kiss him.

"You okay?" she teased when he cursed against her mouth.

"No." Sweat bloomed on his forehead. "I need you to start moving."

Jen squeezed her inner muscles.

He swore again, loud and tortured.

"Like that?" she asked sweetly.

"Among other things."

She squeezed again.

He groaned.

"You know, this is really fun," she remarked. "You've got this vein in your forehead that looks like it's about to burst."

"That's not the only thing about to burst," he grumbled.

"I thought we were practicing the art of patience."

"I thought you were going to fuck my brains out," he countered, eyes blazing with pure agony.

She laughed. "Nobody said anything of the sort, cowboy. I was only instructed to ride you."

Cash dug his fingers into her hips, bringing a sting of pain. He tried thrusting upward, but she locked his thighs between hers and made a *tsk*ing sound.

"Quit being a pain in the ass, McCoy. If you don't let me do my thing, I'll climb right off you and make myself come in private."

He immediately stilled.

Jen grinned. "That's what I thought."

And then she started to move. In earnest. Lifting off his dick and then slamming down on it. Over and over, fast and hard, until the couch protested the ferocity of her movements. Cash reached up to play with her breasts, pinching her nipples, rolling them between his fingers. His hips came up to meet her. Their breathing became labored, choppy, as she rode him.

The throbbing between her legs took a critical turn. "Touch my clit," she said, surprising herself with the bold order.

His lips formed a sensual smile. "Yes, ma'am."

He placed his palm on her navel, fingers circling her belly button before traveling south.

Jen exploded the second he touched her. A wave of sensation slammed into her. Her mind splintered into a million pieces, and white dots assaulted her vision. Crying out, she grinded into him, vaguely aware of his hoarse shout as he came.

It took her a while to recover this time. Sagging onto his

chest, she just lay there and waited for her heartbeat to regulate and her breathing to steady.

Why hadn't anyone ever told her that sex could be this good?

And why did she get the feeling that three weeks in Cash's bed wouldn't be nearly enough?

She lifted her head and peeked up at him. "Again," she said with a groan. "We need to do that again."

His guttural laughter tickled her forehead. "I think I've created a monster."

CHAPTER TEN

As far as Cash was concerned, Sundays were sacred. Sundays meant watching football, drinking beer, and eating junk food. And he never strayed from that routine, not if he could help it.

So why was he finding it impossible to focus on the television screen?

For the hundredth time in the last hour, his gaze moved away from the TV and landed on the blonde across the room. She had a pair of earbuds in and was listening to music. She hadn't voiced a single complaint when he'd laid down the Sunday football law. Instead, she'd spent the past hour transferring photos from a very expensive-looking camera to her laptop.

He had no idea what was up with him, why he felt the strongest urge to pull up the chair next to Jen's and find out what she was working on. To spend the day sitting and talking. Maybe steal some kisses.

Talking. Stealing *kisses*.

What was he, a teenaged girl?

This need to get to know the woman he was sleeping with was disconcerting as hell.

Curiosity had him grudgingly rising from the couch. Jen's gaze flicked up at his approach. She pulled out her earphones. "What's up? Did your team lose or something?"

"No." He rounded the table and plopped down beside her. "I was curious about what you're working on."

She blinked in surprise. "Oh. Nothing really. I'm just uploading some pictures."

Cash inspected the Nikon on the table. "Shit, this camera is hardcore. When you said you liked messing around with photography, I figured you had one of those point-and-shoot cameras."

"I used to, but there's no fun in that." She shrugged. "It's more satisfying adjusting the settings yourself and capturing something unique."

"Can I see some of your pictures?"

Now she looked uneasy. "Why?"

"Why not?"

She chewed on her bottom lip as if trying to decide whether or not he was genuinely interested, and Cash suddenly remembered the comment she'd made when they'd first met, about how nobody in her family took her seriously. Maybe she was worried he'd make fun of her work?

"Come on," he pressed. "I'd love to take a look."

"Um. Okay." She shifted the laptop so they could both see the screen. "These are some shots I took in January when I went to a resort in Jamaica."

Cash leaned in, expecting to find postcard-perfect shots of swaying palm trees, sandy white beaches, and a calm ocean, but that was not the case. At all.

"What the hell kind of resort did you to go?" he asked suspiciously, his gaze focused on the desolate scene before him.

She offered a sheepish look. "I didn't spend much time on the resort. But don't tell my brother," she added quickly.

"Carson and my parents think I take these yearly sun-and-fun vacations for the, well, sun and fun."

Her fingers traveled over the track pad to scroll through the pictures. Cash was blown away. Some of the pictures were in color, others in black and white, but all displayed images he hadn't expected. Several featured a little boy, not older than five or six, with crooked teeth bared in a big grin. In one photo, the boy sat in the dirt, playing with marbles. In another, he dashed toward a small hut with a tin roof and made of rotting wood that looked about to collapse. The last shot showed the boy weaving through piles of garbage, while black flies hovered around him.

Cash frowned. "Where was this taken?"

"In a little town outside of Kingston. Poverty is their way of life. But Marcus—that's the kid in the picture—he was the sweetest kid I'd ever met. Smiling all the time, despite it all."

"What the hell were you thinking, walking around in places like these? You should've stayed at the hotel where it was safe."

She didn't even have the decency to look contrite. "There's only so many times you can *ooh* and *aah* at the ocean. Besides, I'm easily bored. Lying on the beach all day for a week isn't my thing. I want to see and do things I've never experienced before. So if it means stepping out of my comfort zone and visiting a village, or checking out the ganja shops in Kingston—"

"What?"

"Or visiting sugar cane fields in Haiti, ancient ruins in Mexico..." She trailed off with a shrug. "You've got to admit, it makes for more interesting pictures."

She kept scrolling through photos. Cash couldn't fight the concern in his gut. When he saw a series of photographs that looked like they'd been taken in the middle of a full-blown riot, he let out an expletive and scowled at Jen.

"So you take these trips, tell your family you're suntanning at a resort, and then you disappear into some of the most dangerous areas in those countries?"

"Pretty much."

"That's beyond foolish, Jen. It's downright reckless."

"I'm careful," she insisted. "I hire a respectable driver recommended by the resort staff. I don't go off into dark alleys alone—I don't go out after dark at all, in fact. And I've been trained in self-defense. I'm not some weak little twit who can't take care of herself."

"Then why are you lying to your family about what you really do on these trips?"

"Because unfortunately, *they* think I'm a weak little twit who can't take care of herself. So instead of trying to change their minds, I let them think what they want and do my own thing." She studied his face. "Disapproval of my tactics aside, what do you think of the pictures? Honestly?"

Cash sighed. "They're incredible."

A blush dotted her cheeks. "Are you just saying that?"

"No. If anything, I'm tempted to tell you they suck ass, just so you'd quit putting yourself in potentially dangerous situations," he grumbled. "But I can't lie to you. These are amazing."

The joy that flooded her eyes bugged him a little. Was this the first time anyone had complimented her work? If so, that was a damn shame. The pictures on the screen were crisp, stark, unforgiving—she didn't use any fancy techniques or filters to pretty up her subjects. She simply captured what she saw and forced you to look at it. Really look at it.

"Why aren't you working for some big-time magazine or newspaper?" he asked in bewilderment.

She looked startled. "I do this for fun. I have a blog where I upload pictures, but it's just a hobby. Other than the people who go on my blog, you're the first person I've ever shown my pictures to."

"You seriously haven't shown these to anyone other than me?"

Her brows furrowed. "Why do you look so pissed?"

"I'm not pissed. I'm surprised." He shook his head. "You should be doing this professionally. Forget blogging, your work needs to be hanging in a gallery. Or on the cover of *National Geographic* or something."

She stared at him as if he'd just told her she'd won the lottery. "You really think that?"

"Hell yes."

"I never thought..." Her voice wobbled. "Thank you."

"You're welcome." His expression clouded over. "But I'm still pissed you're exploring all those foreign countries without a single concern for safety."

"Isn't that your job? Exploring foreign countries without a single concern for safety?"

She had him there.

Before he could point out that he was *trained* for that kind of shit, Jen's phone broke out in an ear-shattering military march, complete with pounding percussion and a lot of horns. The sound was so intense it shook the dining room table.

She grinned. "That's my dad's ringtone. He programmed it for himself because he thought my other ringtones were too girlie." Rolling her eyes, she lifted the phone to her ear and said, "Hi, Dad." She paused, and then all the color drained from her face. "Are you serious? Did he hurt her?"

Cash's shoulders went rigid.

Next to him, Jen breathed a sigh of relief. "Oh thank God... Yes... Dad, I just said yes, okay? I'll be there in thirty minutes." She mumbled something unintelligible under her breath. "Yes, Dad, he'll come with me. Tell Carson he doesn't have to—oh fine, whatever." Her jaw tightened. "Yes, sir."

She hung up and turned to him with a flat, angry expression. "Brendan showed up at my parents' house an hour ago."

"What did he do?"

"Nothing crazy, which proves he's not a total moron. You don't mess with the admiral, and Brendan knows it. But he did yell a little and demand to know where I was. Carson already told our parents that Brendan and I broke up, but he didn't give them any details. Now they have an idea, because Brendan mentioned the restraining order during his rant." She scraped her chair back and stood with a scowl. "He scared my mom—and trust me, she doesn't scare easily. And he pissed off my dad, who is now requesting our presence."

Wariness climbed up Cash's throat. "*Our* presence?"

"Carson told him I'm staying with you, so he wants you there. Be prepared, because he'll probably grill you."

Cash felt shell-shocked as he watched Jen scurry off toward Matt's bedroom. He had to meet her *parents*? Now?

He ran a hand over the stubble coating his jaw. Normally he had no problem charming a girl's folks, but if Admiral Scott was anything like both Carson and Jen described, then no amount of charm would work on the man. Shit. And he didn't even have time to shave, damn it.

Cash sprang to action. In his bedroom, he rummaged through his dresser drawers for some presentable clothing. Showing up in sweatpants and a wife-beater definitely wouldn't make a great first impression. He settled on a pair of wrinkled khakis he hardly ever wore, hence the wrinkles, and a blue button-down shirt. Forgoing his trademark shitkickers, he shoved his feet into a pair of brown loafers he found in his closet, which made him take pause because he had no idea how they'd gotten there.

He looked—and felt—like a total tool in the getup.

When he stepped out of his room, he collided with Jen, who

took one look at him and burst out laughing. "Are you wearing khakis? And *loafers*?"

He gritted his teeth. "I'm trying to look presentable."

"Why?" It dawned on her. "For my parents? Oh, that's sweet. But unnecessary—they'll be too busy lecturing me to notice what you're wearing."

He cast a longing look at the television before walking over to turn it off. So much for his sacred Sunday ritual. Instead of football and beer, he was about to spend the afternoon with Jen's parents.

And Carson.

Shit, he'd forgotten all about Carson.

"By the way—not one word to your brother about what we've been doing all weekend," Cash said as they left the apartment.

Jen was walking ahead of him, and she spared him a pithy look over her shoulder. "Gee, really? I was planning on giving him a play-by-play of every orgasm I had."

They reached the stairwell door. Before she could walk through it, he grasped her chin with one hand and glared at her. "I'm serious."

She frowned. "What exactly did Carson threaten you with when he told you to keep your hands off me?"

With a sigh, he dropped his hand from her face. "I'm planning on doing the officer training this year, and I need a recommendation from him. He implied he'd give me a bad one if I got involved with you."

Jen's jaw fell open. "Cash, if my brother denies you a good recommendation based on who you're sleeping with rather than your skills as a soldier, then he's a really shitty lieutenant."

"Maybe, but I can't risk it."

It was her turn to sigh. "Fine, my lips are sealed. But I can't promise I won't tell him off for all the other ways he's been interfering in my life lately." She paused. "Not today, though. I'll already have my hands full dealing with my dad."

She reached for the door handle, then stopped abruptly. She surprised him by looping her arms around his neck, standing on her tiptoes, and giving him a long, open-mouthed kiss that left him breathless.

As their tongues met, Cash's anxiety vanished, replaced by a blast of molten heat that sizzled from his mouth straight down to his dick. He couldn't get enough of this woman. She was like a new drug he hadn't known existed. Every kiss, every touch and mind-numbing release, fueled the addiction.

"There," she said, pulling her mouth free. "That ought to tide us over for a while."

Hardly. That one kiss had made his groin throb like a motherfucker. It took all his willpower to banish the surge of lust buzzing in his veins.

They left the building through the rear doors that opened onto the parking lot. Neither of them said much during the drive, the silence broken only by the occasional direction from Jen. Cash absently tapped his fingers on the steering wheel as he drove north on the I-805, wishing he knew what to expect from this visit. He hated going into situations blind, and by the time he exited the interstate and followed Del Mar Heights toward Jen's parents' house, he was feeling tense and subdued again.

The Scott family home was nestled away from the road in a residential area. Modest-sized houses, towering oaks, and well-maintained sidewalks flashed by. It was a nice area, and family friendly, judging by the multitude of bicycles and kiddie pools littering the lawns.

Cash pulled into the driveway and parked behind a very familiar Range Rover. He smothered a curse. Great, the LT was already here. Hopefully Carson didn't possess some freaky sex radar that would start beeping the second he saw Cash's face.

But hell, Jen had raised a damn good point before. Carson had no business basing his recommendation on Cash's sex life. So what if he'd given in to his attraction to Jen? He was a damn good SEAL, and his dick played no part in that equation.

The front door swung open the second they climbed the porch. Carson's tall frame filled the doorway, his gloomy expression serving as an omen of what lay behind the door. He nodded a distracted hello at Cash, then glanced at his sister.

"How pissed is he?" Jen asked.

"Scale of one to ten? Seven, maybe eight." Carson dragged a hand through his blond hair. "But it's not directed at you. Mostly Brendan, and then me, for handling it on my own and not telling them."

Jen frowned. "*I'm* handling it on my own. They should be mad at me, not you."

Her brother shrugged. "Come on, let's get this over with. They're out on the patio."

Neither Scott sibling paid Cash much attention. They simply marched down the wide hallway, leaving him to steal a quick glance here and there as he trailed after them. Family photos lined the cream-colored walls in the corridor. There was an obscene amount of shots featuring Carson in his uniform, and Cash also glimpsed a portrait featuring an older version of Carson clad in full navy regalia.

The hallway spilled into a spacious, country-style kitchen with gleaming appliances and an enormous butcher-block work island. A glass sliding door across the room led out to a cedar deck ringed by a slatted wooden railing. As they neared the door, Cash gazed beyond the deck at the manicured lawn and kidney-shaped swimming pool.

Jen's parents were out on the deck, sitting on white wicker

chairs. Both jumped to their feet when they spotted the new arrivals, and a little blonde cyclone dashed over to embrace Jen. Jen had inherited her tiny stature and perfect features from her mother, who looked so much like her they could have been twins.

The admiral waited his turn while his wife hugged their daughter, but the hard line of his square jaw belied his patient pose. The second Jen's mother released her, the admiral pulled her into a tight embrace.

The Scotts looked Jen up and down as if gauging her physical and mental state. Their scrutiny lasted so long Jen finally sighed. "I told you I'm fine. Stop looking at me like I'm not."

Jen's mother peered at Cash. "Is this him?"

"Yes," Jen replied, sounding both irritated and amused. "Cash McCoy, these are my parents, Laura and Gary Scott."

Cash approached the couple and stuck out his hand. "Pleased to meet you, Mr. and Mrs. Scott," he said gruffly.

Laura shook his hand first. Her smile was genuinely warm. "Call me Laura, please."

Gary leaned in for the handshake, his lips curled in a frown as he said, "Call me Admiral. Or sir."

From the corner of his eye, Cash saw Jen rolling her eyes.

Jen's father still had a death grip on Cash's hand. He didn't want to pansy out and be the first to end the shake, but he knew the older man expected it of him, and the need to get in the man's good graces beat out Cash's macho instincts.

He withdrew his hand, then studied Gary Scott. Six feet tall, blond hair threaded with silver, the shoulders of a linebacker and a handsome yet stern face. *Commanding* was the first word that came to mind. Followed by *terrifying*.

The admiral narrowed his pale blue eyes. "So you're the one entrusted with the task of keeping my daughter safe."

"Yes, sir."

The man continued his slow appraisal, then nodded as if Cash had passed his test. "You seem competent."

Relief flickered through him. "Thank you, sir."

"With that said, know that if any harm comes to my daughter, I will drown you."

Huh. So that's where Carson got it from.

"Dad!" Jen chided, but her father had already turned away from Cash.

"Why don't we all sit down?" Although he formed it as a question, it was clearly an order.

And although the admiral wasn't his CO, wasn't even active duty, Cash's butt landed in the chair before the man even finished his sentence. So did everyone else's butts. Which made one thing very clear—the admiral ran a tight ship here.

This was going to be a long afternoon.

CHAPTER
ELEVEN

As expected, her parents almost had a coronary when Jen reluctantly detailed Brendan's stalker activities of late. When she reached the part about the rose petals in her apartment, her father looked so livid she thought he might actually grab his favorite rifle and go after Brendan. Thankfully, Carson managed to talk the admiral down, assuring him that Jen was safe at Cash's apartment and would remain that way until Brendan left town.

The discussion lasted for the better part of an hour. When her parents finally eased up and stopped trying to coerce her to move back home, she breathed a sigh of relief—only to get annoyed all over again once they started harassing her about her current state of unemployment.

Her mother mentioned nursing again.

Her father pointed out there was no shame in enlisting in the military at twenty-five.

They both remarked that she spent too much time taking "silly" pictures.

Her brother tried to run interference.

And through it all, Cash sat there, looking so uncomfortable she felt truly bad for him. The only time her father acknowledged him was to bark out questions about Cash's training and offer pointed reminders that his "little girl's" safety was in Cash's hands. Talk about pressure, but it was all you could expect from the mighty Admiral Scott.

By four o'clock, her parents had calmed down, and she was anxious to get the hell out of there. So was Cash, judging by the way he kept tapping his loafers on the floor of the deck. Carson had gone inside by then to check his email, though Jen suspected he'd used that as an excuse to disappear.

Abruptly, she pushed her chair back and stood up. "Okay, I think it's time for us to go. I want to clean up my resume tonight."

That earned her a frown from her mother. "Where are you thinking of applying?"

"Not sure yet. I'll take a look at the listings, maybe hit up Horton Plaza and Fashion Valley to drop off resumes."

Her mom made that familiar *tsk* of disapproval. "Wouldn't you rather do something useful, Jennifer? Something that makes a difference?"

"Sales makes a difference," she said lightly, hoping her parents wouldn't notice the annoyed tic in her jaw. "I help people pick out that perfect outfit or find the perfect gift."

"Honey, can't you just *consider* the idea of nursing school?"

Fighting the urge to rip out her own hair, Jen managed a nod. "Sure, Mom. I'll consider it." She turned to Cash. "Ready to go?"

He was on his feet in a nanosecond. "Sure. If that's what you want."

Suck-up. Leaving it up to *her* when he was clearly dying to escape. There was a reason she hadn't brought many guys home. Her mother wasn't so bad, aside from the not-so-veiled criticism, but her father? He was a force to be reckoned with: authoritative, strict, and with no tolerance for error.

"I want a daily check-in," the admiral said after Jen gave him a goodbye kiss on the cheek.

"Weekly," she countered.

"Twice a week."

She rolled her eyes. "Yes, sir."

Leaving her parents on the deck, she and Cash headed back inside. In the hallway, she stopped and touched his arm. "I just need to use the bathroom," she said.

"I'll meet you in the car." His strides were eager as he hurried off.

Jen was eager to get going too, but after she left the bathroom, she ended up getting sidetracked on her way to the front door. Hearing Carson's voice drifting out of the den, she halted midstep. Her brother sounded...agitated.

She wasn't a snooper by nature, but Carson's strained voice compelled her to creep closer to the den.

"I know, but I really need to see you."

Jen froze.

"Maybe a quick cup of coffee tomorrow?" Carson paused. "No, Holly doesn't know. I haven't told her yet."

A sick feeling settled in the pit of her stomach.

"Okay...sure...tomorrow at noon. The Starbucks on Market? See you then, angel."

Angel?

Jen shook the WTF cobwebs from her head. When she heard footsteps nearing the door, she snapped out of her trance and darted back to the bathroom. Sucking in a few deep breaths, she tried to control the confusion and suspicion flying through her.

Exhaling slowly, she stepped out of the bathroom, running into Carson just as he strode into the hall.

He flashed her a tired look. "All done with the Spanish Inquisition?"

"Yes, thank God." She hesitated. "Why didn't Holly come with you today?"

"She's at the restaurant."

"I thought she doesn't work Sundays."

"She doesn't, but the weekend chef called in sick, so she had to go in."

Jen narrowed her eyes. "What's this I hear about Holly staying with her sister the other night?"

Carson's lips tightened under her scrutiny. "It was no big deal. We got into a little fight, that's all."

"A fight over what?"

"Over none of your damn business."

He made a move to march off, but she latched her hand onto his defined upper arm. "Carson. What's going on?"

"Nothing," he muttered. "Just husband and wife stuff, okay?"

"Should I be worried?"

"No." He slowly uncurled her fingers from his biceps. "So how you doing at Cash's? Is he being a gentleman?"

His transparent attempt at deflection annoyed her. "He's being very hospitable."

"He hasn't put the moves on you, has he?"

No, I put the moves on him.

"Of course not," she replied, but only because she'd promised Cash she wouldn't say anything.

Still, the lie left a bitter taste in her mouth. She was twenty-five, for God's sake. Her brother had no say in her love life. Her safety, fine, she'd give him that, but she'd only bended to Carson's will and agreed to move out of her apartment because he'd raised legitimate concerns. What if Brendan *did* violate the restraining order and show up at her door? That wasn't so farfetched anymore, considering he'd just confronted her parents.

But while her brother's concerns about Brendan were valid, she didn't agree with his high-handed attitude about Cash.

"I'll talk to you later."

She snapped out of her thoughts in time to see her brother's retreating back. Rather than call after him, she let him go, unable to fight the feeling of foreboding climbing up her spine. What on earth was up with her brother?

And why the hell had he called some other woman *angel*?

"I swear to God, if you're cheating on your wife..." She couldn't even finish that sentence. The thought of Carson stepping out on Holly made her blood boil.

Squaring her shoulders, she marched to the front door and practically sprinted outside. She slid into the waiting SUV, slamming the door so hard Cash jumped.

"What's wrong?" he asked immediately.

"Nothing." She buckled her seatbelt. "Can we stop at my sister-in-law's restaurant on the way home?"

"Sure. Why?"

"I just want to say hi to Holly."

As Cash started the engine and reversed out of her parents' driveway, Jen fixed her gaze out the window, still troubled by the conversation she'd overheard.

The idea of Carson cheating on Holly continued to burn a hole in her stomach, but she didn't want to share her suspicions with Cash. Maybe if she didn't voice them out loud, they wouldn't feel real.

Angel.

Who had Carson been talking to?

Whoever it was, this didn't bode well for her brother's marriage. At all.

By the time Cash pulled up in front of Primrose, the restaurant where Holly worked, Jen was anxious to see her sister-in-law and make sure everything was okay.

"You can wait in the car," she told him. "I wouldn't mind some girl time."

A perplexed groove dug into his forehead. "All right."

She hopped out and hurried toward the restaurant's entrance. When she strode inside, she had to let her eyes adjust to the dim lighting. As usual, she was taken aback by the elegance of the place. Primrose was owned by a renowned West Coast chef, and Jen remembered Holly having to endure a three-month-long interview process to snag the prestigious sous-chef position.

The lanky young man at the hostess stand waved her in the direction of the kitchen once she told him Holly was her sister-in-law. Thanking him, she bypassed the main room and made her way down a wood-paneled hallway.

She hesitated in front of the swinging doors, then entered the enormous kitchen, where she earned a few quizzical looks from the kitchen staff. She immediately spotted her sister-in-law by a gleaming stainless steel counter across the room.

"Hey sis," she called.

The petite brunette spun around, her catlike green eyes filling with surprise. "Jen? What are you doing here?"

"Just stopped to say hello," she said lightly.

Holly saw right through her. "What's wrong?"

"Nothing's wrong," Jen lied. "I really came by to say hi."

Wiping her hands with a dishrag, Holly stepped away from the counter, abandoning the onions she'd been mincing.

"Don't you have to finish those?" Jen asked.

"It's just prep work. It can wait a few minutes." Untying her white apron, Holly tossed a glance at the dark-haired man by the grill. "Luis, I'm taking a break."

"Sure thing, sweetie."

Holly took Jen's arm and practically dragged her out of the kitchen and into the employee lounge, a large space with two couches, a kitchenette, and a bank of lockers spanning one wall.

Under Holly's piercing gaze, Jen felt like a little kid again. She and Holly were the same height, but the brunette triggered the same urge to cower that the admiral evoked in her.

"Are you okay? Did something happen with Brendan?" Holly frowned. "Did you come here alone? Because Carson said you weren't supposed to go anywhere without Cash. What's wrong?"

She had to smile. "I'm fine. Nothing happened with Brendan. Cash is outside waiting in the car. And nothing's wrong." She gave Holly a pointed look. "Not with me, anyway."

"What does that mean?"

"Why didn't you tell me you and Carson were having problems?"

After a beat of stunned silence, Holly's shoulders sagged. "You talked to Annabelle."

"Yes. And Carson, though he didn't say much."

Holly drifted over to one of the couches and sat down. She rubbed her eyes, then lowered her hands to her lap and started fidgeting.

Jen sat next to her. "What's going on?" she prodded. "Come on, Hol, talk to me. You know I'm a good listener. And if it's confidentiality you're worried about, don't. I won't breathe a word of what you tell me to Carson."

Holly worried her bottom lip with her teeth. "It's not a big deal. Carson and I are just going through a bit of a rough patch."

"A few more details would help."

Holly seemed reluctant, but then she opened her mouth

and a stream of words gushed out. "We're not connecting, okay? He was gone for six months, and ever since he got back it's like we're on a different wavelength. It always takes a while to readjust once he comes home, but this time...it's a little harder, I guess. He comes back and expects everything to be the same, but he doesn't realize that each time he leaves, it's like our entire relationship was put on hold.

"He complains that I work too much, but what else am I supposed to do? When he's away, I have to do *something* to occupy myself, and I can't just drop what I'm doing when he gets back." Holly let out an anguished breath. "I know this is what I signed up for. I knew being married to a SEAL wouldn't be easy, but your brother is so...*infuriating* sometimes. It's different for him—when he's out of the country, he's not thinking about me. He's focused on the job, the mission, staying alive. But me? All I do is think of him, and worry, and stress, and pray that he's safe."

Tears slid down Holly's cheeks, which startled Jen. She'd never once seen her feisty sister-in-law cry.

She reached out and gripped Holly's hand. "Hey, it's okay."

"No, it's not. He doesn't understand that I get used to being alone when he's gone. It's like I have a part-time husband. We didn't even have a honeymoon, for Pete's sake! We had to cancel it because he got sent on some mission I'm not even allowed to know about. Don't get me wrong, I love him. I love him so damn much. But sometimes it feels like I spend our entire marriage waiting for him to come home. And this time, he comes back and tells me he wants to have a *baby*."

Jen's jaw dropped. "Seriously?"

"Yes, seriously. The big oaf wants a baby, but who'll be the one raising it? Me. Doing it alone half the time." Holly huffed. "He suggested that I quit the restaurant and focus on Prestige Events with Annabelle, since that's only a weekend gig. So he comes home after six months, barely says hello before he carts me off to bed, drops a baby bomb and asks me to quit my job! Am I the only one who sees something wrong with that?"

Jen's heart ached. But how was she supposed to comfort her sister-in-law? Everything Holly just said was the reason Jen had vowed not to get involved with a military man. A part-time husband didn't sound all that appealing to her either.

At a loss for words, she searched her brain for something reassuring to say, but Holly shot to her feet, looking mortified. "Shit. I'm sorry. I didn't mean to unload all that on you."

"It's okay. I'm glad you told me."

Holly's face scrunched up in misery. "I love him. You know I love him, right?"

"Of course you do. Everything will work itself out, Hol. But you need to talk to Carson about all this."

"I have, but the stubborn jackass doesn't seem to hear me."

"So keep at it. Make him hear you. Carson can be a pigheaded asshole, but he loves you."

Her brother's conversation with his *angel* suddenly flashed through her mind, but Jen forced it away.

"Talk to him," she urged again. "You two can fix this. I know you can."

Hope shone in Holly's eyes. "You really think so?"

"I really think so."

Swallowing, the other woman wiped her eyes with the sleeve of her shirt. "Fuck. I should get back to work. But thanks for coming by, Jen. I really needed this."

"You're not off the hook yet. Annabelle and I are organizing a girls' night, so you'll have another chance to rant." She grinned. "I hear Savannah gives good advice."

Holly snorted. "Only if it's about sex. But yeah, I'm totally up for a girls' night. Text me with the details, okay?"

"Definitely."

They parted ways in the corridor. Jen's heart continued to ache as she walked outside. Cash had been fiddling with his phone, but he tossed it into the cup holder when she slid into the SUV.

"Everything okay?" he asked.

"No."

He pinned her down with a hard stare. "What's going on?"

She hesitated, knowing she probably shouldn't say anything about her suspicions, but the need to confide in someone was too strong. With a heavy breath, she told him what she'd overheard earlier.

Cash instantly shook his head. "No way. Carson would never cheat on Holly."

Jen envied his conviction. "Then why did he call that woman *angel*? And what about the *Holly doesn't know* part?" Nausea scampered up her throat. "Holly fully admitted they're having problems. What if Carson got tired of fighting with his wife and found some outside comfort?"

"No way," Cash said again. "Whatever you heard, there has to be an explanation for it. Carson's not the fucking-around type."

"You never knew him in his manwhore days," she countered. "Fucking around was his middle name."

"*Was*. He loves his wife, Jen. There's an explanation, trust me."

She wished she could. Wished she could feel as certain as Cash sounded.

And she really wished she could erase Holly's miserable expression from her mind.

I knew what I signed up for.

Yep, Holly had known, but that didn't make it any easier, did it? Loving a SEAL was no walk in the park, and Carson and Holly's marital problems were proof of that.

Jen studied Cash from the corner of her eye, watching his strong hands move over the steering wheel as he pulled away from the restaurant. She'd been staying with him for five days now, they'd been having sex only two of those days, but already she felt herself getting attached to him. She loved his heart-stopping grins and rough voice. The way he'd fallen asleep last night with one arm carelessly flung over her, as if he were trying to protect her even in her sleep. How he smiled at her when she'd opened her eyes this morning. And his genuine praise for her photographs earlier had made her heart soar like a damn helium balloon.

But seeing Holly's ravaged face had reaffirmed her decision to avoid relationships with military guys. That meant she needed to nip this growing attachment in the bud and remember that they were just having a fling. Some hot sex, some laughter, some fun, and in two weeks, they'd say goodbye.

Keeping his eyes on the road, Cash dropped one hand from the steering wheel and rested his palm on her jeans-clad thigh, lazily stroking her over the denim. The gesture felt so natural that Jen gulped.

Two weeks.

Biting her lip, she forced herself to cling to that reminder. Two weeks. That was all the time they had left, all the time she would allow herself. No matter how much she enjoyed being with Cash, she couldn't risk forming an emotional attachment to him.

Because there was no doubt in her mind that if she let herself, she could fall head over heels in love with Cash McCoy.

CHAPTER TWELVE

Cash had just dunked his head under the shower spray when the curtain was ripped open and Jen appeared like an apparition.

"Hurry up," she ordered. "We're going out."

He wiggled his eyebrows. "Why don't you join me instead?"

"We're going out," she repeated.

Then she disappeared, leaving a cloud of steam in her wake.

Bewildered, Cash rinsed the shampoo from his hair and shut off the faucet. Water slid down his naked body and dripped onto the fluffy blue bath mat as he grabbed a towel. He quickly dried off, wrapped the towel around his waist, and wiped the foggy mirror so he could see his reflection while he shaved.

Since his electric razor was busted, he was using disposables until he got around to buying a new one, but he'd run out of those too, so for the past couple of days he'd been stealing Jen's lady razors, which drove her nuts. When he opened the medicine cabinet and reached for her stash of pink razors, he found a yellow Post-it note taped to the package.

The words "NO MEANS NO" glared accusingly at him.

Grinning, he ignored the permanent-marker warning and

swiped a razor. He shaved in a hurry, knowing that Jen was probably pacing the bedroom while she waited for him. Probably biting on her bottom lip the way she did whenever she was upset.

And he knew she was upset, because she'd been nibbling on that sexy lip ever since they'd come back from Del Mar yesterday. He'd tried assuring her there was no way Carson would cheat on his wife, but Jen remained unconvinced. She'd stewed about it all night.

Though if Cash were being honest, he was less upset over what was no doubt a misunderstanding with Carson, and more upset about the way Jen's parents had behaved. They'd treated her like she was a huge disappointment to them, a total failure because she hadn't found her career path yet.

And the admiral's barbed remark about Jen's "silly" pictures had seriously grated. After seeing her photographs, Cash knew there was nothing silly about them. He still couldn't believe she wasn't doing it professionally, and now that he'd seen firsthand how talented she was, he planned on encouraging her to look into photography opportunities. *Someone* needed to offer some encouragement, seeing as how she didn't get any from her folks.

It bothered him that she let them undermine her confidence and make light of her skills. But when he'd asked her last night why she didn't stand up to her family, she'd shrugged and said something about "picking her battles."

Yup, she was indeed pacing when Cash entered the bedroom a couple minutes later. She fired an impatient look in his direction and said, "I picked out an outfit for you."

He glanced at the bed—shit, she'd actually laid out some clothes—and raised his eyebrows. "Um. Okay."

"To save time," she added hastily. "I'm not making some controlling statement about your fashion sense."

Speaking of fashion sense, he suddenly noticed what *she*

was wearing, and his brows rose even higher. Rather than the tight-fitting jeans, cute tops, and sexy shoes he'd become accustomed to, she wore black yoga pants, black Adidas, and a snug hooded sweatshirt in a dark shade of blue. And a baseball cap.

An alarm went off in his head. "Where exactly are we going?"

"The Gaslamp. I wanted to drop off a few resumes."

"Then why are you dressed like Sporty Spice?"

She huffed out a breath. "I'm applying to a sporting goods store. I figured I'd dress the part, show them that, ah, I'm into sports."

Suspicion swarmed his gut. His gaze shifted to the clothes she'd picked out for him—jeans, black hoodie, and yup, a baseball cap. Okay, this was weird.

Deciding he didn't like the WTF nature of the situation, Cash dropped his towel and flashed a grin. "Why don't we do the resume thing tomorrow and spend the day in bed instead?"

Jen didn't bat an eyelash, not even when he gave his hardening dick a long, firm stroke. Huh. No reaction at the sight of his goods. She was definitely a woman on a mission today.

"Or...we can hand out resumes," she said before turning to the door.

Sighing, he reached for a clean pair of boxers from the laundry basket on the floor, then dressed in the clothes Jen had left on the bed. He even put on the damn hat, mostly because he was curious to find out where Jen was taking him that would require them to wear matching hoodies and caps. Sporting goods store, his ass.

His unease grew once they left the apartment and got into his car. Jen seemed even more agitated now—avoiding his eyes, biting her lip, tapping her short fingernails on the stack of resumes in her lap.

"Okay," he grumbled. "Why are you acting like a crazy person?"

"What are you talking about?" she said in an overly cheerful voice. "I'm acting normal."

He shook his head, deciding to give up. Might as well let this insanity unfold naturally.

Ten minutes later, they reached the Gaslamp District. Cash lucked out and found an empty parking space in front of a meter, but not even his impressive, borderline-superhuman parallel parking job inspired a reaction from Jen.

After he fed the meter and locked the SUV, he glanced at the small coffee shop they'd parked in front of. "Want to grab a coffee?"

She looked so thrilled that he grew even more suspicious. "Yes! I would love a coffee."

Cash made a move toward the café, but she quickly grabbed his arm. "Not from here. I'm in the mood for Starbucks."

He shot her a strange look. "Okay."

They took off down the sidewalk, dodging pedestrians as Jen set a brisk pace more suited for running the Boston Marathon.

"What's the rush?" he asked in annoyance.

"Craving an iced mocha, that's all," she said cheerfully.

The Starbucks was five blocks away, but at the breakneck speed they were going, they reached it in three minutes flat. Cash headed for the door, but Jen yet again intercepted him. Her eyes were glued to the storefront, scanning the glass like a hawk focusing on its prey. All of a sudden, a cross between a squeak and a hiss flew out of her mouth, and then she tugged on his hand and dragged him toward the side of the building.

Just like that, Cash had officially had enough.

"What the *fuck* is going on?"

Shamefaced, she met his frazzled gaze. "Okay, so... Don't be mad."

He groaned. Someone starting a sentence with "don't be mad" was never a good sign.

"Why are we here, Jen?"

"Look in the window."

Frowning, Cash peered around the corner. Every table in the coffee shop was occupied and he scanned the patrons with military precision. Three older women laughing over iced coffees, a lone student reading a thick textbook, a group of businessmen chatting.

Son of a bitch.

He rapidly moved out of sight and glared at Jen. "Are you fucking kidding me? We're spying on Carson?"

"Don't think of it as spying. We're...discreetly monitoring his movements. You know, doing some recon."

Cash raised his hand to run it through his hair, only to collide with the brim of his baseball cap. Make that his disguise. And he noticed that Jen wasn't carrying her resumes. She'd left them in the car, which confirmed she'd had an ulterior motive this entire time.

"This is ridiculous. Let's go. I'm not spying on your brother."

Her lips tightened in an angry line. "Did you happen to notice that he's not alone?"

"He was sitting alone at the table."

She crept along the brick wall and peeked around the building again, then beckoned him. "Look again," she said flatly.

Cash stole another glance and cursed under his breath. She was right. Carson's back was to the window, but Cash had a clear view of the auburn-haired woman now occupying the small table. She must have stepped away when he'd looked over the first time.

From his vantage point, he noted that Carson's companion was average looking, but those long auburn tresses and the remarkable rack beneath her V-neck top definitely upped her hotness factor.

Jen sidled up to him and made a dismayed noise. "What the hell is he doing with that woman?"

"Maybe they're just friends."

No sooner did he finish that sentence than the redhead reached across the table and gripped Carson's hand. Her face took on an intense expression as she said something to the blond SEAL.

Cash caught Jen's look of outrage. "Friends hold hands sometimes," he said feebly.

She ducked back into the alley, a cloud darkening her face. "I've seen enough. Let's go."

He didn't argue. He also didn't sing what was becoming his new favorite tune: *there has to be an explanation*. So what if the cute redhead had taken Carson's hand? That didn't mean a damn thing.

Still, he couldn't shake the uneasiness in his gut as they walked back to the car.

After he settled in the driver's seat, he glanced over and sighed when he noticed the stiffness of Jen's shoulders. "This doesn't mean anything, sweetheart. I'm sure if you ask Carson about it, he'll have an explanation."

"And what if the explanation is that he's cheating on Holly?"

Cash had no answer for that. Damn it. What the hell was Carson doing? All this sneaking around wasn't painting the guy in a positive light.

"Poor Holly. Do you think I should tell her?"

"No," he said immediately. "Talk to your brother first. If this is all a misunderstanding, you don't want to cause any more problems by getting Holly riled up."

"Yeah, you're right." She went quiet again. "Seeing that sucked, Cash."

He swallowed. "I know."

"But...but at least it kind of reaffirms my decision, you know?"

"What decision?"

"Not to be a military wife. I mean, look at what Holly and Carson are dealing with. Fighting, unable to connect or communicate." She rubbed her temples as if warding off a headache. "My parents' marriage was the same. My dad was always gone, and Mom had to do everything on her own. It got better once he retired, but his being home now doesn't make up for all the times he wasn't. And yeah, I get that relationships require work and compromise, but relationships should also be a partnership. How can that happen when one partner is gone half the time?"

He didn't have an answer for that, either.

"At least we won't ever get to that point."

His mouth went dry. "What do you mean?"

"Because we're just having a fling. We don't have to worry about ending up in a Carson-and-Holly situation." She reached for the stack of resumes she'd left on the dash. "Anyway, there's no point in going home just yet. Since we're already here, I may as well hand out some resumes, right?"

With that, she hopped out of the car, leaving Cash feeling unsettled. He knew her words shouldn't bother him. It was just a fling, exactly like Jen said.

So he got out of the car and followed Jen down the sidewalk, trying not to dwell on the confusing emotions spiraling through him, or the way his chest constricted when he thought about having to say goodbye to this girl.

CHAPTER THIRTEEN

Jen spent the rest of the afternoon updating her blog and trying not to stress over what she and Cash had seen earlier. The idea that Carson might be an adulterous jackass made her want to drive to his apartment and lay into him, but Cash had convinced her not to talk to her brother until she cooled off a little.

Probably a good idea. She and Carson rarely saw eye to eye on anything—get them in the same room together and they were bound to argue. But she didn't want to fight with him about this. She wanted a mature, adult conversation, in which he explained why the *hell* he'd been holding hands with another woman.

"You okay?" Cash asked as he collected the cardboard containers from the dining room table.

They'd ordered Chinese for dinner, but Jen hadn't tasted a thing. She'd spent the entire meal staring at her phone and battling the urge to call Carson.

"Nope. Maybe I should call him now."

"Or maybe you should call him tomorrow like we agreed. You're still too pissed—I can see it in your eyes."

"Aren't *you* pissed?"

"No, because I maintain there's a reasonable explanation for what we saw."

She helped him clear the table, wishing she shared Cash's confidence. Cash, however, hadn't been around when Carson was in his manwhore prime, while Jen had had a front-row seat.

Her mouth flattened as she carried the leftovers into the kitchen. First thing tomorrow, she was confronting her brother, and he'd better have a damn good explanation.

Cash must have sensed that she'd boarded the angry train again, because he held out his arms and said, "C'mere."

As if a magnet drew her to him, she sank into his strong embrace, shivering when his lips brushed over the top of her head. His woodsy scent enveloped her, his powerful arms providing the rush of comfort she'd needed. God, whenever he held her, she turned into a puddle of mush.

"No more thinking," he said, running his hands over the small of her back. "Let this go until you talk to Carson, okay?"

She exhaled slowly. "Fine, but I might need you to distract me. Like a sexy kind of distraction."

He laughed. "The sexy distraction will have to wait. Dylan's on his way over, remember?"

"Oh yeah, football. I forgot."

"You don't mind, do you? I could cancel."

"No, don't do that. He's already on his way." She planted a kiss on his cheek and stepped out of the embrace. "I'm going to hop in the shower. If you want some guy time, I can hang out in the bedroom tonight."

Cash tugged on her ponytail and brought her mouth to his again. "No way. You're hanging out with us and watching the game. It'll help get your mind off this Carson situation."

"You sure I won't be intruding?"

He chuckled again. "Trust me, Dylan will love having you around."

Right. Dylan, AKA Cash's go-to threesome pal. At the memory, a flush heated her cheeks.

Cash clearly didn't miss the blush, because he offered a dry grin. "No threesome tonight," he assured her. He arched a brow. "Unless you want one."

Her whole body tingled in response. "Are you serious?"

He shrugged. "Just throwing it out there. Dylan's a bit of a slut, so you never know what'll happen when he's around."

Jen studied his face, realization dawning. "You'd be up for it."

Another shrug.

"You totally would," she exclaimed. "I can see it on your face."

"Sure, I'd be up for it."

His light admission startled her. "Wow. You're really into it, aren't you?"

The molten heat in his eyes disrupted her pulse and sent it careening. "Of course. There's nothing sexier than a woman turning her pleasure over to two men." Without letting her digest that, he gave her butt a little smack. "You taking that shower?"

"Oh. Um, yeah."

She felt slightly dazed as she wandered off toward the bathroom. What did it say about her that the thought of being with two men turned her on?

And Cash would actually be up for sharing her with another guy? It continued to surprise her how open-minded he was about sex. He didn't balk at anything.

Her nipples puckered as the idea crept into her mind once more. She banished it, ordering her head out of the gutter. Cash's friend was coming by to watch football, not to ravish her, for fuck's sake.

She ended up taking a long shower, allowing the hot water

to ease the muscles that had been tied in knots all day. She washed her hair, shaved her legs, lathered lavender-scented body wash on her skin. By the time she toweled off and walked into Cash's room, she felt loose and relaxed.

She spent the next ten minutes blow-drying her hair, then brushed it until it shone and left it loose. She dressed for comfort—leggings, sports bra, and a turquoise top with a wide neckline that caused the soft material to fall off one shoulder. After a moment of hesitation, she applied some make-up. Mascara, subtle eye shadow, a dab of lip gloss.

The effort she went to for her appearance was more for her own sake than Cash and Dylan's. She always felt better when she looked her best, and there was a spring to her step as she left the bedroom.

Male voices sounded from the living room. Jen's pulse quickened, a reaction that had her rolling her eyes. Okay, enough. Just because Cash had broached the subject of threesomes didn't mean one was in the cards. Besides, she didn't know a thing about this Dylan guy, save for the fact that he was a SEAL, and, apparently, a slut. For all she knew, he was completely unattractive and someone she would never dream of—

The thought died when she entered the room and laid eyes on their guest.

Okay. Well. Unattractive was *not* the adjective to describe Dylan Wade.

Movie-star gorgeous was more apt. Or maybe *female wet dream*.

"Hi. You must be Jen," he said in a deep, easygoing voice. His expression was downright smoldering as he unabashedly checked her out.

A bolt of heat struck her as the golden Adonis rose from the couch. He was around the same height as Cash, six-foot-plus, but fair where Cash was dark. Jen couldn't hide her appreciation as she swept her gaze over his chiseled face—green eyes the shade of ripe limes, a killer grin, sexy dimples.

His body didn't disappoint, either. Long muscular legs were encased in dark-blue denim, and a 49ers jersey stretched over a sculpted chest. The sleeves of his shirt revealed corded biceps and roped forearms.

She was tempted to ask him to do a little twirl so she could assess whether the back of him was as delicious as the front, but she had no doubt that it was.

Jen finally found her voice. "Hey. And you must be Dylan."

She stuck out her hand, but rather than shake it, he grasped her fingers with his and raised her knuckles to his lips, brushing a fleeting kiss over them.

"It's a pleasure to meet you," he drawled.

From his spot on the couch, Cash snorted. "Laying it on a little thick, don't you think?"

"Can't help it," Dylan called without taking his eyes off her. "I'm overwhelmed by her beauty."

Another snort cut through the air.

Dylan ignored his friend and gave Jen a long once-over. "I'm serious. You're beautiful."

Her cheeks warmed. "Um. Thanks."

"Hey Romeo, how about you sit your ass back down so we can watch my boys claim victory?" Cash suggested.

Dylan shot her a lopsided grin. "McCoy actually believes his shitty team stands a chance of defeating mine. Clearly, he lives in a fantasy world." He took her hand and led her toward the couch. "Come on, let's watch his bubble burst."

The next thing she knew, Jen was sandwiched between two SEALs, who proceeded to spend the next fifteen minutes trash-talking each other as their respective teams took the field. Their good-natured taunts and creative insults kept her in a state of much-needed laughter. By the time the game's first quarter came to a close, she'd managed to put all thoughts of Carson and his marriage out of her mind.

When Dylan disappeared into the kitchen to grab some beers, Jen glanced at Cash and grinned. "I like him."

"Everyone likes him," he answered dryly. "I can honestly say that motherfucker's the most charming person I've ever met in my life."

She couldn't disagree. Those laughing eyes and devilish grins were definitely having an effect on her.

"Look what I found," Dylan announced. He held up a bottle of Patrón, grinning like the cat who'd swallowed the canary.

"What happened to beers?" Cash asked. He'd slung his arm over Jen's shoulder, and she was enjoying the way he carelessly dragged his fingers over the top of her arm.

"You want a beer? Fridge is that way," Dylan replied, jerking a thumb at the kitchen. "But I'm gonna get my Patrón on. Who knew O'Connor had such good taste?"

Retaking his seat, he unscrewed the bottle and brought it to his lips. He swallowed with a contented sound, then held out the bottle.

"What do you say, Blondie? You gonna pansy out and stick to beer, or are you in the mood for something that'll make you burn?" Dylan waggled his eyebrows in challenge.

A smile stretched across her mouth. "I guess I could use a burn." When Cash frowned, she offered a little shrug. "I need a distraction, remember?"

"Fine, but you're not allowed to pass out, okay?"

"Deal." She accepted the outstretched bottle and took a small sip. It burned, all right, all the way down to her stomach. But almost immediately, warmth spread through her and buzzed pleasantly in her veins.

She handed Cash the bottle. After a beat, he slugged back some tequila.

"Oh, get ready for it," Dylan said with a whoop, his eyes focused on the TV. "Ten yards...five...touchdown!"

A new round of heckling ensued, courtesy of Dylan as San Francisco scored. But then Arizona answered with a touchdown of their own and it was Cash's turn to deliver some verbal abuse.

Jen couldn't remember the last time she'd had so much fun. During halftime, Dylan regaled her with stories, everything from childhood anecdotes to bad dating experiences. The guy was charismatic as hell, not to mention gorgeous as all get-out. She couldn't help checking him out, admiring his classically handsome face, his ripped arms, those hypnotic dimples.

Cash caught her ogling more than once, but he didn't seem put off by it. He simply grinned knowingly before taking another shot of tequila. Dylan had brought out three shot glasses sometime during the second quarter, and the amber liquid in the bottle had slowly begun to dwindle.

Jen definitely had her buzz on, but she also knew her limit, so when Dylan tried coaxing her into another shot, she shook her head and raised her hands in surrender. "One more and I'll go from tipsy to flat-ass drunk."

"Maybe I'm trying to get you drunk," he responded, his dimples making another appearance.

"Why, so you can talk me into a threesome?" The words flew out before she could stop them.

"Why, is that something you'd be interested in?" he countered.

She felt herself blushing. "No," she lied.

His grin widened. "I think you would." He glanced at Cash. "You didn't tell me the LT's sister was such a bad girl. If I'd known, I would've come over days ago."

Cash rolled his eyes.

Dylan shifted, leaning into the arm of the couch. Expression gleaming with mischief, he locked his gaze with Jen's and said, "So, the idea of being with two dudes turns you on?"

"Maybe a little," she relented.

He cocked a brow. "What else turns you on?"

She shrugged. Her cheeks were scorching. And somehow, in the span of a few seconds, she'd become wildly aroused. She squirmed on the couch, tried to ignore the zip of heat moving between her legs. From the corner of her eye, she caught Cash grinning at her again. Bastard was enjoying watching her squirm.

"Come on, Blondie," Dylan prodded, "tell me all your turn-ons."

When Cash had the nerve to chuckle, she scowled at him. He thought it was funny, huh? Letting his friend tease her like this? She swallowed to bring moisture to her dry mouth, deciding that maybe Cash needed to do some squirming of his own.

"Well," she said slowly, "I've always wanted to watch two men together."

Although Dylan's eyebrows soared, he didn't blanch or seem the slightest bit horrified by the idea. If anything, he looked intrigued. "Really," he mused.

"It doesn't freak you out?"

"Why should it?"

Before she could blink, he tugged her toward him. She squeaked in surprise, her pulse racing when he touched her cheek. His palm was callused, fingertips rough as he skimmed them along the curve of her jaw.

"So you wanna see me and Cash get it on, huh?"

Had he really just said that?

Her heartbeat thudded at triple speed as his words generated a slew of images in her mind. Images of these two sexy guys touching and kissing and... Oh boy.

"What do you say, McCoy? Should we give Blondie a show?"

She twisted around, needing to see Cash's expression. She figured he'd recoil at the idea, but he looked more bemused than appalled. "How drunk are you exactly?" Cash asked his friend.

Dylan just laughed and wrapped his arms around Jen. Rough hands stroked her shoulders, and his touch unleashed a flurry of shivers, leaving little flashes of heat in its wake. She locked eyes with Cash, but he didn't seem at all bothered that his friend's hands were all over her.

Her mouth ran dry again. Dylan's hands traveled down to her waist, teasing the sides of her breasts on their southward journey. She shivered again. Every muscle in her body coiled tight with...anticipation?

Lord, what was she anticipating would happen?

The alluring possibilities swirling through her mind got her so wet she clenched her thighs together and slid off Dylan's lap, afraid he'd feel the dampness of her panties right through her leggings.

Sucking in much-needed oxygen, she stumbled to her feet. "I'm craving ice cream," she blurted out. "Anyone else want some?" Without letting either man respond, she fled to the kitchen.

As Cash watched Jen hurry off, he was unable to resist a low chuckle. He glanced at Dylan, who seemed equally amused. "Quit toying with her," he told his buddy. "You're making her nervous."

"I'm making her hot," Dylan corrected with a barely contained grin.

Yeah, no doubt about that. Cash hadn't missed the flush of arousal on Jen's cheeks or the way she kept shifting in pure sexual discomfort. His dick stirred as he imagined the wetness he'd find if he slipped his hand between her legs.

Now he was the one shifting around, a motion Dylan didn't miss, judging by his husky laughter.

Jen returned with a carton of Choctastic Verryberry Swirl and a spoon. Rather than rejoin them on the couch, she settled in one of the recliners, as if a distance of four feet would alleviate the hot promise of sex thickening the air. She stuck her spoon into the carton, her gaze darting from Cash to Dylan, her cheeks an enticing shade of pink.

Cash glanced at the game flashing on the screen, but found he could no longer concentrate. Jen and Dylan were now engaged in an unmistakable eye fuck that should've made him jealous, but didn't.

"You know, sitting all the way over there won't save you, Blondie," Dylan said lightly. "You opened this can of worms."

"Why, because I dared to say the word *threesome*?"

"Yep."

Jen glanced at Cash as if to ask for help.

He shrugged. "Sorry, sweetheart. I warned you he's a slut."

Looking frazzled, she swallowed another spoonful. Cash was tempted to march over and kiss her. Her lips would be cold from the ice cream, but he'd warm them up, no problem. Nibble on her bottom lip for a bit. Lick his way into her mouth and taste the chocolate and strawberries on her tongue.

He quelled the urge. Truthfully, he was curious to see how far she'd let this go. He hadn't been lying before—he found threesomes hot as hell. He knew some guys didn't like sharing, but Cash didn't see it that way. A woman's pleasure mattered more to him than his own, which was why he'd been so dismayed to hear that Jen's former boyfriends hadn't bothered to make her come. Hearing a chick cry out in orgasm was the ultimate turn-on for him, and he knew from experience that women lost their fucking minds when they had two men dedicated to driving them over the edge.

And he knew the idea intrigued Jen. She'd dropped so many hints about it she might as well have advertised her curiosity on a billboard.

"Come back to the couch," Dylan urged.

Jen's gorgeous tits heaved as she drew in shallow breaths. "I'm good here, thanks."

She scooped out some more ice cream. All the blood in Cash's body pooled in his groin as he watched her suck on that spoon.

"What'll it take to get you back here?" Dylan asked with a taunting lilt in his voice.

Once more, Jen turned to Cash.

He suppressed a laugh. "Hey, you were the one who gave me the rock-your-world and try-new-things speech. Everything that happens next is up to you."

She gulped.

Dylan patted the couch cushion. "Your call, honey. But you should know—Cash and I have a lot of experience in making a woman feel good."

Cash sized up her expression, noting the temptation flaring in her eyes. She wanted this. Anyone could see it. All the same, he refused to push her into doing something she wasn't comfortable with, and he knew Dylan wouldn't be insulted if she chose not to go through with it.

But he hadn't anticipated his friend's determination to lure Jen to the dark side.

"If you won't join us, maybe we'll just have to entertain ourselves," Dylan announced.

Wait, *what*?

Dylan slid across the couch toward him.

He blinked. "What are you doing?"

"Fulfilling the lady's fantasy." Dylan was so close Cash could smell the guy's aftershave, see the five o'clock shadow rising on his jaw.

"I think you've had a little too much to drink," Cash said gruffly. When Dylan's hand reached for his zipper, his brows shot up. "You can't be serious." And yet neither of them missed the note of interest in Cash's voice.

Hiss. Dylan dragged down the zipper, shooting him a look loaded with an unexpected amount of heat. "Come on, McCoy, you know I'm a firm believer in the try-anything-once philosophy."

Next thing he knew, his friend's hand slid beneath the waistband of his boxer briefs and...yup, Dylan's fingers were wrapping around his dick.

Which hardened.

Like instantly.

And not just in a semi, look-at-that-someone's-touching-me way. It went stiffer than a flagpole, rising from zero to full mast in two seconds flat.

His gaze flew to Jen, whose eyes had grown wide. Her mouth slackened as if she couldn't fathom the scene in front of her.

He couldn't quite fathom it either, but God help him, he couldn't seem to stop it. When Dylan squeezed his shaft, his body arched involuntarily, his erection eagerly jutting into that rough hand. A drop of precome beaded at his tip, and he saw Jen's eyes fix on that pearly drop.

"You like it," she accused, sounding both awed and aroused.

"He likes it," Dylan confirmed with a chuckle.

The base of his spine began tingling as Dylan jacked his cock. His friend's hand was bigger, rougher than a woman's, his strokes more forceful. But it didn't hurt. Dylan knew exactly how much pressure to exert, which didn't surprise Cash—he supposed only a man would know how much force another man could take.

What did surprise him was his visceral reaction to the feel of a strong, masculine grip on his dick. Mouth dry, pulse racing, palms damp. Dylan kept pumping his cock, squeezing the head on each upstroke. It felt so damn good, Cash let out a groan.

Dylan studied his face, green eyes darkening with arousal and flickering with an unspoken question.

Cash responded by easing his pants down his hips, giving his friend a better handle on his package. Dylan swiped his finger over the moisture seeping from Cash's tip and spread the sticky substance along the rock-hard shaft.

"This is the hottest thing I've ever seen in my life," Jen moaned.

Dylan released him and gave a half-smile. "Should we make her hotter?"

When his friend moistened his lips with the tip of his tongue, Cash knew exactly what he planned to do. The urge to resist warred with the need for release. He sat there. Torn. Turned on. Ready to explode.

He thrust his dick back into Dylan's hand, then groaned when his friend squeezed so hard it ached. He closed his eyes for a moment, but they snapped open when the couch squeaked and that wicked hand disappeared.

Dylan had slid onto his knees on the floor, and Cash glanced down in time to see his friend's lips close over his engorged head.

He jerked, overcome with sensation. Oh, fuck. That felt criminally good.

He groaned when Dylan sucked harder, each wet tug stoking the fire. The lust pulsing in his veins was so powerful, so startling, that he pulled out of the other man's mouth.

"You okay?" Dylan rasped, peering up at him with heavy-lidded eyes.

Just like that, his resolve crumbled. Screw resistance. If Dylan was into it, and Jen was into it, then he might as well go with it.

"I'm good," he said hoarsely. And then, shoving his hand in Dylan's hair, he guided that hot male mouth to his cock and settled back to enjoy his first blowjob from another guy.

CHAPTER **FOURTEEN**

Jen was seconds away from spontaneous combustion. She'd never seen anything hotter than the unexpected scene unfolding four feet away from her.

Dylan was on his knees, with Cash's cock buried deep in his mouth.

How was this real?

Her clit swelled and throbbed, but she was too stunned to do anything about it. Struggling to breathe, she set the ice cream carton on the table, unable to take her eyes off the two guys. Dylan made low growls in the back of his throat as he sucked Cash in slow, deep pulls. The pleasure etched onto Cash's face stole the breath from her lungs. He rested one hand on his friend's head, the other curled into a fist at his side. But silent and passive he wasn't—even with another man, he had no problem vocalizing the rough, sexy demands she'd become accustomed to.

"Tease my balls," he ground out, rocking his hips as he fucked Dylan's mouth.

She nearly passed out when Dylan followed his friend's orders. He squeezed the heavy sac, then released the dick in his mouth, skimmed his tongue down the length, and buried his face in Cash's balls.

"Oh fuck," Cash mumbled. "Yeah, that's good."

Heat rolled through her, tingling her nipples, scorching her core. Pressure built inside her. Moaning, Jen slipped a hand into her leggings, inside her panties.

She couldn't believe she was watching another man going down on Cash. And Dylan seemed to be enjoying the hell out of himself; his muffled groans filled the air, combining with Cash's ragged breaths.

Her eyes nearly popped out of their sockets when Cash tangled both hands in his friend's hair and brought Dylan's mouth back to his cock. "Take me deep. Fuck, man, suck harder."

Dylan's cheeks hollowed as he gave Cash what he wanted. When Jen lowered her gaze to the floor, she saw the unmistakable bulge in Dylan's jeans. He was hard.

She stroked herself, her clit throbbing so hard she knew she was two seconds away from orgasm. But she didn't want to come yet. She wanted to see Cash explode first. She watched as his eyes squeezed shut, as he bumped his hips into Dylan's face, and when he moaned again, she knew he was getting close.

Jen was startled when his eyes suddenly popped open and focused on her. "Does this turn you on?" he growled.

She nodded numbly.

"You gonna come, watching Dylan suck me?"

Another nod.

He fisted his friend's hair and thrust deeper. "Take it all. Show Jen how much you like doing this to me."

Dylan groaned. He took Cash's dick so deep that his nose brushed Cash's abs.

She couldn't take it anymore. The pressure inside her was

too much. She rubbed furiously on her clit, grinding wildly into her hand.

"You want me to come in your mouth?" Cash asked in a guttural voice.

Dylan peered up, his lips stretched wide over the thick shaft. When he nodded, Cash growled again, then turned to meet Jen's eyes.

His expression glazed over, his features grew taut, his hips rocked faster.

They came at the same time. Cash groaned as he climaxed, and her own orgasm intensified when she saw Dylan's throat working to swallow every drop.

Ragged breathing cut through the air. Dylan glided his tongue over Cash's glistening shaft before releasing him, then turned to look at Jen. Holding the gaze, he swept his tongue over his glossy lips.

It was the most erotic thing she'd ever seen in her life.

"How was that?" Dylan said silkily. "Did it live up to your fantasy?"

Dazed and wide-eyed, she managed a nod.

The blond SEAL stood up, unzipped his jeans, and strode toward the armchair like a predator homing in on its prey.

"I'd ask McCoy to return the favor, but he looks like he needs some time to recover." Dylan's eyes glittered as he tossed a glance at Cash, who was struggling to regain his breathing. "So I think I'll have to put your mouth to use instead."

He opened the flaps of his jeans and his cock sprang up. Commando. She should've known.

Jen's pulse drummed in her ears as he stepped toward her, his dick jutting in her direction. He was longer than Cash, not as thick but equally tantalizing. Saliva flooded her mouth the closer he came. She stayed seated, which put his erection at mouth level when he reached her. Fisting his shaft, he guided it to her face and prodded her lips.

"Open," he murmured.

She opened, and he slid into her mouth in one smooth motion.

"This'll be fast, honey. I just need to take the edge off."

As she wrapped her lips around him, she peered past him and met Cash's eyes. His heated gaze told her he liked what he saw. A lot. His reaction spurred her on, had her suckling on the crown of Dylan's cock. She curled her fingers around the root of him and pumped, enjoying the low noise that exited his lips.

He wasn't kidding. It only took a few long strokes, a few persistent sucks, before he spilled into her mouth and coated her tongue.

After he'd caught his breath, he brushed his fingers over her cheek, stroked her lips where they circled his dick, then withdrew slowly and dropped to his knees. When he leaned in to kiss her, she welcomed his mouth, her heart pounding. His kisses weren't as dominating as Cash's; they were sweeter, lazier, as if he had all the time in the world. His tongue tasted and swirled, his lips teasing her to the point of breathless, mindless sensation.

When she felt herself being yanked to her feet, she opened her eyes. "What now?"

"Now it's your turn." He glanced at Cash. "Bedroom?"

Cash was already on his feet.

A thrill shot through her as the men ushered her toward Cash's room. Once there, she barely had time to blink before their hands were all over her. God. She'd never been so excited in her life. Her leggings came off, followed by her panties, her shirt, her bra. When she stood naked before them, both their gazes smoldered with appreciation.

"Damn, you are so fucking pretty it hurts to look at you," Dylan breathed.

"Isn't she?" Cash agreed, his eyes burning as they rested on her bare breasts.

She suddenly felt the urge to cover herself up. It was too much. Their hot, hungry gazes branding into her skin. The thick, erect cocks jutting from their unbuttoned pants. And then they started to strip, and she forgot all about her own sense of modesty. Shirts and pants hit the floor, Dylan's belt buckle jingling when it connected with the hardwood.

Jen gawked at their bare chests, trim hips, muscular legs—pure sensory overload. She'd never seen so much smooth, tanned skin and bulging muscles. They were so utterly *male* that all the moisture left her mouth. Her throat felt like it was coated with sandpaper.

"On the bed," Cash ordered.

The low, sexy command made her shiver. All uncertainty forgotten, she got on the mattress and stretched out on her back. A second later, there was a SEAL on either side of her, and two hot mouths latched onto her breasts.

Her hips shot off the bed.

Dylan chuckled. "Everything okay, Blondie?"

"Mmm-hmmm."

Her eyes fluttered closed as the guys feasted on her. Two tongues darted out to lick her nipples, and when she bucked in surprise, two sets of hands dug into her hips to keep her still. They suckled her, twin groans of approval vibrating in her breasts and bringing goose bumps to her skin.

The mattress dipped, and cool air met her nipple as Cash's mouth left it. She shivered when his lips grazed her ribcage, then her navel, her pubic bone, her inner thigh. While Dylan continued playing with her breasts, Cash crouched at the foot of the bed and spread her legs. His hot breath tickled her core. Anticipation poured into her.

When his tongue flicked over her clit, she moaned with abandon and shifted restlessly on the bed.

"You like how Cash licks your pussy?" Dylan whispered before moving his mouth to her neck and nipping her flesh.

"Mmm-hmmm."

"You want my tongue down there too?"

She trembled uncontrollably, unable to believe this was actually happening.

Without awaiting her reply, Dylan joined Cash between her legs. Cash immediately retreated to let his friend have a taste.

Jen groaned at the sudden change of pressure. "Oh...*God*."

Dylan's mouth was gentler, teasing her with feather-light kisses and long, drawn-out licks. As shivers danced over her naked flesh, she released a soft sigh of sheer contentment. Yet the moment she relaxed, losing herself in the sweet, gentle ministrations, he licked his way down her slit, speared his tongue into her core, and made her cry out with pleasure.

She'd barely recovered from the shocking invasion when he lifted his head to give Cash another turn.

Jen looked down, her heart pounding like a jackhammer. One dark head, one blond one. Between her legs. It was too much. They took turns teasing her into oblivion. Slow, fast, gentle, rough. A whirlwind of sensation fogged her brain and racked her body.

"Too much," she choked out. "It's so good...so...good. You're going to make me explode."

"That's the point." Cash laughed, then slid two fingers into her sopping wet channel and she nearly bucked off the bed.

Dylan captured her clit with his mouth and started to suck in earnest, his low groans vibrating in the sensitive nub.

And just when she thought she'd reached the ultimate pinnacle of arousal, she heard Cash mutter, "Want a taste?"

Dylan's mouth abruptly left her.

Jen's eyes flew open in time to see Cash slide those two long fingers directly into his friend's mouth. Dylan sucked on them and growled with approval. "Fuck, she's sweet."

Cash caught her expression and grinned. "You okay, baby?"

"I...God, I..."

No words. She had no words. The guys chuckled before resuming their posts—Cash filled her with his fingers, Dylan tended to her clit, and it wasn't long before every muscle in her body tightened and she came in an explosive rush. It was so intense she tried to wiggle away, but squirming proved to be an exercise in futility. Strong hands held her in place, husky voices murmured encouragement as wave after wave of pleasure crashed into her.

When she was able to function again, she found both men kneeling in front of her, sporting matching grins.

"Don't you dare high-five," she grumbled.

"We already did. You were coming too hard to notice." Dylan's green eyes gleamed with sinful promise. "Ready for round two, or did we wear you out?"

Gulping, she eyed the blatant evidence of their arousal, the unconcealed hunger in their expressions. She was unable to fight the resulting burst of panic as she realized she really hadn't thought this through.

Cash laid his palm flat on her belly. "What's wrong?"

"I...um..." She licked her lips. "I'm not sure about the whole, um, double penetration thing."

Dylan chuckled. "Not into ass play, are you?"

Her cheeks heated. "I've never tried it. I guess we could, if you—"

"No," Cash interrupted. He moved his hand over her

stomach in a tender caress. "This isn't about us. It's about you, and if you're not comfortable with something, then it's a no-go. Right, Dylan?"

"Right." The other man didn't even hesitate.

Relief trickled through her. As incredible as this entire encounter was, she wasn't ready to jump into the darkly unfamiliar.

The bed creaked as Cash climbed off and walked over to the dresser. He opened the top drawer and grabbed a couple of condoms.

"How about Dylan watches for now?" he said roughly, rolling on a condom as he met her eyes. "Does that sound good?"

She nodded, overcome by a fresh surge of anticipation.

The bed squeaked again. Cash got on his knees and positioned himself between her thighs. Keeping their gazes locked, he drove into her, filling her completely.

Jen gasped.

Dylan, who was on his knees beside them, seemed to enjoy her reaction. With a faint smile, he tweaked one of her nipples and said, "Does he feel good inside you?"

She choked out an assent.

Dylan brought his hand to the juncture of her thighs and idly stroked her clit. With his other hand, he pumped his shaft, watching Cash's cock tunnel in and out of her. Having another man there, touching her while Cash moved inside her, was so deliciously surreal.

As Cash slowed his pace and shortened his strokes, Dylan lowered his mouth, laving her clit with his tongue. His face was inches from Cash's cock, and he must have been licking more than her clit because Cash suddenly released an agonized groan.

"That is one talented tongue," he rasped at his friend, eyes dark with desire.

"You know it." Chuckling, Dylan sat up and began stroking himself again.

Jen reached for him, more than happy to help him out, but to her surprise, Cash's hand beat her to it.

He pumped his friend's cock harder than she would've ever dreamed of doing, but Dylan didn't seem to mind. He groaned, his head lolling to the side as he pushed his erection into Cash's hand.

Heat pulsed between Jen's legs. These guys were going to kill her. They weren't fulfilling just one of her fantasies, but two, and as unbearable tension seized her core, she rocked her hips to meet Cash's hurried thrusts. It didn't take long for her to explode, and Cash wasn't far behind.

"Fuck. *Fuck.*" His big body trembled, his expression filling with rapture.

The climax had him sagging forward. His cheek brushed over her nipple, tongue darting out to lick the tight bud as his breath warmed her skin.

When he withdrew, she whimpered in disappointment, longing for that feeling of completion. Then, remembering she had another man just dying to complete her, she turned to Dylan with a faint smile. "What are you waiting for?"

"You sure, Blondie?"

"Mmm-hmmm. I want you inside me."

His green eyes burned. "Roll over. On your hands and knees."

Despite the fact that her muscles had turned to jelly, she managed to roll onto her stomach and prop herself on her hands and knees. The mattress shifted again. Cash knelt in front of her and brought his semi-erect cock to her mouth.

"Tease me for a bit," he said huskily.

Her tongue came out to explore just as Dylan moved behind her. She moaned when his tip brushed over her swollen opening. She had no idea how many times she'd come already, but the second he drove into her, she knew another orgasm was imminent, especially when he adjusted his angle and hit a sweet spot she hadn't known existed.

"Oh, honey, you're tight," Dylan mumbled.

He rammed into her with absolutely no finesse, while Cash rubbed his hardening cock against her lips. The mattress squeaked out a reckless rhythm as Dylan pumped into her, hitting that spectacular spot with each stroke. Ripples of pleasure gathered in her belly, growing stronger when Dylan reached beneath her and strummed her clit with his thumb and forefinger.

Jen came with a loud cry. The second her lips opened, Cash pushed his now-stiff cock into her mouth. He pumped his hips, once, twice, and then he moaned and come spurted onto her tongue. A third groan joined the mix and Dylan's sweat-soaked chest layered over her back as he shuddered with release.

Erratic breathing heated the air as the three of them recovered from the sexual tornado that had just swept through the room. As she fell forward on her elbows, Jen heard hoarse laughter—it took her a second to realize it had come from her.

"Are you all right?" Cash asked in a surprisingly gentle voice.

She lifted her head, another laugh tickling her throat. "Three words," she croaked, her entire body throbbing with lingering pleasure. "Best. Ménage. Ever."

CHAPTER FIFTEEN

"You realize you haven't stopped smiling all morning?" Cash leaned in the bathroom doorway, watching Jen brush her hair in front of the mirror. That shit-eating grin on her face widened when their eyes met in the reflection.

"I can't help it," she answered. "I keep thinking about last night."

So was he, but he doubted the reason for his preoccupation aligned with Jen's. The threesome had taken things to a whole new level for Cash—he and Dylan had crossed a line he hadn't dreamed they'd ever cross.

Sure, there hadn't been any awkwardness last night when Dylan left, but the tequila was still burning a path through Cash's veins at that point.

Now, sober and in the light of day, he didn't feel as confident.

Memories of last night kept flashing across his mind: Dylan's mouth surrounding his dick, the hard length of Dylan's erection pulsing in his hand...

Christ. How would he ever look his friend in the eye again?

"You're not happy."

Jen's strained voice interrupted his troubled thoughts. He met her eyes, confused by the flicker of shame he saw there.

"You think less of me, don't you?" she blurted out.

"*What?* Of course not."

He came up and wrapped his arms around her from behind, lacing his fingers over her stomach as he leaned in to kiss her neck. Her silky hair tickled his chin, the sweet scent of it filling his nose.

Jen continued to watch him in the mirror. "So you don't think I'm a huge slut for sleeping with your best friend last night?"

He had to smile. "Not at all."

Distress crossed her face. "Having sex with two men at the same time isn't normal, Cash. It's...deviant."

Now a laugh escaped. "Deviant? Come on, you don't actually believe that, do you?" He hurried on before she could answer. "You know what kind of raunchy shit happens behind closed doors? What we did last night was probably vanilla in comparison to what other 'deviants' do."

Her lips twitched. "I guess."

"We're adults. We can invite whoever we want into our bed, and as long as everyone involved is into it, then there's nothing wrong with that. Okay?"

"Okay." She bit her bottom lip. "Then why did you look so unhappy before?"

Cash hesitated. "I was thinking about Dylan. Me and Dylan...what we did."

She set the hairbrush on the edge of the sink and turned to face him. "Fooling around with another guy doesn't take away from your hetero masculinity, you know that, right? It's perfectly healthy to explore some bi-curiosities."

"That's not it."

"So you're not embarrassed about what happened?"

"No. I'm just wondering if this will change anything between us," he admitted. "He's my best friend. I don't want things to get...weird."

"He seemed fine when he left last night."

Cash smiled ruefully. "Alcohol has a remarkable way of making everything seem like a good idea."

She stepped forward and looped her arms around his neck. He had to tilt his head to look down at her, which continued to surprise him. He kept forgetting how tiny she was. Probably because her sunny smiles and big heart seemed to fill up any room she was in.

When she stood on her tiptoes to kiss him, he experienced a rare burst of tenderness. His chest tightened, his brain going fuzzy when she deepened the kiss. As much as he loved having sex with this girl, it was her kisses he was growing addicted to. Her sweet taste, her pliant lips, the tiny moan she let out each time their tongues met.

She'd gotten under his skin. He couldn't deny it any longer, and he couldn't pretend their conversation in the car yesterday hadn't affected him. He'd tried to brush it off. Told himself he wasn't bothered by Jen's reminder that the fling would end as scheduled when three weeks were up. But hell. It *did* bother him. He didn't like having an end date looming over him like a thundercloud.

He broke the kiss, trying not to dwell on his thoughts. "What's on the agenda for today? I'm meeting the guys around four to work out, but what should we do until then?"

Her expression instantly hardened. "I want to talk to Carson."

"Did you call him?"

She nodded. "His cell went to voicemail. I left a message. I was tempted to say it had to do with Brendan, just to guarantee he'd call back, but I felt bad making him worry so I said I needed to see him ASAP but that everything was okay. He hasn't called back yet." Her face clouded over. "Maybe he's busy with his *angel.*"

"Jen," he chided.

"I know, I know. There *must* be an explanation," she mimicked.

Cash stifled a sigh and changed the subject. "Okay, so what do you want to do until he gets back to you?"

She grabbed an elastic band and twisted her hair into a loose bun. "I guess I can hand out some more resumes."

"Nobody's gotten back to you, huh?"

Her frustration was evident. "Nope."

"Well, it's only been a day."

"Maybe it's for the best. I wasn't thrilled about any of the stores we went to. Besides, I hate sales." She shoved the hairbrush in her toiletry case and blew past him.

Cash noted the droop of her shoulders as he followed her into the kitchen, where she grabbed a bottle of water from the fridge.

"Maybe I should apply for more office jobs," she said after taking a sip of water. "I worked as a receptionist at a dental office a few years ago, and it wasn't so bad."

"Or you could do something with photography," he suggested.

She faltered. "Like what?"

"Apply at the local papers, submit your stuff to magazines, contests." He met her baffled eyes. "You're a damn good photographer. Why don't you find out if you can make a career out of it?"

"A career?" She looked surprised. "I'm not good enough to be a professional photographer, Cash."

"Says who?"

Her brows puckered. "It's only a hobby. I've never taken any classes or studied photography. I don't know any fancy techniques, or even the proper names for half the stuff I do on my camera."

"So? Your work speaks for itself. At least put yourself out there before you decide you're not good enough."

"I guess." She chewed on her bottom lip. "It's just not very practical. I can't see how I'd make enough money to support myself."

"Says who?" he repeated. "Because you're sounding a lot like your parents right now."

He tried to mask his anger, but it was difficult when he remembered the condescending way her parents had spoken about her photographs. Or the way they'd treated Jen—like she was a failure, a disappointment to them.

"I..." She swallowed. "It's...a hobby, Cash. And I'm not good with rejection—what if I send work out and everyone hates it?"

"Then everyone hates it." He shrugged. "At least you'll know that you tried."

"And failed," she muttered.

"That kind of attitude isn't conducive to success, babe. See, you've got yourself failing before you've even given it a shot. Coming up with excuses not to go after what you want won't achieve a damn thing."

"Excuses? I'm not—"

"Yes you are," he interrupted, his tone coming out harsher than he'd intended. "You're scared to put yourself out there. I get it. And I'm not surprised it never occurred to you to turn your hobby into a career. I think your parents commented on your 'silly' pictures half a dozen times when we went over there. Don't tell me that didn't annoy you."

Her shoulders sagged. "Of course it did, but—"

"But nothing. Your parents act like you're disappointing them because you aren't doing what *they* want you to do, and all that criticism can't be good for your self-esteem. But I've seen your photographs, and trust me, they *are* good enough. So man up and go after what you want, Jen."

His speech was rewarded by deafening silence.

Jen stared at him.

Fuck. Had he really just told her to *man up*?

His tendency not to sugarcoat was the reason his past relationships had failed. He'd discovered a long time ago that women didn't want the truth—they wanted a man who showered them with compliments and told them everything was fine and dandy. But Jen was so open and honest with him that he'd let down his guard. He'd stopped carefully weighing every word and started openly speaking his mind.

Cash cleared his throat. "I'm sorry. That might have come out a little harsh."

She opened her mouth to reply, but then her phone rang.

"Um, I'll just...get that."

He winced as she bulldozed past him. He knew he'd screwed up, but damn it, she was too talented to let her parents' criticism deter her from doing what she loved.

Too bad he hadn't been able to convey that with a little more tact.

Jen answered the phone with an overly cheerful, "Hey Tessa, what's up?" She paused, then said, "*What?*"

Cash went to her side and made out a tinny female voice on the line, talking a million miles a minute.

"Speakerphone," he said.

Jen clicked a button, and the panicked voice became audible.

"—I gave him your number. I'm so sorry. I panicked, and he was so angry I thought he might hurt me. I've—"

"It's okay," Jen interrupted. "I understand—"

"—never seen anyone look so crazy. I know I shouldn't have

given him your new number, but you should've seen his face. He had crazy eyes and he was breathing hard, like he'd just run a marathon or something. It was the freakiest thing—"

Jen cut in again. "Tessa...*Tessa*...calm down."

A heavy breath sounded on the line.

"You were scared," Jen said gently. "I totally understand. Where are you now?"

"Back at the office. I ran all the way here from the restaurant. My boss will never invite me to lunch again, that's for sure."

A beep cut through Tessa's last sentence. Call waiting.

Squaring his jaw, Cash signaled for Jen to ignore it, then leaned into the mouthpiece to address her friend. "Tessa? This is Cash McCoy. Jen's staying with me until Brendan leaves town. Do you feel like he might come after you again?"

"No," was the wobbly response. "He was adamant about getting Jen's number, that's all. He also demanded to know where she was staying, but I pretended I didn't know. I made up a story about her brother whisking her off and how none of her friends have had contact with her for a week."

"Good," Cash said. "Stick to that story if he bothers you again. Your office has security?"

"Yes."

"If he shows up there, get security involved. If he approaches you outside of work, call the police. I don't want him making a habit of hitting you up for information."

"Okay. Thanks," Tessa said. "Jen?"

"I'm here," Jen spoke up.

"I'm so sorry. I panicked."

"Hey, I told you, it's fine. Brendan is my problem, not yours. I'm sorry he cornered you like that."

"It's not your fault, hon." Tessa sighed. "That man is certifiable, huh?"

"Tell me about it."

After they said goodbye, Jen checked the screen to find out who'd called. Her scowl was all the answer Cash needed.

"Brendan's office number," she muttered, releasing an annoyed breath. "Looks like I have to change my number. Again."

An idea niggled at the back of his mind. "Call him back."

Her eyes widened. "Why would I do that?"

"Because enough is enough," Cash said tersely. "This creep showed up at your parents' house, and now he's harassing your friends. Someone needs to have a little chat with him."

"And, what, that someone will be you?"

"Yup."

"Forget it. The best way to get him off my back is to ignore him. If you confront him, you'll only rile him up."

No, but he might *rough* him up.

Probably best not to mention that, though. Using violence as a method of problem solving wasn't something he did often —not in his personal life, anyway. But Psycho McGee had already scared Jen out of her apartment, bombarded her email inbox with his nonsense, harassed her parents, and now he was causing trouble for her friends? The dude was long overdue for a wake-up call, and Cash had no problem giving it to him.

"Call him back," he repeated, his tone brooking no argument.

Jen looked frazzled. "And say what?"

"Tell him you want to meet him when he gets off work."

"What? No."

He ignored her protest. "Say you want to sit down and hash all this out. Arrange to meet at the Gaslamp Tavern."

"Cash—"

"Just do it, Jen."

"This is insane," she said, but she still reached for her phone.

"Be polite, tell him it's time for the two of you to talk, but don't lead him on," Cash warned.

"Lead him on? It'll be a challenge not to yell every swear word in the book at him." She lifted the phone to her ear.

"Speaker," he ordered.

Rolling her eyes, she pressed a button and lowered the phone.

Jen's ex picked up on the first ring, sounding overjoyed. "Jen! Oh, baby, I'm so glad you called."

Cash's shoulders stiffened. *Baby?*

No fucking way, buddy. She is not *your baby.*

Her lips tightened. "Hello, Brendan."

"You spoke to Tessa, didn't you?" Brendan's deep, slightly gravelly voice held a note of unmistakable guilt. "I know I scared her, and I regret that. I was just going out of my mind not knowing where you were. I get why you moved out and why you filed the restraining order. I know you were freaked out about the notes and the flowers, but I didn't mean to frighten you. I wanted to make a grand romantic gesture, you know? Show you how much I still love you."

Jen listened to the entire speech without comment. The angry glint didn't leave her eyes, but her voice remained cordial as she said, "Well, I *was* freaked out. Forgive me if your grand romantic gestures were a tad overwhelming."

"I know. I'm sorry," he said again. "But you called back, so that means you're not angry anymore, doesn't it?"

"No, I'm still angry," she answered coolly.

Cash sent her an unspoken warning with his eyes.

"But I do think we should meet," she added in a forced voice.

"You do?" He sounded overjoyed.

"We need to sit down and talk about this, Brendan."

"That's a good idea. When do you want to do it?"

"As soon as possible. Maybe today when you're done work?"

The muffled sound of typing filled the line. "My last appointment is at five. I'll be finished by six. Should I come to you?"

"No." Her tone came out sharp. "I'd rather we meet somewhere public."

A pause. "I understand."

"Meet me at the new bar on Market and 5th. The Gaslamp Tavern," Jen said. She shot Cash a brief look, and from her pink cheeks, he knew she was remembering the night they'd met. "How about six thirty?"

"Six thirty is perfect." Brendan sounded choked up. "Thank you. I know if you just give me a chance to explain, we can fix this."

As promised, Jen didn't lead him on. Not even an inch. "I'll see you later, Brendan." Then she disconnected and turned to Cash. "Happy?"

"No, not really," he said darkly. "He's clearly obsessed with you."

"You're the one who wants to meet him." She dropped the phone on the table and took a step away.

"Wait." He gulped. "About what I said before. I know I was harsh, but—"

"It's fine," she cut in. "Let's not talk about it anymore."

Cash reached out for her, but she sidestepped him and put a few more feet of distance between them. "I'm going to work on my laptop for a bit. I want to look through some more job ads."

Guilt pricked his insides as she stalked toward the bedroom. Shit. He'd definitely hurt her with the accusation that she didn't have the guts to follow her dream, but as usual, his brain-to-mouth filter had failed him.

Frustrated, he ran a hand over his scalp. Times like these, he wished he possessed Dylan's charm or the ability to sweet-talk the birds out of the damn trees like Jackson. But no, apparently he was destined to wreck every relationship by being too damn blunt.

This isn't a relationship. It's a fling with an end date, remember?

The reminder only sent his spirits plummeting even lower.

A FEW HOURS LATER, CASH TRUDGED DOWN THE BEACH TO meet the guys. His mood hadn't improved as the day dragged on. He'd tried apologizing to Jen, but she'd brushed it off, saying it was no big deal. But clearly it was because she'd barely uttered ten words to him all afternoon. He'd almost blown off this workout to stay home and make things right with her, but slacking off wasn't an option in his line of work.

As he approached his teammates, he pushed all thoughts of Jen from his mind. Seth and Jackson walked up to greet him, but Dylan hung back, averting his eyes.

Shit. So this *was* going to be awkward.

"'Sup, Wade," he said tentatively, sticking out his hand.

After a beat, Dylan lifted his head. Rather than the discomfort or embarrassment Cash expected to see, Dylan's green eyes displayed a twinkle of humor. "'Sup, McCoy."

As they bumped knuckles, the tension in Cash's body eased, replaced with a tremor of relief that last night's activities hadn't fucked up their friendship.

"How's Jen?" Dylan asked with a faint grin.

"Pissed. Her psycho ex got ahold of her cell number."

"Did she talk to him?"

"Yeah, but only because I forced her to." He glanced at the

other two. "I need to be out of here by six, so let's get this show on the road."

They stuck to the same routine as last time. But Cash was preoccupied about his impending meeting with Jen's ex, which allowed all three of his buddies to kick his ass in the push-up competition Seth challenged everyone to after the swim.

It was quarter to six when they finished up. Carrying their sneakers, the foursome walked soaking wet to the parking lot, drawing several appreciative glances and a few come-hither smiles from a group of female tourists loitering near the Hotel Del.

While Seth and Jackson walked ahead, Dylan sidled up to Cash. "What's going on? You've got the expression you wear when you're in ass-kicking mode."

He lowered his voice. "I'm paying a visit to Jen's ex."

Seth overheard and turned to stare at him. "What the hell you doing that for?"

"Because I'm tired of this asshole not getting the message. Someone needs to make it clear that Jen doesn't belong to him."

"And that someone has to be you?" Seth asked, perplexed.

They reached the cars. Cash popped the trunk of his Escape and grabbed a few towels and four water bottles. He tossed the others one of each, then dried up and chugged some water. Normally he drove back to his apartment in his wet trunks, but since he was heading straight to the bar, he'd have to change in the parking lot.

"Make sure nobody's looking at my bare ass," he called as he grabbed a pair of cargo pants from the duffel bag in his trunk.

He ducked behind the open driver's door, quickly shucked the swim trunks, and yanked his pants on, commando. His black T-shirt went on next, and rather than sneakers, he grabbed a pair of clean socks, rolled them on his feet, and put on his boots.

When he turned around, he noticed the other guys

rummaging through the duffels in the back of Seth's Jeep. Trunks were stripped off, pants and shirts came on, and all three opted for shitkickers as well.

Cash frowned. "You all live around the corner. Why're you getting dressed?"

"We're coming with you," Dylan answered.

"Duh," Seth said in a dry voice.

"You think we're going to let you confront the dude without backup?" Jackson piped up as he bent to lace his boots.

"I'm only going to talk to the guy."

"Talking's for pansies," Seth replied. "If you want him to get the message, you've gotta rough him up a bit."

"It might come to that. But you guys don't need to get involved. It's not your fight."

"Like hell it isn't," Dylan shot back. "Your fights are our fights. Besides, I wouldn't mind giving that asshole a warning of my own. Considering what happened last night, I'm feeling invested in Jen's safety too."

Seth's head swiveled from Cash to Dylan. Then he started to laugh. "Son of a bitch. You tag-teamed the LT's sister?"

"No," they said in unison.

"Wow. Just...wow." Seth doubled over, gripping his side as he laughed. When he finally settled down, he sent a mocking look in Cash's direction. "You realize you went from begging us to help you not screw her, to screwing her, to screwing her with Dylan. What's next? Can me and Texas join in next time?"

Jackson's slow drawl joined the mix. "Yeah, can we? I still haven't had the pleasure of meeting the mysterious Jen."

Cash glared at Dylan, who seemed to regret opening this can of worms. "No one is joining in. But if you're serious about coming along, I'd appreciate the backup. I haven't met this guy, so I don't know what to expect."

"Where we going?" Seth tossed his wet trunks in the back of the Jeep.

"The Gaslamp Tavern."

Seth headed for the driver's door with his badass swagger, while Jackson walked around to the passenger side. "We'll meet you there."

After the Jeep sped out of the lot, Cash glowered at Dylan. "Did you have to drop that *last night* comment? I didn't exactly want those two knowing about it."

"Sorry. I wasn't thinking."

"Clearly. Way to blow it."

"Actually, I blew you," Dylan said glibly.

They looked at each other for several long beats.

Then they burst out laughing.

When the laughter died down, Cash gave his friend a somber look. "We cool? You're not going to get all weird around me now, are you?"

"Nah, we're cool."

Relief fluttered through him. "Good."

Dylan smirked. "You were actually worried, huh? What, you thought I'd morph into a teenage girl and never talk to you again?"

"The thought crossed my mind."

"Aw, you love me, don't ya? You would've missed your bestest friend ever."

Cash gave him the finger. "Get in the car, jackass."

CHAPTER **SIXTEEN**

Cash slowed the car in front of the Tavern. There was no meter parking outside the bar, so he had to drive to the next block to find a spot. He and Dylan strode down the sidewalk a few minutes later, scanning both sides of the road for Seth's Jeep.

"There they are." Dylan shoved his fingers in his mouth and whistled to get Seth and Jackson's attention.

The after-work happy hour was in full swing when the four men entered the bar. Cash took the lead, pausing at the edge of the main room to search the crowd for lone male patrons. All he saw were groups of three or four, clad in business attire and chatting over beers and cocktails.

His gaze shifted toward the bar, the haven for single males. Out of the dozen people occupying the tall stools, most were older men who wore weathered, tired looks as they silently nursed their drinks. One man seemed around the right age, but his gleaming shaved head and plethora of tattoos, including one circling his thick neck, told Cash the guy was no investment banker.

He continued his inspection. Bingo. A man in his late twenties or early thirties sat at the far end of the counter. He had a slick look to him—perfectly styled brown hair, clean-shaven face, expensive Rolex on his wrist. He wore a black suit, no tie, with an open-collar white shirt. Cash couldn't deny the guy was handsome, but something about those sharp clothes and deep smirk rubbed him the wrong way.

"Nine o'clock," he murmured.

The others followed his gaze. "That him?" Seth murmured back.

"Let's go and find out."

They started walking. The bartender lifted her head at their approach, her eyes lighting with unconcealed appreciation, but as they got closer, her expression faded to wariness.

Her concern didn't surprise Cash. The four of them made an intimidating sight. Six-feet-plus, two hundred pounds of muscle, and in military-issued shitkickers.

They moved toward Mr. Slick the way they moved on an op—with single-minded focus and a helluva lot of aggression.

The man looked startled when he noticed them. He set down the wine glass he'd been sipping. "Can I help you?" he asked coolly.

Cash instantly recognized the gravelly voice. "You Brendan?" he said, equally cool.

"Who's asking?"

"My friends and I were hoping to have a little chat with you."

Brendan's shoulders stiffened. "Screw off. I'm waiting for someone."

Cash bared his teeth in a not-so-pleasant smile. "Yeah, about that... I'm afraid Jen won't be coming."

Surprise flared in Brendan's dark eyes. "What are you talking about? Who are you?"

Behind the counter, the bartender frowned.

"I've got this," Jackson said. He moved toward the pretty brunette, resting his elbows on the counter and flashing that *aw-shucks* smile of his. "Don't worry, sugar, there won't be any trouble," he drawled. "Just a few friends shootin' the breeze."

"Who are you?" Brendan repeated, beginning to look irritated.

Cash's smile widened. "Oh, I didn't introduce myself? I'm Jen's boyfriend."

The other man's jaw went slack. Then he scowled. "Bullshit."

"Sorry, but it's the truth. And see, as her boyfriend, I've gotta admit I'm getting really fucking annoyed with your harassment."

Brendan slid off the stool in a huff. "I don't believe you. Jen would never go out with someone like you."

He raised a brow. "Someone like me?"

"Yeah, the dumb muscleman type." Contempt dripped from Brendan's voice. "Military too, from the looks of you. Jen doesn't date military muscle heads."

Cash exchanged a grin with Dylan and Seth. Jackson turned away from the bartender and flashed a grin of his own before resuming his flirting.

"Military muscle heads, huh?" Cash shrugged. "Well, these military muscle heads want to talk to you outside."

"Fuck off."

Brendan tried to take a step, but he hit a wall of—surprise—muscle. Dylan and Seth flanked Cash, and all three crossed their arms over their chests.

"Get out of my way," Brendan said through visibly clenched teeth.

"That's not gonna happen," Cash replied. "Not until we get some things straight. You've got two options here. Either you calmly follow us outside so we can continue this discussion, or I drag you out by the collar of your shirt."

"I'd choose option one," Dylan suggested.

"Yeah," Seth agreed. "That shirt looks expensive. Wouldn't want it getting ripped when Cash hauls you outta here."

Brendan took another step forward. Hit another wall of muscle. Bitterness crept into his tone as he capitulated. "Fine. Let's go."

Cash clapped his hand on the guy's shoulder and led him to the hallway at the rear of the bar. They received a few odd looks from the wait staff as they crossed the employees-only area.

A metal door met them at the end of the corridor. It led out to a narrow alley separating the Tavern from the neighboring Chinese restaurant. Dumpsters cluttered the space, and the smell of garbage and urine wafted in the air. The sun hadn't completely set yet, but the sky was cloudy, casting gray shadows over the alley.

Once outside, Brendan got a taste of freedom and took a few steps forward, his gaze glued to the opening of the alley.

Cash stepped in his path. "Hey now, no running off," he said pleasantly. "We haven't had a chance to talk yet."

Seth and Dylan flanked him again, while Jackson remained near the door.

"Look," Brendan blurted out, "I don't know who you are, but my relationship with Jen is none of your business."

"Relationship?" Cash made a *tsk*ing noise. "She dumped you, and instead of handling the breakup like a mature adult, you decided to play these sick games with her. But it stops tonight, understand?" Tightening his jaw, he got right in the other man's face. "Stop emailing her. Stop calling. Stop harassing her family and friends. As of this moment, Jen does not exist to you."

Brendan looked livid, but his jaw remained shut.

"She doesn't want to see you, she doesn't want to talk to you. Hell, she doesn't want to *think* about you. It's time for you to get the message. Go to Oakland, do your investment banking thing, and leave Jen alone."

Brendan's nostrils flared. "Who the hell do you think you are, ordering me around? I don't know you, asshole. And you know *nothing* about my relationship with—"

"Again with this relationship bullshit?" Cash sighed. "Just nod and tell me you understand, bro. If you don't, the only relationship you'll be having is the one with my fist."

Dylan snickered.

On Cash's other side, Seth reached into his pocket for a pack of Marlboros. He extracted a smoke and lit up, looking bored as he inhaled. But the deadly look in his eyes belied the casual pose. Seth could rip Brendan to pieces in a nanosecond, if provoked.

Brendan went silent, his gaze shifting from one man to the other. Then, knowing he was beaten, he mumbled a curse and said, "Fine. I won't bother her again. Happy, asshole?"

"Ecstatic. Now that we've cleared all this up, you can—"

The right hook blindsided Cash.

Fortunately, he saw the fist coming at his nose at the last second and shifted his head so that Brendan missed the intended target. The blow sliced into the corner of Cash's mouth instead. His bottom lip snagged on his teeth and the coppery taste of blood filled his mouth.

Oh, *hell* no.

As Jen's ex charged forward with a second attack, Cash struck him with a jab that made the man's head snap back. With a roar, Brendan threw another punch, which Cash easily blocked. Blood continued to pour from the side of his mouth, but he didn't bother wiping it away. Blocking the fists swinging in his direction, Cash sidestepped and got his arms around the guy from behind.

"Are you done?" he demanded as he secured Brendan in a chest lock.

"Screw you!" was the sputtered response. And then the guy elbowed him in the jaw before spinning around and landing a lucky kick on Cash's groin.

Years of training had taught him to ignore the pain zipping through his balls. Without so much as flinching, he drew his arm back, but Seth's fist beat him to it.

A sickening crunch sounded in the air.

Blood erupted from Brendan's nose. His hands flew to his face. "You fucking asshole!" he shouted. "You broke my nose!"

Seth just chuckled. "Shouldn't have played dirty, going for McCoy's balls like that."

Seth retreated and walked over to Dylan, who'd watched the entire scuffle with visible amusement.

Cash got in Brendan's face again. "This is your last warning. Stay away from Jen. If you try to make contact again, my boys and I will pay you another visit, and trust me, next time you'll have a lot more than a broken nose."

He stepped back just as sirens wailed.

Shit.

Cash caught the flicker of alarm on Dylan's face, the resignation in Seth and Jackson's expressions.

A moment later, a car door slammed and footsteps thudded into the alley.

He didn't need to turn around to know what awaited them.

"This is the San Diego PD! Hands in the air!"

CHAPTER SEVENTEEN

Coming up with excuses not to go after what you want won't achieve a damn thing.

Jen couldn't get those words out of her head as she wandered around the apartment. After Cash left, she'd tried occupying herself by posting some photos on her blog, but her heart hadn't been in it. Sifting through her photographs, she'd kept thinking back to everything Cash had said. Stop making excuses and *man up*. Accusing her of letting her parents' criticism erode her self-esteem.

His words had hurt, but not for the reason he'd believed. He hadn't damaged her pride or hurt her feelings. No, what he'd done was voice the truth she'd been too blind to see.

She'd always told herself that photography was just a hobby. The thought of pursuing it on a professional level had crossed her mind once or twice, but her lack of experience and education had held her back. Better to call it something she did in her spare time and leave it as that.

But who was she kidding? Photography was her one and only passion, the only thing in her life that made her feel fulfilled and confident. Cash was right. She couldn't make excuses anymore. She chose to work at pointless dead-end jobs not because she didn't have any other options, not because she sucked at everything else, but because she was too scared to pursue the one thing that made her happy.

Biting her lip, she paused in the middle of the living room, wishing Cash would come home already so she could explain that she wasn't angry with *him*, but with herself. For being a damned scaredy-cat and letting her parents and her own self-doubt hold her back for so long.

Where the hell is he?

She stalked into the kitchen to check the time, frowning when she noticed it was past eight already. He was supposed to meet Brendan at six thirty, and she couldn't imagine the confrontation lasting this long.

And that was another thing. Why had he insisted on confronting her ex-boyfriend? Cash possessed some serious protective instincts, but she got the feeling this was about more than protecting her. This was about him...staking a claim.

Her teeth dug deeper into her lower lip. Was Cash developing feelings for her?

Was she developing feelings for *him*?

No, of course not. This was just a fling. A fling that would end in a week and a half.

Does it have to?

Did it?

Yes.

Well, maybe.

She took pause, weighing the notion in her head. Her cheeks heated as she thought about all the spectacular sex they'd been having. And the threesome... God, the threesome. Her body still tingled at the memory. But as amazing as last night had been, she wasn't looking for a repeat performance. A fantasy fulfilled, that was how she viewed it, and she couldn't see the whole ménage thing becoming a habit.

Besides, Cash didn't need outside assistance to satisfy her. The man was perfectly capable of driving her wild all by his lonesome.

But his superior bedroom skills weren't the only things she liked about him. He might be gruff and intense at times, but he was also funny, sweet, smart...

...and a military man to the core. He'd confessed his desire to go to officer school, which told her he was committed to the military life. And he was still young, which meant he had at least another decade or two before he rode a desk at the base.

Regret rippled through her. No matter how much she liked Cash, she didn't want that kind of life. She'd already watched her mother struggle, and now she had to watch her sister-in-law suffer the same fate, spending long stretches apart from her husband, unable to talk to him anymore because they felt like strangers.

When a knock came on the door, Jen made a beeline for the front hall, needing the distraction. She peered into the peephole and found her brother's cloudy blue eyes staring back at her. Instantly, her mood sank even lower. She hadn't spoken to Carson since she and Cash had witnessed his coffee date with that redhead, and she was not looking forward to the argument that lay ahead.

"What's up?" Carson said once she let him in. "Your messages sounded cryptic. All seven of them."

He looked annoyed as he followed her into the living room. "Want something to drink?" she asked, stalling.

"No." He flopped down on the couch and glanced around warily. "Where's McCoy?"

She sighed. "Being a hero."

"What does that mean?"

"It means the big, bad soldier is determined to have it out with Brendan." She settled in the armchair and tucked her knees into her chest, wrapping her arms around them. "Brendan managed to get my number from Tessa."

"Psycho McGee was bothering Tessa? And Cash is meeting with him ? Where?"

When her brother started to get up, Jen said, "Oh, sit down already. Cash is probably on his way home, so you'd be too late to back him up."

"Why?"

"Why what?"

Suspicion crept into his voice. "Why did McCoy go after Brendan?"

"He's just being a good friend." She quickly changed the subject before he could grill her further. "I talked to Holly, by the way."

Carson's shoulders stiffened. "When?"

"Sunday, after we left Mom and Dad's house. She told me you two aren't connecting."

"I don't want to talk about it, Jenny."

"Tough shit, because you're going to." She took a breath. How on earth did she even start?

Hey, big brother, are you cheating on your wife? The direct approach probably would be best, but a part of her didn't want to ask the question for fear of what his answer would be.

Exhaling, she slid her knees down and placed her palms on her thighs. "Look, I need to ask you something. I know it's none of my business, but I—"

A phone rang.

She suppressed a groan as Carson held up his hand. "I gotta get this." He fished his phone out of his pocket. "Hey, Beck, what's doing?"

Jen's heart dropped. Beck. AKA Thomas Becker, Carson's CO.

Carson listened for a few seconds, frowning. The frown deepened the longer Becker talked, and then Carson said, "Fucking hell!" and shot to his feet. "Yeah, I'll meet you there."

Jen stood up too, fighting a tremor of panic. "What's wrong? Are you going overseas?"

"No," he said in a clipped tone.

"Then what's going on?"

"What's going on? McCoy and his band of idiots got arrested, *that's* what's going on."

"*What*?"

Carson was already marching to the door. "I've gotta go. Someone needs to bail their sorry asses out of jail."

"Wait, I'm coming with you!"

He glanced over his shoulder and shot her a firm look. "Out of the question. You're staying here and locking the door behind me. I'll call you when I know more." He strode out the door, slamming it loudly behind him.

"Great job, McCoy. Great fucking job."

Cash scowled at Seth from across the holding cell. "Nobody asked you to join in and defend my honor."

"They would've hauled me in either way. Texas and Wade didn't take a swing and they're still in jail."

Seth was sprawled on one of the long metal benches, his stormy gray eyes fixed on a cracked piece of plaster on the ceiling. On the other side of the cell, Cash and Jackson sat side by side, their heads resting against the cement wall, legs stretched out. Dylan had been pacing the concrete floor for the past hour.

The four of them were the holding cell's sole occupants. Ironic, how the asshole who'd thrown the first punch was conspicuously absent. But when the cops showed up in the alley, Brendan had sprinted toward the cavalry and proceeded to spin a sordid tail in which he, the poor victim, had been jumped by four goons who'd broken his nose. The two uniformed officers took one look at the four SEALs and the cuffs had come out.

The last thing Cash heard before being carted toward the squad car was Brendan's announcement that he was pressing charges against his assailants. Lying asshole.

Across the cell, Dylan finally quit pacing and turned to face the group, his broad shoulders slumped. "We're totally gonna do hard time for this."

Cash rolled his eyes. "We won't do hard time. It was just a brawl."

"Didn't you ever see *Con Air*? Nicolas Cage ends up in prison for a *brawl*. Know why? Because his body is considered a lethal weapon thanks to his military training."

"But didn't he kill a bunch of dudes?" Jackson pointed out. "And then there was that scene where Harrison Ford is all *Get off my plane*. Best movie line ever."

"That's *Air Force One*, dumbass," Seth said with a grin. "But yeah, I think Nic Cage accidentally killed someone. See, Wade, we're fine. Nobody got accidentally murdered tonight."

Dylan wasn't listening. Scraping a hand through his blond hair, he glared at Cash. "I can't go to prison. It'll break my mother's heart. And you know I'll be fighting off would-be rapists left and right."

Seth snorted. "You already like it up the ass, so what's the problem?"

"Ha ha. I'm dying of laughter here." Dylan looked frazzled. "Fuck, those inmates will be all over me. I'm too good-looking to resist."

Cash snickered.

"Conceited much?" Jackson drawled.

Dylan stared down the Texan. "You saying I'm not good-looking enough to attract a bunch of lonely, horny prisoners?"

"No, just saying if we're basing it on looks, I think I'd be the one holding the rapists at bay," Jackson replied. "The ladies never stop raving about my face. And my fine ass."

"My ass doesn't get any complaints," Dylan shot back. He narrowed his eyes, then glanced at Cash. "Who do you think? Me or Texas?"

Cash shook his head in bewilderment. "How the hell do I know?"

"I'm sure you'd both be equally violated," Seth said helpfully.

"*Ahem.*"

They swiveled their heads toward the bars to find Lieutenant Commander Becker standing there.

For the first time all evening, Cash experienced a flicker of anxiety. Shit. The arresting officers had called their CO?

And the CO's XO, he realized with growing dismay when Carson appeared next to Becker.

"Hey, Commander," Dylan said with a sheepish look.

"You our ride home?" Seth piped up.

Becker sliced a hand through the air. "Not one word from any of you."

A uniformed officer approached the cell with a heavy key ring. The keys jingled in the silent space as he unlocked the door. "You're free to go," he said in a monotone voice.

Trudging out of the cell, Cash felt like a kid about to get grounded for sneaking out of the house. They strode down the fluorescent-lit hallway of the police station toward the processing area. Their keys, wallets, and other belongings were returned to them, and as they signed some paperwork, Becker stood there with his arms crossed, a vein throbbing in his forehead.

They'd been ordered to stay silent, but Seth, being Seth, couldn't help himself. "Is the asswipe pressing charges?"

Becker glared murder at him. The vein throbbed harder and faster.

But Carson answered. "No. There's a witness on the record saying that Psycho McGee threw the first punch. No assault charges will be brought against you."

Witness? Cash glanced at Jackson, who'd been their lookout, but he just shrugged.

"Waiter at the restaurant next door came out to have a smoke just as the action went down," Carson explained.

They left the station and still Becker didn't say a word. From the daggers in his eyes, the CO was clearly on the verge of exploding. Cash had two inches and about twenty pounds on the commander, but he felt five feet tall in the man's presence. Beck was a man of few words, but when he spoke, you paid attention. And with those waves of intensity rolling off him, he could scare the shit out of you with one look.

They stood on the front steps, nobody making a move. Becker kept staring at them as if he wanted to kill them, and even though he'd expected it, Cash was still startled when the explosion came.

"What the *hell* is the matter with you?" Becker roared. "A bar fight? Really?"

"Well, it was more like an alley fight," Seth said.

Becker ignored him. "Here I am, enjoying a lovely evening with my wife and daughter and then the phone rings and who's on the other end of the line? The *police*. Telling me four of my men decided to rough up some businessman in frickin' public. Were you idiots born stupid or is this something you've worked on your whole life? Brawling in public! Jesus fucking Christ!"

Cash's jaw went slack. He'd never seen Becker so pissed off or heard him utter so many words at one time.

"This is the last time I bail you out, understand?" Becker barked.

"Technically, you didn't bail us out," Seth pointed out. "No charges were pressed."

Becker once again ignored the resident smartass. "If you ever pull another stunt like this, I'm filing a disciplinary report. No brawling, hear me? I don't give a shit if you were provoked—you find yourself in this position again, you walk away. Understood?"

"Understood," they answered in unison.

Becker crossed his arms over his massive chest and glared at them, one at a time. "And to solve your who-gets-violated puzzle? Based on looks alone—Pretty Boy over here." He jammed a finger in Dylan's direction. "Based on personality? Texas, because he's too damn nice. Based on attitude? This guy," he pointed at Seth, "because he'd probably piss off an inmate named Bubba with his smart mouth and Bubba'll have to punish him." Beck cocked his head at Cash. "And McCoy would quietly serve his time and probably avoid any ass shenanigans."

A silence fell.

"Well," Dylan spoke up. "Thanks for settling that, Commander."

Becker's eyes flashed. "Now, Carson and I will drive you dumbasses back to your cars, and then I'm going home to read a bedtime story to my daughter and pretend this bullshit never happened. Pretty Boy, Smartass, you ride with me."

He marched off without waiting to see if Dylan and Seth were following. Which they were. Running after him, more like it.

Cash let out a relieved breath that he didn't have to sit in the same car as Becker. He glanced at Carson, who'd stayed silent during Becker's entire tirade. "You don't have anything to add?"

"Nope." Carson's eyes twinkled as he gestured toward the Range Rover at the curb. "Come on, dumbasses, let's get your car. Texas, you're riding in the back."

Jackson slid into the backseat as ordered. Cash reached for the passenger door, but Carson came up beside him before he could open it.

"Did the creep get the message?" Carson asked, steel in his eyes.

Cash nodded. "I think he did, LT."

"Good." The man's lips twitched. "Don't think I'm condoning brawling in public, but I appreciate what you did, McCoy. Looking out for my sister like that."

"Jen and I are friends," he said with a shrug. "I don't like it when people harass my friends."

Carson slanted his head, suspicion entering his expression. "Friends," he echoed.

"Yup." Cash was tempted to avert his gaze, but he knew that would only raise a red flag. So he met the lieutenant's gaze head on, daring him to challenge that.

Hell, he kind of wished Carson would. Cash didn't like lying to the guy, especially now that his feelings for Jen were... changing. This didn't feel like a fling anymore, not by a long shot.

But Carson didn't push the subject. Instead, he changed it, studying Cash's face. "Bastard got you good, huh?"

He brought a hand to his mouth and touched the swollen bump. He felt the dried blood caked there. "Yeah, but I got him better."

Carson grinned. "Good. But if you tell Becker I said that, I'll deny it. My official stance on what you did tonight is the same as Becker's—foolish as hell."

"And your unofficial stance?"

"My unofficial stance is...hoo-yah."

JEN WAS CLIMBING THE WALLS BY THE TIME CASH WALKED through the door. She was at his side in two seconds flat, gasping when she noticed the red bump at the corner of his mouth. And was that blood on his lip?

"Are you okay?" she demanded, her hand flying up to his face.

He winced. "I'm fine." His fingers circled her wrist and he slowly moved her hand away. "Just a little bruise."

She studied him, trying to decide if he was downplaying his injury in an attempt to act macho, but the lack of pain and discomfort in his eyes said he was telling the truth. Still, she couldn't help but sweep her gaze over him to make sure he hadn't been hurt anywhere else. He seemed fine, though. Pretty damn fine, in fact. His T-shirt hugged every delicious muscle of his chest, his scuffed-up boots added to his tough-guy look, and the swelling at the side of his mouth lent him a dangerous vibe.

He was so hot her mouth went dry, and he must have sensed where her thoughts had drifted because he cocked an eyebrow and grinned.

"You finished ogling me, Ms. Pervy Eyes?"

She laughed. "You complaining?"

"Nope. I love having your eyes on me. Especially when I'm naked."

"You look really good naked," she conceded.

Cash promptly reached for the hem of his shirt.

"What are you doing?"

"Giving you what you want."

She intercepted his hand before he could remove his shirt.

"Hold your horses. If you get naked now, I'll totally lose my train of thought."

"I'm that distracting, huh?"

"You know you are. Now come sit down and tell me what happened. How on earth did you wind up in jail?"

They settled on the couch, where Cash released a breath. "The boys and I went to the bar. We politely asked Brendan to come outside and I told him in no uncertain terms to leave you alone. He didn't like that. He threw a punch. Things escalated from there."

She had to laugh at his matter-of-fact recitation. "That's it? He punched you, you punched back?"

"Yep." Cash eyed her warily. "You're not going to lecture me about violence and not solving problems with your fists, are you?"

She mulled that over. "No." A grin sprang to her lips. "Honestly, the thought of you kicking his ass is hot as hell."

Cash took that as his cue to reach for his shirt again.

This time, Jen didn't stop him, and sure enough, when he exposed his chest, his six-pack distracted her for several seconds. Snapping herself out of it, she placed her hand in the center of his chest and said, "Wait. There's something I wanted to say to you."

"Fuck. It's about earlier, isn't it?" He hesitated. "I'm sorry, I was insensitive. I told you, I don't know the first thing about talking to women—"

"Don't apologize. I'm not mad at you."

"You're not?"

"No. I spent the whole day thinking about what you said, and I realized you're right." A twinge of embarrassment colored her cheeks. "I could have been submitting my work to magazines and newspapers years ago, but something always stopped me. The truth is, I'm scared. I'm scared people won't like my pictures, scared they'll tell me not to quit my day job, scared my parents will say I told you so."

Cash stroked her cheek with his knuckles. "It's okay to be scared."

"Maybe. But it's not okay to not try." She shook her head. "I'll never know if I'm any good unless I put myself out there."

"Is that what you're planning on doing?"

She nodded. "I made a list of publications I think I'd be a good fit for, but most of them require a portfolio, so I need to put one together." Excitement trickled through her. "And then I'll start submitting and lining up interviews. I want to try to make my hobby into a career. I *have* to try."

His answering smile warmed her heart. Despite everything he'd said earlier, she'd half expected him to say it was a bad idea or give her that patronizing stare her parents had perfected. But he didn't. All she saw in his eyes was encouragement, and before she could stop herself, she launched herself at him and pressed her lips to his.

She kissed him, cupping his stubble-covered jaw with her hands. Cash groaned and parted his lips, but it wasn't until she tasted copper on her tongue that she remembered he'd been hurt.

She drew back and gently touched the bump. "Sorry, I forgot."

"I already told you, it doesn't hurt."

She gazed into his eyes, experiencing another rush of amazement. "I can't believe you beat up Brendan for me."

"Does the thought of me defending your honor turn you on?"

"Mmm-hmmm." Jen pressed her face to his neck and kissed him, then tasted him with her tongue, enjoying the masculine flavor of his skin. "You taste good."

"I taste like saltwater," he corrected. "I swam two miles

earlier and haven't showered yet." He made a move to get up. "I should probably do that."

"Later. I'm trying to properly thank you for what you did with Brendan."

She gave him a little push so that he lay on his back, then lowered her head and kissed the hollow of his throat. When she felt his pulse hammering beneath her lips, she smiled. It was so liberating knowing she affected him as much as he affected her, that her kisses excited him, made his heart race.

As excitement quickened her own pulse, she roamed the spectacular expanse of Cash's chest with her hands, tracing each hard ridge, gliding over every inch of smooth, tanned skin.

When she circled his nipple with her tongue, a husky sound escaped his lips. "That feels good," he mumbled.

"Yeah?" Intrigued, she kissed her way to his other nipple and flicked her tongue over the flat brown disc. It stiffened, and Cash moaned again.

She hid a smile, enjoying having him at her mercy. Loving the way his muscles quivered beneath her touch. She kissed a path down to his abs and rubbed her cheek over his tight six-pack like a contented cat. The man was all muscle, all raw power and masculinity. Her fingertips skimmed over those delicious abdominal muscles before dipping down to the waistband of his cargo pants.

Unzipping him, she eased the pants down his long, muscular legs. He wasn't wearing any boxers, and his erection sprang up to greet her, long and thick, a glistening drop pooling at the tip.

Jen practically purred with pleasure. "I could probably come just from looking at you."

Male arrogance hung from his voice. "You like looking at my dick that much, huh?"

"God, yes." She swallowed. "I wish I was as good at dirty

talk as you. I'd tell you all the naughty things I want to do to you, how hot you make me, how badly I want you."

"Well, damn, that's something I definitely want to hear. Come on, baby, talk dirty to me."

Ribbons of heat uncurled inside her, spreading to every erogenous zone in her body. "I want to lick you," she told him. "I want to suck on the head of your cock and feel you pulsing against my tongue."

"Yeah?" He made a growling noise. "Do it."

As her heart pounded at triple speed, she licked his shaft from root to tip. The heady taste of him made her head spin. She encircled him with her fingers and pumped slowly, continuing to lavish him with long swipes of her tongue before closing her lips around him and sucking hard.

"What else?" he said in a raspy voice that made her shiver. "What else do you want to do to me?"

"Ride you. I want to ride you."

A strangled noise left his lips. "Do it."

Trembling wildly, she released him and climbed onto the couch. Rather than straddle him, she scrambled up his body and positioned her knees at either side of his head so that her aching core hovered over his face. "I want your tongue on me first," she said huskily.

Cash didn't hesitate. His tongue swiftly connected with her clit, spearing the swollen bud with absolute precision.

Jen cried out and grabbed the arm of the couch to steady herself. The satisfied growling sounds Cash made as he licked her teased her hypersensitive nerve endings. He feasted on her like a starving man, his strong hands digging into her ass, as she ground into his face with complete abandon. She should've been embarrassed by her excitement, the all-consuming desperation, but her brain became a black hole void of all thought, any sense of decency forgotten. All she knew was that she had to come. *Needed* it, the way she needed oxygen and sustenance.

But just as the orgasm rose to the surface, just as her muscles turned to limp noodles and her pulse grew erratic, she managed to wrench herself away and stave off the release.

Breathing hard, she flung an arm in the direction of the coffee table. They'd formed a habit of leaving condoms all over the apartment in the event that a crazy case of lust overtook them, which seemed to happen often. She'd tucked a condom underneath the *Sports Illustrated* magazine on the table and her fingers shook as she grabbed it. Somehow she managed to tear it open and roll the condom onto his erection. Then she sat astride him, her breaths coming out shallow.

"I should warn you, I'm going to explode the second you're in me."

"I look forward to it," he said solemnly.

Sucking in a burst of air, Jen sank onto his thick, hard cock.

As she'd warned, pleasure blasted through her the moment he filled her, her inner muscles clenching even as they stretched to accommodate him. The orgasm sent her soaring into oblivion. Gasping, she collapsed on his chest, her hips moving in a frantic rhythm as she rode out the release.

When she crashed down from the orgasmic high, she felt Cash shuddering beneath her. His upward thrusts contained no finesse, just short, erratic strokes emphasized by his hoarse grunts as he came hard and fast.

Sometime later, when their breathing steadied and their pulses regulated, Cash gently moved her off him so he could ditch the condom, then brought her body back to his and cuddled her close. Jen rested her cheek on his chest, sighing in sweet contentment.

God, this felt good.

It felt *right*.

Apprehension gnawed on her insides when she realized where her thoughts had drifted. She tried to wiggle out of Cash's embrace, but he held her tighter, his laughter tickling her forehead. "You're not going anywhere, sweetheart. I haven't gotten my cuddling fill yet."

An unwitting smile tugged on her lips. She forced herself to relax, trying not to overthink things. Snuggling after sex was perfectly acceptable fling behavior.

But...yeah, she definitely needed to work a little harder on the not-falling-in-love-with-him part.

CHAPTER EIGHTEEN

Four days later, Jen's confidence in her ability to control her emotions began to crumble. Keeping an emotional distance from Cash was harder than she'd thought, especially when he was intent on being so wonderfully *wonderful*. He cooked for her, offered encouragement while she worked on putting together a portfolio, made her breathless with his kisses and dizzy with desire.

They'd spent nearly every waking moment together, except for the night Dylan came over to watch football again. There'd been no follow-up to their threesome, though. As fun as it had been, Jen only wanted Cash in her bed now. Thankfully, Dylan hadn't seemed to mind that sex wasn't on the table. Which didn't surprise her—she got the feeling nothing fazed that guy.

"I get it, Mom. She's unhappy."

Cash's mumbled voice drifted into the room, breaking Jen's concentration. She lifted her gaze from the laptop screen and spotted him pacing the hallway in front of the open bedroom door.

"I'll do it now, okay? Uh-huh...uh-huh...got it. I'll email you later. Uh-huh... Love you too... Say hi to Dad."

Silence ensued, finally broken by a soft expletive from Cash, who entered the room, sank on the edge of the bed and dragged a hand through his hair.

"What's wrong?" Jen asked. "What was that phone call about?"

He set his jaw. "That was my mother."

"Is she okay?"

"Yeah."

Jen waited for him to continue. When he didn't, she rolled her eyes. "Come on, cowboy, spit it out."

"I..." He was gritting his teeth now. "I need a favor."

"Okay..."

"I wouldn't ask you this if it wasn't important."

A million possibilities ran through her head. "Let me guess—you need me to serve as the getaway driver for the bank robbery you're planning." She paused. "Wait, that makes no sense. Your parents are loaded."

"Right, *that's* why it makes no sense."

"Fine, then you need me to...kill someone for you? Wait, no. You could easily kill someone all by yourse—"

"I need you to take my picture," he interrupted.

She gawked at him. "Seriously? That's what's getting your panties in a knot? Don't tell me you've never had your picture taken."

Misery clung to his voice. "It's not that."

"Then what is it?"

"My birthday was last month."

"Happy belated birthday?"

Cash scowled. "I wasn't done. Anyway, the team was OCONUS so I didn't get to spend my birthday with my family, but my parents flew in for a visit a few weeks ago, and they brought a present my grandmother made me. Now she keeps harassing them, wanting to know if I liked it."

"What was it?"

"A sweater." He didn't elaborate. "I called to thank her, but apparently she doesn't believe I like it. She's demanding I send photographic evidence of me wearing the sweater so she knows I'm not lying."

"That seems a little...strange."

"She's a strange woman," he muttered. "Scratch that, she's absolutely nuts. That's one of the reasons my mom left home when she was a teenager. My grandmother has some issues. Serious case of OCD, gets hysterical at the drop of a hat, disapproves of anything she doesn't understand. I'm not looking forward to spending the holidays with her this year, that's for sure."

"Let's not get ahead of ourselves. We'll deal with this picture problem for now." She closed her laptop and climbed off the bed. "I left my camera in the living room. Why don't you put on the sweater and meet me out there?"

As she headed for the doorway, she noticed Cash hadn't budged.

"What now?" she asked with a sigh.

His cheeks hollowed and she could practically hear his molars grinding. "Before we do this, you have to promise me something."

She waited.

"You can't laugh," he said in a deadly voice.

"I won't laugh. What's the promise?"

"No, *that's* the promise. You have to promise not to laugh."

She wrinkled her forehead. "Oh. Okay. I promise."

She slid out the door, hearing Cash's low curses as he rummaged around in the closet. In the living room, she grabbed her camera and peered through the lens, snapping a couple of test shots to assess the lighting in the room. She adjusted the shutter speed and aperture until she was pleased with the results.

Five minutes passed and Cash still didn't make an appearance.

"You coming?" Jen called.

Heavy footsteps thudded from the hall, then ceased.

"I promised I wouldn't laugh," she told the empty doorway. "Now get that sexy ass out here and let's start this photo shoot before I change my—"

Her words died in her throat when he stepped out.

And God help her, but even though she'd promised not to laugh, she couldn't help herself. Doubling over, Jen laughed so hard she thought her ribs would crack. When she started wheezing, she clutched her side and dropped her gaze to her feet.

"I'm going to pee my pants," she choked out between giggles. "I can't look at you."

"Thanks, thanks a lot," he muttered. "I'll just go hang myself now."

"No, don't. I'm sorry, I couldn't help myself." She wiped the corners of her eyes. "I'll be good now, I swear."

He tilted his head in the most adorable way. "It's not that bad, is it?"

"It's the most bizarre thing I've ever seen."

She gave the sweater a long once-over, trying to figure out what the hell she was seeing. It'd been knitted out of pink and green wool, clearly handmade judging by the uneven stitching and lopsided neckline. And as if the pink and green stripes weren't distracting enough, Cash's grandmother had stitched an image in the center of the sweater. Jen suspected it was supposed to be Cash, since the disproportioned male figure wore a uniform. A red uniform. With a black helmet. And she didn't even want to know what he was holding in his hands.

She started to get dizzy from all the colors flashing at her. Pink, green, red, black. She swallowed another gust of laughter. "Is that you?"

His jaw was tighter than a drum. "Yes."

"Why are you holding a dildo?"

Cash briefly closed his eyes, as if trying to talk himself out of murdering her. "It's a shotgun."

"Why would a Navy SEAL carry a shotgun?"

"Because she couldn't find a pattern for an assault rifle."

"Oh." Jen clamped her lips together to stifle another giggle. "And why is the uniform red? Are you supposed to be a guard at Buckingham Palace?"

"Can you just take the fucking picture?"

She was still giggling as she picked up the camera and aimed it at Cash. She took a candid shot, then glanced at the digital display and laughed at the stony expression on his face.

"You have to smile for the next one. Otherwise your grandmother will know exactly what you think of her sweater."

For the next twenty minutes, Jen had an absolute blast ordering him around. She snapped far more shots than necessary, but she couldn't help herself. The sight of tough guy Cash in that pink and green sweater was too tempting an opportunity to ignore. She made him pose by the window, in the living room, in the kitchen. Sitting, standing, striking a thoughtful finger-on-the-chin pose.

But all bets were off when she tried to persuade him to lie on the couch in the ultimate male pin-up pose. That's when he promptly grabbed the camera from her hands and announced he'd had enough.

"We're done," he declared, then proceeded to strip off his sweater as if it was covered in ants. "And I'm officially *never* wearing this thing again." To punctuate the declaration, he whipped the sweater on the couch. "Now, do you want to grab some lunch at the grill on 4th? I'm in the mood for a steak."

"At three o'clock in the afternoon?"

"After what you just put me through, I feel like a juicy T-bone is the only thing that will reaffirm my masculinity."

With a sassy smile, Jen stalked over and cupped his package over his pants. "Mmm. I could go for a juicy T-bone myself."

He rewarded her with a wicked grin. "Baby, I like the way your mind works."

"How about my mouth? Do you like the way that works too?" She dropped to her knees and unzipped his pants. He'd gone commando and his erection sprang out with an excited bob.

Licking her lips, she dipped her head and licked a little circle around the head of his cock.

Cash groaned, his hands immediately moving to tangle in her hair. His hips thrust forward, the hard length of him seeking her mouth.

She swiftly pulled back. "Uh-uh, you don't get any sexy time until you do one thing for me."

His eyes narrowed. "What's that?"

"Put the sweater back on."

SADIE BECKER'S FIRST BIRTHDAY PARTY WAS IN FULL SWING when Cash and Jen arrived the next afternoon. Becker and Jane lived in a modest, two-story home in Coronado, and though the house itself was smaller than most in the area, the backyard made up for that. The large, perfectly manicured lawn was big enough to house a decent-sized swimming pool, a swing set, an enormous pine deck with a table that seated ten, and a stone patio littered with children's toys.

Bright pink balloons hung from the tall fence surrounding the yard, and tables laden with food had been set up on the patio. A few dozen people milled around the yard, most of whom Cash recognized. Stepping onto the deck, he and Jen dropped Sadie's gift off with Jane's older sister, Elizabeth, a tall, slender blonde who looked nothing like her curvy, redheaded sister.

Speaking of the curvy redhead, Cash spotted Jane holding court by the refreshment table, chatting with a few women Cash had never met. She had one-year-old Sadie propped on her hip, and now there was a clear resemblance. The baby had a head of shocking red hair and big blue eyes just like her mother, but the expression of intense consternation on the kid's face was all Becker.

"Let's go say hi to everyone," Jen said, searching the crowd.

Cash longed to hold her hand, but he resisted the urge. They'd already agreed there'd be no PDA today, or anything else that could reveal they'd been sleeping together for the past two weeks. The last thing he wanted to do was get into it with Carson, not in a backyard full of people they knew. Besides, keeping the fling on the down-low was probably for the best, considering it was supposed to end soon.

Supposed to being the operative words.

Because no way was Cash letting this end. For the first time in his life, he'd found a woman he actually connected with. A woman he had no problem communicating with. A woman who captured his attention in *and* out of bed.

Jen was the quirkiest, funniest, most amazing person he'd ever known. He loved the sound of her laughter. Her sunny smiles. The way she left yellow sticky notes all over the apartment to remind herself to do things. And she'd started leaving *him* notes, too—this morning he'd found a Post-it on the bathroom mirror, with Jen's feminine scrawl saying, "Top of the morning to you, cowboy!"

Yeah...he wasn't ready to let her go yet. Not by a long shot.

"Jen, Cash!" On the steps of the deck, Annabelle waved them over. Next to her were Savannah Harte, Shelby Garrett and a woman Cash didn't recognize.

"Cash, do you know Mackenzie?" Annabelle asked, gesturing to the woman at her side. "She's married to Will."

"It's nice to meet you." As he shook Mackenzie's hand, he couldn't help but notice what a knockout she was. Tall and slender, with long black hair and blue eyes that sparkled when she smiled at him.

"Will told me about you," Mackenzie said warmly. "He said you were one of the most determined men he's ever met and that you kicked ass during BUD/S training."

Cash hid his surprise. Will actually said that? Receiving a compliment from the brooding SEAL, who was now an instructor on the base, occurred about as often as an eclipse. It surprised him that Lieutenant Will Charleston had mentioned Cash to his wife at all.

"I had no choice," Cash replied ruefully. "He was too intimidating. Every time I got tempted to quit, I pictured myself ringing that bell while the LT stood there glaring at me, and I knew I couldn't live with that kind of embarrassment. Is he here today?"

Mackenzie pointed to the pool deck. "Over there."

He followed her gaze, instantly spotting Will. The mirrored Aviators and unruly black hair were a giveaway, but the menacing air the man exuded during Cash's training was missing. Probably because Will held a wiggling dark-haired toddler in his arms: his son, Lucas.

John Garrett stood next to Will, also with his hands full—

two-year-old Penny kept grabbing at the beer bottle in her father's hand, which he kept moving out of her grasp.

Garrett's wife, Shelby, giggled when she saw what her daughter was up to. "She's got a fascination with bottles of all things," the blonde revealed. "She tries jamming all her fingers into the bottle like she's digging for treasure."

Smiling, Jen searched the yard again. "Hey, are my brother and Holly here?"

"They were," Annabelle replied. "I don't know where they disappeared to."

From the refreshment table, Jane suddenly caught Cash's eye and flashed him a delighted smile.

"We should say hi to the birthday girl," Cash said as he waved hello to Jane.

He and Jen drifted away, passing several men Cash knew from the base. He said a few hellos, then caught sight of Dylan and Jackson near the swing set, holding paper plates and munching on appetizers. Ryan and Matt stood a few feet away, beers in their hands, heads bent in deep conversation. He looked around in search of Seth, but their resident badass was MIA. No surprise there—Seth's dislike of kids was no secret. No doubt he'd already come by to drop off a gift, said a quick hello, and hightailed it home.

"I'm so glad you could make it," Jane said when they approached.

Baby Sadie made a delighted gurgling sound as her big eyes focused on the new arrivals.

"Hey there," Jen crooned, leaning in to kiss Sadie's forehead. "Happy birthday, cutie."

"Gah!"

Jane grinned. "That means *thank-you.*" She shifted Sadie to her other hip and gestured to the food table behind her. "We decided not to barbeque—" She rolled her eyes, "—because Becker is scared the smoke from the grill will give our daughter cancer. But Holly prepared a bunch of yummy dishes—there's like five different kinds of salad, mini sandwiches, apps and a bunch of other finger foods. So help yourself, okay?"

"Everything looks delicious," Jen said, reaching for two plates. "Where is Holly, by the way?"

Jane wrinkled her brow. "I don't know. I haven't seen her since she set up the tables."

Carson was noticeably absent too. Cash wasn't sure if that was a good sign, or a bad one. As much as he didn't want to imagine his lieutenant screwing around, he hoped Carson and Holly were inside getting it on somewhere. At least that would mean they were on their way to fixing the problems between them.

"I'm sure they'll turn up soon," Cash said, catching Jen's frown. "Come on, let's have something to eat."

They spent the next twenty minutes chatting with Jane while they scarfed down some food. People drifted over to say hello, including Dylan and Jackson.

"So you're the Texan," Jen said, giving Jackson a thorough once-over.

Cash knew she liked what she saw. Women went wild for the smooth-talking Texan, with his wavy brown hair and tall muscular frame. The guy lived in faded blue jeans, plaid shirts and combat boots, which made him appear laidback but at the same time tough.

Jackson winked. "And you're even more beautiful than everyone described, sugar."

"What the hell, Texas?" Jane grumbled. "Why don't you ever call *me* sugar?"

"Why don't I call you sugar?" Jackson hooked a thumb behind her. "*That's* why."

Next thing Cash knew, Becker was barreling toward them with a surprising spring to his step. "There's my little angel," he said happily, in no way resembling the man who'd picked them up at the police station the other night. This Becker was relaxed and overjoyed, smiling broadly as he greeted his kid.

Sadie wiggled in her mother's arms and stuck out her chubby fists in Becker's direction. "Gah!" she cried.

Becker gave everyone a brisk nod. "That means *dad*." He promptly scooped Sadie out of Jane's arms and tucked her against his chest.

"It means everything," Jane muttered under her breath. "It's the only word she says."

"Thanks for coming," Becker told the guys. He glanced at Jen. "You too, Jen. I'm sorry to hear about the troubles you've been having with your ex-boyfriend."

She shrugged. "Thanks, but I think the trouble's come to an end."

Cash casually squeezed her arm before she could say more. He didn't want her bringing up the bar fight and reigniting Becker's anger.

"So the little princess is growing up," Cash said, reaching out to touch one of Sadie's tiny hands.

She immediately curled her whole fist around his index finger and squeezed. Man, the kid was strong. Then again, she was the offspring of Thomas Becker, so no surprise there.

"She sure is." Becker planted an indulgent kiss on the tuft of red hair atop Sadie's head. "And she's smart as a whip. She—" He halted, his eyes narrowing as he gazed at something behind Cash. Then he made an annoyed sound and turned to glare at his wife. "Why the fu-*fudge* did you invite Steven?"

Jane was clearly braver than Cash and the others, because she didn't cower under Becker's hard stare. "It was the polite thing to do."

"Polite? That lunatic nearly killed our child."

Cash and Jen exchanged WTF looks.

"It was harmless fun!" Jane shot back.

"Who's Steven?" Jen asked tentatively.

Becker jammed a finger across the backyard. Everyone followed his gaze, but the only person in their line of sight was a chubby woman with a cherub-cheeked infant in her arms.

"Wait—Steven's the baby?" Dylan said, looking confused.

"Spawn of Satan," Becker corrected.

Jane sighed. "Beck tags along for my Mommy and Me program." Which she sounded incredibly *un*thrilled about. "Last time we were there, Steven crawled over to Sadie and knocked her over. It was nothing. They both got giggly about it and wiggled around on the floor afterwards."

Becker looked livid. "That baby had malevolence in his eyes, Jane. He knew exactly what he was doing when—"

"Who wants to help me refill the beer cooler?" Jane interrupted, turning away from her husband.

Cash spoke first. "I'll do it."

He resisted doing a victory dance as Dylan, Jackson, and Jen all scowled at him in betrayal. Whatever. He didn't feel the slightest bit of remorse over saddling them with Becker. Babies with malevolence in their eyes? Fatherhood had clearly turned the commander into a crazy person.

Besides, Cash had been hoping to get Jane alone today. Now that the opportunity had presented itself, he pounced on it, trailing after the redhead as she headed for the house.

"We stored all the alcohol in the fridge in the basement." Jane opened a door in the hallway, pulled a metal string, and light illuminated a narrow staircase.

"I'm glad we have a moment alone," Cash said as they trudged down to the basement. "There was something I wanted to talk to you about."

She looked intrigued. "Okay."

The Beckers' basement was unfinished, a large dusty room cluttered with boxes. Jane walked over to a large freezer against the far wall and leaned in to grab a case of beer, which Cash promptly took from her hands and set on the floor. "Let me do it. How many cases do you want to bring out?"

"Two or three should be fine."

As he grabbed two more and added them to the pile, Jane leaned against the wall. "So what did you want to talk about?"

He hesitated before reaching into his back pocket for the flash drive he'd shoved there. Guilt pricked his gut. He hated going behind Jen's back, but he knew that if left to her own devices, she would keep stalling, the way she had for the past five days.

Despite her insistence that she was ready to seriously pursue photography, she'd already started second-guessing herself again, this time with the photos she wanted to include in her portfolio. Since no papers or magazines in the area had any open full-time positions, her best bet was to submit work to a bunch of places in hopes of landing a freelance gig, but the way she was agonizing over this portfolio, it would take years before she sent any submissions out.

That's why he'd wanted to talk to Jane. Before marrying Becker, she'd worked for a big-time magazine in L.A., and Cash was hoping she could put feelers out with her former editor. But he knew they'd need to see Jen's work, and he also knew Jen wouldn't dream of sending stuff to such a prestigious publication.

Cash shifted his feet. "You still keep in contact with your editor at *Today's World*, right?"

"Yeah, why?"

He rolled the flash drive between his fingers, battling another pang of guilt as he remembered how he'd snuck onto

Jen's laptop when she was in the shower earlier and copied her entire picture folder onto this drive.

"Jen's a photographer," he started. "And she's damn good."

"Really? I had no idea."

"She doesn't advertise it. And I don't think she realizes how talented she actually is, but trust me, she's the real deal. The thing is, she's too scared to show her work to anyone. She just started researching where she can submit to, but I remembered that you worked at *Today's World* and I figured it wouldn't hurt to ask you to take a look at this." He held out the USB stick. "All her stuff is on this."

Jane tucked it in her front pocket. "Sure, I'd be happy to take a look. And if her photographs are as good as you say, I'm happy to forward them to the photo editor at *TW*. He's always on the lookout for talented freelancers."

"Wow, that would be amazing. Thanks, Jane."

She tilted her head pensively. "Why didn't Jen just ask me herself?"

"Um...well, she doesn't exactly know I'm talking to you. Actually, if you don't mind, I'd like it if we kept this between us."

Her bewilderment grew. "Why?"

"I don't want her to think I'm overstepping my bounds and messing around with her career. She's got this blog where she posts her pictures. I can send you the link, and if your editor likes her work and wants to meet with her, maybe he can pretend he came across her blog." Cash offered a sheepish shrug. "That way Jen will feel like she did it on her own, you know?"

Jane stared at him, slack-jawed.

"What?" he mumbled.

"You're sleeping with her," she accused.

"No," he said in a half-ass denial. "We're friends, that's all."

"Bullshit." Jane grinned. "You're sleeping together. And not only that, but you care about her, don't you?"

Continuing to deny it was fruitless. Jane would see right through it.

"Yeah, I care about her."

"A lot."

"A lot," he conceded.

"Oh, Hot Stuff, you've really gone and done it now."

Cash arched a brow. Hot Stuff?

As if reading his mind, she waved a hand. "Yeah, that's what all the wives and girlfriends call you. Deal with it. Anyway, you know Carson will kick your ass, right?"

"I know." He let out a breath. "I tried to keep my hands off her, but she was determined to seduce me."

Jane laughed. "How long did you manage to hold out for?"

"Two days."

"That's actually pretty impressive, considering that...well, that you're a *man*." She paused. "What about Jen? Does she feel the same way?"

Discomfort rippled through him. "She insists we're only having a fling."

"Becker insisted the same thing when we first got together. Don't worry, they always come to their senses eventually."

He had to smile. "That's reassuring."

"She'd be crazy not to want something more. You're a great guy, Hot Stuff. A real catch. She'll figure it out sooner or later."

"I hope so."

Jane stood on her tiptoes and kissed his cheek. "She will. Now, will you be a doll and carry these cases upstairs for me?"

"Sure thing."

Her sandals clicked on the wooden steps as she hurried up

them. Cash bent and picked up the cases, easily carting all three up the stairs. He was two feet from the kitchen when a familiar voice caught his attention.

"Can we please just talk about this?"

Carson.

He followed the voice to a closed door off to the left. The hall bathroom, he guessed, and when a female voice joined Carson's, Cash realized the lieutenant wasn't alone.

"For God's sake, we're at Sadie's birthday party. We can talk about this later."

Holly.

Cash breathed a sigh of relief. Okay, well, at least Carson was in there with his wife, and not some member of the catering staff.

He felt guilty for even considering the latter as a legit possibility, but the memory of Carson with another woman hadn't left Cash's head. Unfortunately, the identity of the woman remained a mystery since Carson was once again avoiding Jen's phone calls.

"You can't tell me seeing Penny and Sadie and Lucas doesn't make you want the same thing for us."

"What I want is to fix this rift between us. A baby isn't the solution, Carson."

"It'll bring us closer together, you know it will. And I'm ready for this." He sounded desperate. "Besides, it'll be nice for our kid to be around other kids his age. He'll have an instant playmate in Penny and—"

Holly cut in angrily. "You want to knock me up so that Garrett and Shelby's daughter has someone to *play* with?"

Cash stifled a sigh. Carson was really digging himself into a hole.

"That's not the only reason. I'm getting older, babe. I just turned thirty-four. I don't want to be an old dad."

"Then you shouldn't have married a woman who's five years younger than you! You should've married one whose biological clock lines up with yours!"

Edging away from the doorway, Cash readjusted his grip on the beer cases. He felt like a shit for eavesdropping, especially now that the argument had treaded into TMI territory.

But he didn't escape fast enough—the bathroom door suddenly swung open and Holly flew into the hall.

She froze when she spotted him, instantly reaching up to wipe the tears welling up in her eyes. Her mouth opened as if she wanted to say something, but then a little sob escaped and she hurried past him. She rushed out the front door, which slammed with gusto.

A second later, Carson burst out of the bathroom, frustration clearly etched into his features.

When he saw Cash, some of the craziness left his eyes. "You heard all that?" he said in a weary voice.

Cash nodded.

"Fuck. *Fuck*. I don't know what to do anymore, man. I can't fucking stand having her mad at me all the time." Carson raked both hands through his blond hair, then took a determined step. "I have to go after her."

Cash hastily moved into the other man's path. "I think you should probably give her some space."

"Space," Carson echoed, his tone wary.

"Hold up, let me put these away." Without waiting for an answer, he quickly ducked into the kitchen and dropped the beer cases on the counter.

When he returned to the hall, he studied Carson's ravaged face and softened his tone. "Let her be for a while. Maybe Jen should go and talk to her. They're close, right?"

"My sister's the one who got my wife riled up in the first place," Carson snapped. "She filled her head with all these ideas about how we're not communicating. Like Jenny's one to dish out relationship advice, for fuck's sake. Any advice, for that matter. Her taste in men sucks, she can't hold a damn job, she's the biggest underachiever I've ever known, she—"

"Enough," Cash growled.

Carson blinked in shock. "What the fuck, McCoy?"

"Don't talk about Jen like that," he snapped, trying to control his anger. "I get that she's your little sister, but she's not a child, Carson. She's a grown woman, and it's pretty fucking sad that you don't know a thing about her. She's intelligent and kind and talented and she deserves a helluva lot more respect than what you give her."

Deafening silence followed.

Cash caught his breath, instantly regretting the outburst, but the damage had already been done.

Understanding dawned on Carson's face, along with the hard glint of accusation. "You're sleeping with her."

Cash held the eye contact. "Yes."

"You're *sleeping* with my *sister*. Jesus Christ, McCoy. I told you I didn't want you messing around with Jenny."

"Jen," Cash corrected. "And yes, I didn't listen to you, okay? But I don't regret getting involved with her. I care about her. She's amazing, and it's a damn shame you can't see that."

Carson clearly heard the possessive note in Cash's voice, because his eyes blazed again. "You care about her? You expect me to buy that?"

"It's the truth."

Carson swore savagely. "This ends now. I don't want you playing games with Jenny."

"I'm not playing games," he said evenly, crossing his arms. "And I'm not ending it. I told you, I care about—"

For the second time that week, a fist came flying at Cash's face.

And yet again, the knuckles caught him in the side of the mouth, ripping open the cut that had just began to heal. Blood spurted and dripped down his chin, but this time Cash didn't fight back.

He just stood there and eyed Carson. "You done?"

The other man was breathing heavily, his fists clenched as he glared at Cash like he wanted to kill him. "Yeah, I'm done," Carson spat out. "And so is your involvement with my sister."

"What the *hell* is going on?"

Both men spun to see Jen standing at the end of the hall. Shock and horror contorted her features. When she caught sight of Cash's face, she raced over and damned if she didn't blot the blood on his lip with the sleeve of her thin blue cardigan.

Keeping her sleeve there to staunch the blood flow, she turned to glower at her brother. "What the hell is the matter with you?"

"Me?" Carson said bitterly. "What's the matter with you? You're the one sleeping with McCoy."

Jen remained completely unfazed. "So what if I am? Who I sleep with is none of your business."

"It is when it's my teammate you're fucking."

She flinched, but recovered quickly. "So what?" she said again. "You just said it—Cash is your *teammate*. He's your *friend*. I don't see how you can be so opposed to this."

"I'm opposed because I know the way he operates," Carson retorted, speaking as if Cash wasn't standing right there. "He doesn't do relationships. One-night stands and casual flings, that's all he's interested in, isn't that right, McCoy?"

Cash decided now wasn't the time to admit he wanted more with Jen, so he wisely kept his mouth shut.

"You deserve better than that," Carson told his sister. "You deserve someone who'll love you and honor you and—"

"Are you kidding me?" she interrupted.

She dropped her sleeve from Cash's mouth and got right in her brother's face—well, more like his chest, seeing as Carson was a foot taller than her. But Jen didn't back down, and her petite frame vibrated with anger.

"You're such a hypocrite, Carson! Love and honor? Isn't that what you promised your wife when you recited those wedding vows?"

Carson jerked as if he'd been shot. "What the fuck does Holly have to do with this?"

"You tell me," Jen snapped. "Were you loving and honoring her when you were sneaking around meeting your little *angel*?"

Her brother's face paled.

"Jen," Cash said cautiously. "Maybe now is not the time to—"

"Now is definitely the time, Cash! He's standing here passing judgment on us when we both know what he's been up to." She glared at her brother. "Who was that redhead you met at Starbucks?"

Carson's ashen face took on a hint of defeat, and his broad shoulders sagged beneath his white button-down.

For a moment, Cash felt a pang of sympathy for the guy, which intensified when he remembered the heart-wrenching argument Carson and Holly had been having only minutes ago. He suspected there was more to the story than he and Jen would ever know, but rather than clarify or explain, Carson simply released a ragged breath.

"I'm not talking about this with you," he mumbled, edging away.

Jen gaped at him. "That's it? You're just going to avoid the subject? Cash and I saw you. And I heard you on the phone with another woman. Not even an explanation?"

"I don't owe you any explanations."

"Well, then apparently I don't owe you one either." She looked at Cash. "We should go."

He touched his swollen lip and his hand came back stained red. "You're probably right."

"Why don't you clean up your face and wait for me here?" she said tersely. "I'll tell Jane and everyone you said goodbye. That way you won't have to go out there and scare the kids with all that blood."

Without sparing a glance at her brother, Jen marched away.

The two men remained, eyeing each other. Cash cleared his throat, knowing he ought to say something, anything, but he couldn't bring himself to apologize. Not about his feelings for Jen, anyway.

Unfortunately, Carson didn't give him a chance to speak. With one final scowl, the man stalked off and then the front door slammed again.

Shit. This was one headache he definitely didn't need.

Cash ducked into the bathroom and studied his face in the mirror. He was no longer bleeding, but his mouth and jaw were bathed in blood, making him look like an extra in a horror movie. Sighing, he turned the faucet and bent to wash the blood off. He dried his face using toilet paper, not wanting to use Jane and Becker's white hand towels in case the cut reopened.

When he stepped back in the hall, Jen was waiting, her mouth set in an angry line. "I can't believe him," she muttered. "I know my brother can be an asshole, but this was something else."

"Don't be too hard on him. I think he was angrier with himself than with me. I kind of showed up at the tail end of his argument with Holly."

"They were fighting?"

"Yeah, and Carson took out his frustration on me. I'm sure he'll come crawling back with an apology once he cools down."

At least he hoped so. Because no matter what Carson thought—or wanted—Cash had no intention of walking away from Jen.

CHAPTER NINETEEN

Two days passed and Jen still hadn't heard from her brother. He was going out of his way to avoid her, which she found not only infuriating, but juvenile as hell. She'd left him several messages, ranging from pissed off to apologetic, but truth was, she didn't feel like apologizing to him. She couldn't believe he'd hit Cash, his own teammate. And then lecturing her about who she got involved with? Seeing as how he'd screwed up his own marriage, he had no right to pass judgment on her relationship with Cash.

Relationship?

Jen's hand froze over the handle of the pot. She'd just filled it with water, but now she set it down, troubled by where her thoughts had gone.

"Fling," she mumbled to herself.

Right, she and Cash weren't in a relationship. They were having a fling. A fling that would be over in less than a week.

So why did the thought of ending it with Cash bring an ache to her heart?

Her ringing phone provided a much-needed distraction. She grabbed it from the counter and looked at the screen, wrinkling her forehead as she studied the unfamiliar number. She didn't think it was Brendan, since it was a Los Angeles area code, but who would be calling her from L.A.?

She answered with a wary, "Hello?"

A male voice met her ears. "May I speak to Jennifer Scott?"

"Speaking."

"Jennifer, hello. This is Rick Martin. I'm the photo editor at *Today's World.*"

Surprise flitted through her. "Oh...hi."

"Jane Becker gave me your number—I hope that's okay. She said you wouldn't mind if I called you directly."

"Ah, no, it's not a problem. What's this about, Mr. Martin?"

"Please, call me Rick." He sounded really pleasant, his voice a deep baritone. "I was hoping you would come in for a meeting to discuss a freelance position with the magazine."

She dropped the phone.

As it clattered to the tiled floor, Jen scrambled to her knees, cursing up a blue streak as she fumbled to retrieve it. When she lifted it back to her ear, she heard chuckling on the other end.

"Sorry about that," she said hastily. "I dropped the phone."

"I gathered."

"I'm a little confused," she confessed. "How did you...I never submitted anything..."

"I came across your blog the other day, and I have to say, I was impressed by what I saw. Your bio mentioned you come from a military family, and the last name sounded familiar, so I called Jane. Turns out I met your brother Carson at Jane's wedding. Her husband and your brother serve on the same unit. Small world, huh?"

"Yeah, small world," she echoed numbly. She was still shocked—the photo editor of one of the most renowned magazines in the country had seen her blog? And it had *impressed* him?

"Anyway, Jane said you'd be open to the opportunity, though she did confess she had no idea you were such a talented photographer."

Jen felt herself blushing.

"Would you be able to come to L.A. this week? I'd love to discuss this further."

"Me too," she said, probably a tad too eagerly. "When would you like me to come?"

"How about Friday?"

Friday? That only gave her three days to put together a portfolio. "Friday's great," she blurted out.

Jen was in a total daze as they went over the details. She scribbled the address and Rick's number on a Post-it note, then thanked him and hung up, staring into nothingness for several long seconds as she tried to wrap her head around what just happened.

When it finally sank in, she let out a shriek of delight.

A second later, a naked, dripping-wet Cash burst into the living room.

"What's wrong?" he demanded.

She gaped at him. "You heard me all the way in the shower? Wow, you've got phenomenal hearing."

He strode toward her. Droplets slid down his bare chest and clung to his eyelashes. His annoyance was written all over his chiseled face. "You screamed. What happened?"

"I shrieked," she corrected.

"Why?"

"Because I just got the best news ever."

She quickly told him about the phone call with Rick Martin, and the next thing she knew, she was in Cash's arms. The front of her tank top promptly got drenched, and drops of water from his nose fell onto her forehead, reminding her of the fact that he was buck naked and soaking wet.

"I'm so proud of you," he said gruffly, then lowered his head to kiss her, and for a second she forgot what they were celebrating. Cash's drugging, toe-curling kisses always had that effect on her.

She sank into his strong embrace, still overwhelmed. Someone had seen her pictures—and liked them. Liked them enough to discuss the possibility of giving her a job.

"I can't believe this," she said, shaking her head. "It's so surreal."

Cash smiled. "We have to celebrate."

She felt a flicker of embarrassment. "It's just a meeting. There's no guarantee I'll even get the job."

Confidence lined his tone. "You'll get it. And we're celebrating." He took a backward step, completely unfazed by his nudity. "Put something nice on," he ordered. "I'm taking you out for dinner."

"But I was about to make macaroni and cheese."

"We can't celebrate over mac and cheese, sweetheart. We're not heathens." He turned on his heel, providing her with a candid view of his taut ass. Man, she could bounce quarters off that thing. "Wear something fancy," he said over his shoulder.

Unable to stop smiling, she hurried into Cash's bedroom and darted toward her suitcases, which sat on the floor. As she rummaged around, she realized with dismay that she hadn't packed anything nicer than a casual sundress.

So she poked her head in the bathroom and said, "I'm going up to Annabelle's. Fashion emergency."

AN HOUR AND A HALF LATER, JEN FINALLY STRODE BACK into the apartment. She knew Cash was probably annoyed that she'd made him wait so long, but when she'd gone upstairs to borrow a dress, Annabelle insisted on helping her get ready. Dress, shoes, hair, makeup—Annabelle had put her through the wringer.

But when Jen walked into the living room and saw Cash's expression, she decided all the effort had definitely been worth it.

"Jesus. You look...incredible."

He couldn't take his eyes off her, and pleasure tickled her skin. Annabelle had loaned her a red dress with a deep vee neckline and a filmy skirt that swirled around her knees. She'd paired it with three-inch black stilettos that added some height to her petite frame and made her legs look long and sleek. Annabelle had curled her hair so that it fell down her back in tousled ringlets, and they'd opted for minimal makeup, save for red lipstick that made her feel bold and wanton.

Under Cash's appreciative gaze, her cheeks warmed, then scorched when she registered *his* appearance.

Oh, sweet mother of God. The man filled out a suit like nobody's business. The black jacket hugged his broad shoulders, and the top two buttons of his white dress shirt were undone, revealing his strong, corded throat. He looked sexy as hell, and he smelled like heaven when he leaned in to kiss her. The scent of his aftershave gave her a head rush; his firm lips as they gently brushed over hers made her even dizzier.

"Are you sure we're not jinxing it?" she asked when they broke apart. "We're kind of putting the cart before the horse by celebrating what might not end in a job offer."

He took her hand and led her to the door. "It's not the job offer that matters. It's that someone recognized your talent. A job would just be the icing on the cake. If you don't get it, then you can apply somewhere else, knowing that you *are* good enough."

His thoughtful words made her heart soar. For a man who

claimed not to know what to say to women, he seemed to be doing a damn good job.

Cash held her hand the entire way down to the parking lot, letting go only to open the car door for her. His long fingers stroked her palm as he drove away from the building.

Ten minutes later, when he pulled up in front of Primrose, Jen looked over in surprise. "How'd you swing a reservation?"

"I know the chef," Cash answered with a grin. He paused. "I know this place probably reminds you of Carson, but everywhere else I called didn't have a table."

She squeezed his hand. "It's all right. But let's promise not to talk about my idiot brother tonight."

"Done."

She felt a bit like Cinderella as she followed him into the restaurant. The place was filled to capacity, but Holly must have pulled some serious strings, because the hostess led them to one of the more secluded tables in the main room. The pristine white tablecloth and glowing candles made Jen smile. Cash pulled out a chair for her, giving her an even bigger princess complex.

"I could get used to all this gallantry," she teased.

His eyes softened. "I could get used to being gallant."

They settled in their chairs and reached for the menus. Jen tried not to raise her eyebrows when she glimpsed the price list. But based on previous visits, she couldn't deny that the food here was to die for, which was probably why it was so damn expensive.

Cash ordered a bottle of red wine and they toasted to her interview. For the next hour, they chatted easily, swiping food off each other's plates and sharing a decadent piece of chocolate cake. At some point, it occurred to her that this was their first real date, a realization that both pleased and troubled her. She decided not to dwell on the latter, choosing to focus on her good news, the great food, and the even greater company. Being with Cash was so...effortless.

By the time they got back to the apartment, Jen had never felt happier or more relaxed.

"Thanks for dinner," she murmured, kissing Cash's clean-shaven cheek. "I had a really nice time, cowboy."

"The night's not over yet," he said, reaching for her hand.

He led her to the bedroom, where Jen gasped. Candles had been arranged all over the room. The yellow glow and the shadows dancing on the walls created a romantic ambience that made her heart do a little flip. The bed was perfectly made with a new bedcover and fresh pillowcases.

When had he done all this?

Probably when she'd been up at Annabelle's, she supposed.

"Did you leave the candles burning the entire time we were out? Because that is such a fire hazard!"

He grinned. "No, I texted Annabelle when we pulled into the lot and told her to light them." He came up behind her and brushed his lips over the nape of her neck. "Sit down."

Jen practically floated to the bed, her pulse speeding up when Cash sank to his knees in front of her. He slid her stilettos off one by one, then moved his fingers beneath the hem of her dress and rolled the fabric up her legs. When her thigh-high stockings were revealed, he groaned.

"Oh, I like these," he rasped, trailing his fingers over the sheer stockings.

Anticipation built inside her as Cash slowly unrolled each stocking, his fingers leaving a trail of heat along her skin. He ran his hands over her bare legs, then bunched the hem of her dress with his fists and slid the fabric up and over her head.

Left in a black strapless bra and skimpy panties, she met his eyes. The longing and appreciation on his face made her palms go damp and her heart beat faster.

"Have I told you how beautiful you are?"

"Only about, oh, a hundred times already."

"Let's make it a hundred and one then. You're beautiful, Jen."

He looked beautiful himself, his eyes shining in the candlelight, his gorgeous face softer than she'd ever seen it.

Her throat clogged with emotion. Her heart squeezed. Her hands trembled. God, something was happening. The way he was looking at her, the tenderness with which he touched her... She sensed something changing between them, but she was too scared to label it, too scared to let it fully sink in.

"Lie back," he said.

Swallowing, she lay back, watching as he stood up and began removing his clothes. He tossed his jacket aside, unbuttoned his shirt, and peeled it off his broad shoulders, leaving him gloriously bare-chested. His trousers and boxers hit the floor. His impressive arousal jutted proudly, making her mouth water.

When he climbed on the bed and stretched out beside her, she tried to reach for him, but he gently moved her hand away. "Not yet. This is about you."

And boy, was it ever.

Cash spent the next hour so focused on her body, on her pleasure, that Jen nearly went out of her mind. His soft lips trailed kisses over every inch of her skin, exploring, teasing, bringing her to the brink only to retreat before she toppled over it. He made love to her with his mouth, his tongue, his hands, and he did it in a slow, thorough pace that threatened her sanity. He didn't leave an inch of flesh unexplored, and each brush of his hungry lips and flick of his hot tongue made her shiver. She was overcome with sensation, gasping for air and mumbling gibberish by the time he gave her what she needed.

He brought her to climax with his tongue, feasting on her until she writhed on the mattress and begged for mercy. Her body hummed, her heart pounded, and she was so sated she could barely move.

"Come up here," she whispered, reaching for him.

He slid up her body and cradled her cheeks with his hands. His eyes glimmered with need, his erection heavy against her stomach. Without a word, he kissed her so deeply and methodically that her brain turned to mush. Despite the fact that she'd just climaxed, tension built in her core again, a dull ache that only Cash could ease.

His powerful chest heaved as he sucked in a breath. "I need you, Jen."

He donned a condom, parted her legs, and slid inside.

The orgasm caught her by complete surprise. She wrapped her arms around him and held on tight while a flood of pleasure swept her away to a plane where only bliss and Cash McCoy existed.

When she opened her eyes, she found Cash watching her with an indefinable expression. "I love watching you come apart like that," he said roughly.

He rolled his hips, hitting a delicious spot inside her, then increased his tempo, but not by much. She was in awe of his control, the restraint he used as he slowly moved inside her. His features were so taut, the tendons in his neck strained, as if he was dying to let go but wanted to make it last. The only sounds in the room were their ragged breathing, the soft squeak of the bedsprings, and the wet suction of his shaft sliding in and out of her.

Jen's heartbeat vibrated against her breasts. "You're not talking," she realized.

He stilled. "What?"

"No dirty talk," she clarified. "The room was so quiet, and I realized it's because you're not talking. You're not telling me all the dirty things you want to do to me or how much you love fucking me." She searched his face. "Why?"

His Adam's apple bobbed as he swallowed. "Maybe because...because this doesn't feel like fucking."

Before she could even attempt to make sense of that, he took possession of her mouth and kissed her, driving his cock into her again and reigniting her passion.

They moved in perfect unison. Mouths locked together, bodies joined, chests colliding. She didn't come again, but when Cash did, groaning out her name as he lost control, the joy that skyrocketed through her and filled her heart rivaled any orgasm.

Cash made a sound of pure contentment as he gently withdrew and rolled them over, tucking her back into his damp chest.

"That was nice," he said hoarsely.

"Yeah," she whispered, unable to fight the unsettling feeling in her gut.

They lay there spooning, and long after Cash had fallen asleep, Jen remained awake, staring at the wall. He was right. This hadn't felt like fucking, and it definitely didn't feel like a fling anymore.

She stirred restlessly, knowing there was really only one question she ought to be asking herself: What on earth was she supposed to do now?

CHAPTER **TWENTY**

Twenty-four hours later, Jen was still riddled with confusion. She'd hoped that girls' night would stop her from overanalyzing what had happened with Cash last night, but the loud chatter of the women around her wasn't providing the distraction she'd needed.

She kept wondering if she'd misinterpreted the look she'd seen in his eyes. The emotions flickering across his face. But why even bother putting a label on it? She didn't need to hear the L-word to know that his feelings for her had evolved.

So had hers. Somehow in the last couple of weeks, she'd stopped thinking about Cash in terms of how many orgasms he could give her or all the naughty things they could do together. Now she associated him not just with sex, but with laughter, support, joy...

He was so right for her in so many ways, except for the grim fact that if she got seriously involved with him, he'd be gone half the time. Or worse, he'd die while serving and shatter her in the process.

God, how did military wives do it?

All the women sitting in Savannah Harte's living room at the moment were in love with navy men. Shelby had lucked out—her husband was now employed by a security firm in San Diego, which meant that Garrett worked nine-to-five and came home to his wife and daughter every evening. *That* was the boat Jen wanted to be in.

"Enough with the long faces, you two," Savannah announced, flipping her long golden hair over her shoulder.

Jen snapped out of her thoughts, realizing she was one of the "two" Savannah had targeted.

"Well, I guess I can let *you* off the hook, since you have a stalker," Savannah amended, grinning at Jen. "But what's your excuse, Hol?"

Shifting her gaze, Jen saw Holly's equally glum look. Her sister-in-law had barely said a word since she'd arrived at Savannah's loft, which was located above Harte to Harte, the flower shop Savannah owned and ran. The change of scenery was nice after being cooped up in Cash's apartment for so long.

"Actually, I don't have a stalker anymore," Jen spoke up, earning a relieved look from Holly, who clearly hadn't wanted to explain the reason for her unhappy mood.

Annabelle frowned. "Just because Cash and Seth beat him up doesn't mean he won't keep causing trouble. Stalkers don't scare off easily."

"But he left town," Jen answered. "My dad was keeping tabs on Brendan ever since he showed up at my parents' place, and this morning Dad found out Brendan's work transfer happened earlier than scheduled. He was on a flight to Oakland last night. I'm hoping that means it's the end of Psycho McGee."

"Fingers crossed." Annabelle held out her shot glass so Savannah could pour another round of tequila into it.

From her spot on the carpet, Jane released a happy sigh. "It's so nice to be out of the house for a while. Sadie was being super cranky today."

"Like father, like daughter," Savannah remarked dryly. "Seriously, though, Becker seems a tad possessive of that cute little baby of yours."

"A tad? Understatement of the year. Sadie is the apple of her daddy's eye. God help that sweet girl when she gets old enough to date."

"John bought a shotgun the day after Penny was born," Shelby confessed. "He's ready to shoot the balls off any guy who looks at her."

Jen laughed. She wondered how Cash would react if he had a daughter—would he be as protective as Becker and Garrett, or more laidback? She held back a snort. Right, like it was even a question. Navy SEAL and protective instincts went together like PB and J.

"What about you and Carson?" Shelby glanced at Holly. "John said you two are talking about having kids."

Holly stiffly rose from the overstuffed couch. "I need to use the bathroom."

She hurried off, leaving everyone but Jen staring after her in shock.

"Shit," Shelby murmured. "What'd I say?"

Jen cleared her throat. "Babies are a touchy subject for her right now."

The other women wore matching frowns. Even the perpetually laidback Savannah looked upset.

"What do you mean?" Annabelle demanded.

Jen hated herself for breaking the confidence, but she didn't know what else to do anymore. Holly was staying with her sister again, and Carson had been ignoring Jen's calls for days. Maybe recruiting some backup would help her stubborn brother and sister-in-law mend this rift between them.

With a heavy breath, she told them everything she knew,

except for the part about seeing Carson with another woman. Everyone in the room was scowling when Jen finished.

"Men," Savannah huffed.

"Like a baby will fix *anything*," Annabelle said with an amazed shake of her head.

"A kid will only bring a whole new pile of problems to the table," Jane grumbled.

"They need to fix their relationship before bringing a child into it," Shelby agreed.

"Ahem."

Five heads swiveled to find Holly standing three feet away. She looked both annoyed and amused at having caught them talking about her.

"We're not gossiping," Savannah said instantly, patting the sofa cushion in a gesture for Holly to sit down again.

"We're venting on your behalf," Annabelle piped up.

Holly sat, her green eyes glittering with fortitude as she picked up the tequila shot she'd yet to take. "So we're all in agreement that Carson is acting like an ass?"

Savannah lifted her own glass. "Hell yeah."

The six of them clinked glasses and threw their heads back as they swallowed the alcohol. Jen felt the burn right down to her belly, and when Savannah tried to refill her shot glass, she shook her head.

"No more for me. My stomach can't handle more than a couple of shots."

"Fill it up anyway," Holly said. "I'll take Jen's shot."

Uh-oh. Jen didn't voice her worry, but the steel in Holly's eyes said she was feeling self-destructive tonight.

For the next hour, they discussed what an idiot Carson was, while Holly continued to slug down tequila. Eventually Savannah had to cut her off, and the conversation somehow turned to sex.

Jen stayed quiet, but Jane sucked her right into the discussion by turning to her and saying, "So how's Hot Stuff in bed?"

"Hot Stuff?"

"Cash," the redhead clarified. With a grin, she turned to the others. "Jen is totally doing the wild thing with Hot Stuff."

That earned her some hoots and catcalls.

Annabelle beamed. "I already knew," she said smugly. "Cash called me yesterday to light candles."

Savannah wrinkled her forehead. "Huh?"

"He took her out for a fancy dinner," Annabelle explained. "And he put candles all over the bedroom and called me to light them before they got back. It was so fucking romantic." She grinned at Jen. "Oh, and Cash made me promise not to tell Ryan what I was doing down there, so I stole a carton of eggs from your fridge to give me an excuse for going downstairs."

Jen rolled her eyes. "So that's where the eggs went."

"Why the fancy dinner?" Savannah asked curiously. "What were you celebrating?"

This time Jane answered. "Our little Jenny has an interview with my old magazine. Am I the only one who didn't know Jen is a kickass photographer?"

"I had no idea," Annabelle said, looking insulted. "You holding out on us?"

She blushed. "I always figured it was just a hobby." She glanced at Jane. "I can't believe your editor stumbled on my blog like that."

Jane got a funny look on her face. "Yeah, that's a stroke of luck, huh?"

The flippant response raised a red flag. Jen studied the other woman with suspicion. "What aren't you telling me?"

Jane's expression epitomized innocence. "I don't know what you mean."

A frown puckered her brows. "Rick found my work on the blog, right?"

"Of course."

"Jane."

The woman released a heavy breath. "Fine. No."

"No what?"

"Rick didn't discover your work on the blog, hon. Your work found him."

"What are you talking about?"

"I'm the one who gave Rick your photographs."

Surprise jolted through her. "What? How's that possible? How did you even get—" Her breath hitched. "Cash."

Jane scrupulously studied the label of the tequila bottle.

"Cash gave you my photographs, didn't he?" Jen demanded.

The other woman lifted her head and offered a sheepish shrug. "He brought over a memory stick with your stuff on it the day of Sadie's party."

"He did?" She had no idea whether to be angry at Cash for invading her privacy or thrilled that he had.

"Don't be mad at him," Jane said quickly. "He had good intentions. He said you weren't planning on submitting work to any of the bigger magazines, but he thought you were too talented not to. He made me promise not to tell you."

"Why?"

"He didn't want you to think he was interfering in your career. And if *TW* was interested, he wanted you to think you'd done it on your own. But I think trying to keep it a secret was silly," Jane said with a shrug. "He went to great lengths to make this opportunity happen for you, and I think you deserve to know that."

Jen's heart constricted. As annoying as it was that Cash had copied her pictures without her consent, his intentions had been anything but malicious. Hell, he clearly knew her better than she'd thought. She'd been second-guessing herself with that portfolio for days—obviously he'd decided to speed up the process.

And now, thanks to him, she might land a job with a magazine she'd never have dreamed of showing her work to out of fear she'd be laughed out of the fancy building.

But Cash had believed she could do it. He'd believed in her from day one.

Savannah grinned. "I might be in the minority here, but I'm pretty sure Hot Stuff is in love with you."

Everyone else nodded.

"Oh yeah," Annabelle agreed. "A man doesn't take on the task of personally getting a girl her dream job if he doesn't love her."

Jen felt like someone had knocked the wind out of her. She wasn't surprised to hear their assessment of Cash's feelings—she already suspected how he felt. But what startled her was the multitude of emotions swirling in her chest. She'd been trying so hard to keep an emotional distance, but who was she kidding? Her emotions had entered the picture a long time ago.

She was in love with Cash.

Her heart felt both lighter and heavier as she absorbed the truth. She loved Cash. She loved his gruff voice and toe-curling kisses and rough hands. She loved his strength and unceasing support and the way he laughed. She loved that he didn't mind the way she stuck Post-its all over his apartment, how he grumbled every time she forgot to hang up her towel in the bathroom, his willingness to cook every time she burned something in the kitchen.

From the moment they'd met, Cash had accepted her for who she was. Supported her. Encouraged her. Introduced her to passion she'd never known and brought all her fantasies to life.

And she knew now, without a shred of doubt, that even one

day with Cash McCoy would be worth however many months without him.

"Holy shit," she mumbled.

From her cross-legged perch on the floor, Annabelle snickered. "You're in love too."

Jen shook her head to clear the fog from it. "Yeah, I think I am. How did that happen?"

"Love has a way of sneaking up on you." Savannah swiped a tortilla chip from the bowl on the coffee table and popped it in her mouth. "Same thing happened to me with Matt."

"I wanted a casual fling. I never expected... I didn't want to fall in love with him," Jen said softly.

Annabelle frowned. "Why not? Cash is a great guy."

"I know, but..." She hesitated, not wanting to talk about her military issues with a roomful of military wives and girlfriends. "I'm just blindsided, I guess. I don't know what this means for us. I went in looking for a fling, and now..."

"I tried to have a fling once," Holly spoke up. "When Carson and I met, all I wanted was to have some fun, but your stubborn brother, Jen, well, he convinced me to give a relationship a shot. And now it's five years later, and look at us."

She swallowed. "Hol—"

"Sometimes I wonder if I should have dug my heels in and left it as a fling. But, fuck, I know that if I could do it again, I'd make the same damn decision." Holly wiped her eyes. "Because no matter how infuriating he can be, I know he's the love of my life."

"ALL RIGHT. THE KIDS ARE ASLEEP AND I'M READY TO ROB you losers of all your money," John Garrett announced, striding into the spacious den with a baby monitor in his hand.

The den was packed with SEALs, beers, and open wallets. Poker night was a monthly tradition, hosted at a different house each time. Cash looked forward to these gatherings. His teammates were damn good men. Good company too, and he felt honored to be included in what had been a tradition long before he'd come on board. Aidan Rhodes was also a recent addition to poker night, but he'd already been close to most of the guys thanks to his tight-knit friendship with O'Connor.

Sitting down, Garrett tossed the baby monitor to Becker, who placed it on the green felt poker table. "The girls went down okay?" the lieutenant commander asked.

Garrett nodded. "Fell asleep holding hands. It was pretty fucking adorable."

On the other side of the table, Seth snorted. "You know, just 'cause you put the word *fucking* in front of it doesn't make you less of a pansy for saying the word *adorable*."

Garrett rolled his eyes. "A man thinking his kid is adorable doesn't make him a pansy, Masterson. You'll find that out one of these days."

"Never," Seth vowed. "No kids for me, thank you very much. I'm getting my tubes tied."

Everyone laughed. Seth's pessimistic position about children was nothing new; the guy was adamant about never siring a child. Which was probably a good thing because the thought of a little mini-Seth with big-Seth's smart mouth was kinda terrifying.

"Where the fuck is Carson?" Garrett suddenly asked. "He's late."

Cash averted his eyes, but nobody glanced his way, which told him that Carson hadn't blabbed about what went down in Becker's hallway over the weekend. Thank God, because the last thing he felt like doing was justifying his feelings for Jen to anyone else.

"Well, we're not waiting for him anymore," Ryan announced, reaching for the deck of cards. "I, for one, am ready to milk Texas for all he's worth."

"Why do you assholes always target me?" Jackson demanded.

"Because your poker face sucks," Matt drawled as he took a sip of beer. "So does McCoy's. You two are easy money."

The banter continued as Ryan dealt the first hand. Jackson, of course, tried bluffing his way into the pot, only to lose five bucks when Ryan and Aidan suckered him into going all in. Laughter ensued, followed by Jackson's grumbling that his poker face had failed him again.

As money changed hands and chips clinked in the center of the table, Cash sipped his beer, his thoughts drifting to Jen. As much as he liked hanging out with the boys, he kinda wished she were here too. He'd grown accustomed to her company over the past few weeks. Not just having sex with her, but simply having her around. Watching TV while she messed around with her camera, cooking dinner while she worked on her laptop. He liked how they could be in the same room and not have to be wrapped all over each other.

Other girls he'd dated expected him to sit there holding their hands and constantly make conversation, but Jen was perfectly content doing her own thing while he did his. She didn't push for them to be joined at the hip or make demands of him. She was happy no matter what they were doing. He appreciated that.

"I swear, if Shelby comes home as drunk as she did last time, I'm divorcing her," Garrett was saying. "I'm beginning to dread the words *girls' night*."

Cash lifted his head. "They don't get that drunk, do they?" he said with a frown.

Groaning, Ryan joined the conversation. "Last time, I spent

the entire night holding Annabelle's hair while she puked out ten gallons of tequila."

"Hey, I love girls' night," Matt argued. "Savannah did the dirtiest striptease for me last time, but then again, my girl's better at handling her liquor than your lightweight ladies."

Becker growled, jabbing a finger at O'Connor. "Don't get me started on Savannah. She and Jane went shopping last week and I got a credit card bill for six hundred dollars. Six hundred dollars' worth of lingerie, for chrissake."

"Oh come on. Like you didn't benefit from that shopping trip."

"I certainly did not," Becker said stiffly.

"I call bullshit. After Savannah modeled what she bought, I didn't let her leave the bed for a week. And she told me she and Jane made identical purchases." Matt cocked a brow. "Did Jane get that lacy black mesh thing with the garter belt?"

"No," Becker muttered.

"No?"

The lieutenant commander sighed. "She got it in red."

As everyone laughed, Cash experienced the most bizarre pang of envy. He found himself wishing that he could contribute to the conversation. Not that he wanted to talk about what kind of lingerie Jen wore, but the idea of calling her his "girl" and sharing stories appealed to him.

Man, he really had it bad.

"All right, enough with the chick talk," Seth announced. "I feel like I'm at a teenage girl's slumber party."

Ryan shuffled the deck, but before he could deal a fresh hand, they were interrupted by the arrival of Carson.

The room fell silent.

"Wow," Dylan remarked. "You look like shit, LT."

Cash wholly concurred. He'd never seen Carson look so... wrecked. Clad in faded jeans and a T-shirt boasting several holes, jaw covered in stubble, blond hair tousled as if he'd repeatedly run his fingers through it. And his expression reflected nothing but sheer misery.

"Sit down," Garrett said quietly. "I'll grab you a beer."

"In a minute," Carson said in a tired voice. His gaze shifted to Cash. "McCoy, a word?"

With a nod, Cash stood up, ignoring the bewildered looks he received from the others. He followed Carson to the kitchen, where Carson made a beeline for the sliding door leading to the backyard. The night air was balmy when they stepped outside.

Carson dropped into a wicker chair and pointed to the chair across from him. "Sit."

Cash sat.

After several long moments, Carson cleared his throat. "How's the lip?"

"It's fine."

A pained look flashed across the other man's face. "I shouldn't have slugged you."

Cash sighed. "Honestly, I'm surprised you didn't do worse."

Carson rubbed his chin in a gesture of pure frustration. "Holly's staying with her sister again."

"Aw, fuck. I'm sorry, man."

"Look, about that woman you and Jenny saw me with," Carson started.

"You don't have to explain. It's none of our business."

"Her name's Angel Whittaker. She's...ah, the therapist I've been seeing."

"Seriously?"

"Yeah, I started seeing her a month or two before we got deployed." Carson hung his head. "Holly and I were having problems then too. And once we got back, things just got worse, so I called Angel. She was on vacation, but I convinced her to meet me for coffee so we could talk about...you know, about everything. Usually I see her at her office."

"Is she helping?"

"Not really, but I've realized that's because I was talking to the wrong person. I *should* have been talking to my wife instead of babbling on to some stranger about how much things suck. Angel told me I wouldn't fix anything unless I start openly communicating with Holly. Jenny said the same thing, but idiot that I am, I'm going around thinking everything will fix itself, or that having a baby might make things better. I'm an asshole, huh?"

"You're not an asshole. Well, not all of the time."

Carson flashed a dry grin. "Thanks."

"So what now?" Cash asked.

"Now I try to convince my wife how much I fucking love her. I know it's tough for her, with me gone for long periods of time, but it's tough for me too. I love that woman to death and I don't care if we have ten kids or no kids. I just want Holly."

"You should be saying this to her, not me," Cash pointed out.

"Trust me, I'll tell her." Carson got that look in his eyes, the determined one he wore during particularly hazardous missions. "I'll keep telling her until she gets sick of hearing it."

"Sounds like a good plan."

"And listen, about you and my sister..."

He winced. "I'm sorry about that, LT. It was a total violation of guy code, I know that, but it just happened. I didn't plan on getting involved with her, and if you want to punch me in the face a few more times, I promise I won't even put up a fight. But..." A heavy breath slipped out. "But if you ask me to end it, I'll respectfully refuse."

Carson tipped his head to the side. "You really do care about her, don't you?"

He nodded. Then he shook his head. "No. I more than care about her. I'm in love with her."

Carson's eyebrows shot up. "For real?"

"Yes."

To his surprise, Carson didn't seem angry. Just oddly sad. "Shit, I'm not just an asshole husband. I suck in the brother department too, apparently. I really do treat her like a child, don't I?"

"Yup."

"It's because I'm used to thinking of her as the baby of the family, you know? And fine, maybe I still see her as a bit of a screw-up. She's smart as hell, but she didn't make any effort in school. She could've gotten As in every fucking class, gone to some Ivy League college and become a big-shot career woman, but she was always more concerned with taking pictures."

"It's what she loves to do. And she's good at it." He told Carson about Jen's job interview in L.A. next week, which brought a crease of shame to the guy's forehead.

"She didn't even call to tell me about it."

"Well, she's not very happy with you at the moment."

"What about you?" A serious note entered Carson's voice. "Is she happy with you?"

"Yeah."

"I'm glad then."

"You are?"

"Don't get me wrong—I'm still annoyed as fuck that you put the moves on my sister after I told you not to, but in all honesty? If there's anyone I could tolerate my little sister with, it's you, McCoy."

Cash swallowed a lump of pain. "As much as I appreciate your blessing, I'm not sure it matters. Jen's not interested in anything long-term. She doesn't want everything that comes along with dating a military guy, and I don't know how to change her mind."

"Does she know how you feel about her?"

He slowly shook his head.

"Then tell her. Trust me, I'm learning that communication is a big fucking deal. Maybe if she knows how you feel, she'll change her mind about her military rule."

"Maybe." He suddenly remembered something. "Hey, by the way, Brendan left town."

"Yeah, I know. The admiral told me."

"Jen's going to stay at my place for a few more days, but then she's moving back to her apartment."

Carson got to his feet. "You're a good man, McCoy. You know that, right?"

"Thanks, LT."

"And if you do end up with my sister, I won't have any complaints." Carson began to laugh. "It's funny, I was so worried about you taking advantage of her, but now I'm starting to think you might be the best thing that's ever happened to her."

CHAPTER
TWENTY-ONE

It was ten thirty when Jen stepped onto the sidewalk in front of Savannah's flower shop. She froze when she spotted the vehicle parked on the curb—not Cash's Escape, but her brother's Range Rover.

The sight of Carson through the windshield had her back stiffening. Why was he here? Holly had left with Shelby ten minutes ago, so he couldn't be here to pick up his wife.

Squaring her jaw, Jen strode over to the car and rapped on the passenger window. When it rolled down, she poked her head in. "Holly went home with Shelby."

Her tone was slightly cool, but it was the most cordial she could muster. She hadn't spoken to Carson since their heated argument on Sunday, and she had no desire to argue with him again.

But his unkempt appearance and the ravaged look on his face told her he wasn't looking for a fight, either. "I'm here for you," her brother answered.

"Why? Where's Cash?"

"He's still at Garrett's. I skipped out early, though. Cash

said he was supposed to pick you up, so I offered to do it." He leaned over and pulled on the passenger door handle.

Jen stared at the open door, debating whether to haughtily announce she'd take a cab, or suck it up and get in the car. After a beat, she slid into the passenger seat and buckled up. Might as well get this over with.

"Should I be worried about the condition Cash will be in when he gets home?" she inquired sweetly.

Carson had the decency to look ashamed. "I deserve that." He moved the gearshift and drove away from the curb. "Look, I already apologized to McCoy. I know I was out of line on Sunday."

"Damn right you were."

"I'm sorry, Jenny. I've been acting like a total asshole the past few weeks."

"No kidding."

"The only excuse I can give you is that I've been upset about Holly."

He sounded so incredibly sad that some of Jen's anger thawed, replaced by a twinge of sympathy. "She's not doing too well herself."

The devastation on Carson's face nearly tore her to pieces. "Did she say anything tonight? About, uh, me?"

"A bit, but I won't break her confidence." Jen paused. "Holly said she's been staying at her sister's for the past couple of days. Have you two even spoken?"

"A couple of times over the phone. I've begged her to come home, but she says she needs time to think. Jesus, Jenny, it scares the hell outta me that my wife has to think about whether or not to come home." His voice cracked. "What if she doesn't?"

"Does she have a reason not to?"

"What the hell does that mean?"

"It means you still haven't explained why you were holding

hands with another woman." Her gaze bore into him. "Straight up, Carson—are you having an affair?"

His jaw dropped. "Are you kidding me? I'm not having a fucking affair. Like I told Cash earlier tonight, I'm seeing a fucking therapist."

"What? Are you serious?"

"Yes, I'm serious." When they neared a red light, Carson hit the brakes and turned to scowl at her. "That woman you saw me with was my therapist. And I wasn't calling her angel on the phone, her *name* is Angel."

Guilt and relief slammed into Jen's chest. "Shit. I'm sorry I thought the worst of you, but you've got to know that sneaking around is never a good idea. Why didn't you just tell me the truth when I brought it up?"

"Because I was embarrassed," her brother muttered. He stepped on the gas and steered through the intersection. "Because I didn't want you to know how bad things with Holly and me had gotten."

Her heart clenched. "She'll come home, Carson. She's just feeling overwhelmed right now and I'm not sure I blame her. You can't come back after six months and start making demands on her. You need to take time and try to reconnect with your wife."

"I know that. Now, anyway," he amended. "Before, I...well, I guess I thought that Hol and me were so rock solid that we didn't need to work on our relationship. I figured everything would fix itself."

"Kind of hard to fix anything when you don't bother listening to what your wife is trying to tell you," she pointed out.

"Yeah, I figured that out too." Smiling, he tilted his head. "When did you get so wise about love and relationships?"

"It just comes naturally, I guess. And you know what? I'm

going to do more than dispense wisdom. I'm going to help you get your wife back."

"And how will you do that? I've been trying for months. Holly doesn't believe me when I tell her how much I love her."

"That's your problem, you're telling, not *showing*." Jen rolled her eyes. "Don't worry, big brother, I know exactly what to do. First thing, you need to—"

"I've been a really crappy brother, haven't I?"

She blinked. "Where did that come from?"

"It's true, isn't it?"

"Not entirely true. You have your asshole moments, but you've always been my biggest protector."

"Yes, but I also don't take you seriously." Shamefaced, he shifted his gaze to her before moving it back to the road. "You're my little sister, and when I look at you, I see the pesky brat who used to eavesdrop on my phone calls and hide under my bed when I had girls over."

"That was a long time ago," she said with a laugh.

"Exactly. But I didn't get the memo. You grew up and became a strong, intelligent woman capable of making her own decisions, but I haven't even noticed because I'm too busy viewing you as a kid. And now you're sitting here and giving me advice after I interfered in your life and annoyed the shit outta you for the last month. You're too damn nice, you know that?"

She sighed. "Yeah, I know."

They neared Cash's building, and Carson turned into the small parking lot. "So...uh...about Cash."

Annoyance rippled through her. "You're not going to lecture me for getting involved with him, are you? Because we just established that I'm a strong, intelligent woman capable of making my own decisions."

"No lecture. And like I said, Cash and I straightened it out.

What I wanted to ask was...uh...okay, fuck, I'm just gonna come out with it—are you planning on dumping him?"

Jen's mouth fell open. "Why would you think that?"

"Because of the whole military thing." Carson absently ran his hands over the steering wheel, his expression growing soft. "I think you were about twelve the first time you told me you hated Dad."

"I never hated Dad," she protested. "You know I wasn't serious."

"No, but you were serious when you said he felt like a stranger to you." He shrugged. "No judgment. The admiral felt like a stranger to me too when I was growing up. Anyway, that time when you were twelve, I came home from college for the holidays, and Dad had shipped out that year, remember?"

"I remember," she said flatly.

"Mom was depressed. I remember she spent Christmas Eve crying in her bedroom. And you and me were downstairs, pigging out on those cookies Grandma brought over, and you turned to me and said that you never, ever wanted to have the kind of marriage Mom and Dad had. I'm pretty sure you gave an hour-long speech about how *your* husband would be home every day, and *especially* on Christmas Eve."

"I hated seeing Mom so sad," she confessed.

"Me too, but I think it affected you more than it did me, huh?" He reached across the seat and ruffled her hair. "I get why you don't want the military life. It's tough, really fucking tough—I mean, look at me and Holly and the rough patch we're going through." He hesitated. "Cash loves you, you know."

Her throat tightened.

"And I think he's good for you," Carson went on. "I was too caught up in big-brother mode to see it—mainly because the thought of any dude touching you makes me furious. But now that I've calmed down, I can see how well you and McCoy fit. He's intense, you're, uh, kind of flighty and weird—"

"Gee, thanks."

"He's not big on talking, you're a blabbermouth. You suit each other." Carson's voice softened. "I think you should give him a chance. Keep an open mind to the whole military thing, because you know what? You've found a man who loves you, a man who'll face his superior officer's wrath to be with you, and you're honestly going to throw that away?"

A ring of pleasure circled her heart. Her brother was right. Cash really had gone above and beyond in proving that he'd be there for her, and although he hadn't said those three little words out loud, Jen knew he cared about her. She knew he wanted more than a fling.

"Don't worry, I'm not throwing anything away."

"Good," he said as he clicked a button to unlock the doors. "Come on, I'll walk you up."

"You don't have to do that."

Carson flung open his door. "Jen, haven't you learned by now that you can't argue with me when I'm in my brotherly protective mode?"

Her jaw dropped. "Did you just call me Jen?"

"That's your name, isn't it?"

A smile tugged at her lips. "Yes. Yes, it is."

Jen was lying on the couch when Cash strode into the apartment. Instantly, his spirits soared, and his heart beat a little faster when she greeted him with a big, beautiful smile.

Shit, he was a total goner for this woman.

"So what can I expect?" he asked as he kicked off his boots. "A striptease, or holding your hair while you barf?"

"Huh?"

Chuckling, he sat at the other end of the couch and lifted her socked feet into his lap. "According to the grapevine, those are the two outcomes of girls' night. You ladies either get drunk enough to strip or puke."

"Sorry to disappoint, but you're getting neither. I only had one drink."

Jen slid closer and leaned her head on his shoulder. Smiling, he slung an arm around her and nuzzled her neck. It felt so natural that his chest grew hot and tight.

"By the way, I'm sorry for springing Carson on you like that," he told her. "He insisted on picking you up and ordered me not to call you and warn you."

"Don't worry, it's fine."

"Did you two talk?"

She nodded. "We worked everything out. And he told me about the woman we saw him with, the therapist."

Cash shot her a smug smile. "Told you there was an explanation."

"Fine. You were right. Is that what you wanted to hear?"

"Yup."

"Well, I'm glad you were right." She exhaled softly. "I just want Carson and Holly to be happy."

"Me too. And I also want..." He trailed off, his confidence wavering.

Just do it already. Tell her you love her.

"Cash? You okay?"

Her worried expression made him smile. "I'm fine," he said gruffly. "There's something I wanted to talk to you about."

"Cash—"

"No, just listen for a minute." He shifted so they were facing each other. "I know we agreed that the fling would have an end date, but...I don't want it to end."

Surprise washed over her face. Surprise, not horror or regret, which was always a good sign. The receptive look in her eyes spurred him to go on.

"I know how you feel about the military life, but I don't think you want this to end either." He reached for her hand, a little embarrassed to discover his fingers were trembling. "We're good together, and it's not just the sex. I've never been able to talk to a woman the way I can talk to you. I love talking to you, actually. I love your sense of humor, I love how big your heart is. I love everything about you." He let out a curse. "Ah, fuck, I'm just going to say it, okay? I love *you*."

She stared at him with wide eyes.

"I love you, Jen," he repeated. "This isn't a fling for me anymore. It's so much more."

As his speech came to a close, Cash studied her and waited for a response. A word. A smile. A squeeze of the hand. Anything would have sufficed, but the longer her silence dragged on, the unhappier he grew.

He'd only ever said those three words to one other girl. Brooke Pollack, who he'd dated in high school. And unlike Jen, Brooke had actually returned the sentiment.

A knot of pain twisted his insides. Fuck, he was such an idiot. He'd really believed they could have more than a fling, but clearly he'd been wrong. Jen wasn't even looking at him, and she kept gnawing on her bottom lip the way she always did when she was upset.

"I get it," he muttered, dropping her hand. "That's not what you wanted to hear." He started to get up. "I'm sorry if—"

"I love you too."

His butt landed back on the couch cushions. "You do?"

Her blue eyes glimmered with certainty. "I love you, and I want to be with you too. I want to give this a shot. I don't care if it's full-time or part-time or even if I only see you one day every other month—I'll take you any way I can get you."

Cash gawked at her. He hadn't been entirely sure what to expect from this heart-to-heart. Rejection had topped the expectation list. Maybe some resistance.

But a straight-up *I love you too*? Nope, hadn't seen that coming.

Why the hell are you sitting here analyzing when you should be kissing the girl?

Good fucking point.

Snapping out of it, he thrust a hand in Jen's silky hair and yanked her mouth to his, swallowing her startled squeak with his kiss. Long, deep, and passionate.When their mouths broke free, the look of joy on Jen's face nearly had him doing a happy little fist pump.

But then her eyes narrowed. "I know what you did, by the way."

"What are you talking about?"

"Going behind my back and giving Jane my pictures?" she prompted.

Guilt slithered up his throat and formed a big lump. "Jane told you? She promised—"

"Don't be mad at her. It just sorta slipped out, and I'm actually really glad she said something." Jen smiled. "Don't worry, I'm not angry at you. I know you were only trying to help. And thanks to you, I have a shot at a freelance position with a great magazine." Her voice wobbled. "You believed in me, Cash. Nobody's ever believed in me before."

"You have a shot because of *you*. I might have given Jane the photos, but you were the one who took them. You deserve this." He had to laugh. "But please, can I be there when you tell your mom and the admiral that your waste-of-time hobby has officially become your career?"

"Wait, you're *volunteering* to be in the admiral's company again? Wow, you must really love me."

"I must really love you," he agreed, smiling. "I'd do anything for you. You know that, right?"

"I know." She swept her fingers over his jaw, her touch making him shiver. "And I'd do anything for you, cowboy, even throw my dating rulebook out the window to be with you."

He searched her face. "Are you sure about this? Can you really handle the whole military thing?"

For a second, uncertainty flickered in her eyes, but then it faded into a gleam of sincerity. "I have to believe we can do it. I know we'll have to work hard on this relationship, and I can't promise that I won't be a bundle of nerves every time you go away, but—"

His cell phone chimed.

"Perfect timing," he said wryly. He pulled his phone from his pocket and glanced at the screen. Son of a bitch.

Next to him, Jen stiffened. "You need to answer it?"

"Yeah," he said grimly.

Rising from the couch, he took the call and listened to Becker's brusque orders, while Jen stayed seated and watched him unhappily.

After he hung up, he couldn't control the frustrated breath that escaped his mouth. "I have to report to the base."

The corners of her mouth strained.

Cash waited for it. The big one-eighty. The moment when she said, *Fuck, I can't do this, after all. I can't wait around for you.*

But the rebuff didn't come. Instead, Jen staggered to her feet and approached him. "It's okay," she said, resting her cheek against his collarbone. "I can do this, Cash."

He cradled the back of her head and tipped it so he could study her expression. "Are you sure?"

"I'm sure. Now, go." She swallowed. "Call me if you can, and if you can't, that's okay. I'll be waiting right here when you come home."

Cash's chest clenched. "You promise?"

"I promise, cowboy."

CHAPTER
TWENTY-TWO

He'll be just fine.

Those four syllables had become Jen's personal catchphrase. Ever since Cash had left, she'd been twisted up in knots, worried out of her mind and constantly questioning her decision to make things permanent with him. How did other women do it, damn it? Cash had only been gone for three days, but it felt like an eternity, and she was going crazy not knowing if he was okay.

Ironically, the woman next to her was in the same boat, yet Annabelle seemed downright chipper as she sat behind the wheel of Cash's SUV and sang along to the White Stripes song blaring out of the speakers. Annabelle was playing chauffeur for the day because Jen was too much of a basket case to make the drive to Los Angeles alone. Her interview with *Today's World* was in an hour, and she desperately wished Cash were here so he could ease her nerves with his distracting kisses.

But at least Annabelle had agreed to accompany her. Well, not so much agreed as *ordered*. After two days of Annabelle popping in every other minute to "hang out," Jen had finally gotten her to confess that Cash and Carson had told her to stick to Jen like glue. Even with Brendan gone, the two overprotective men in her life still thought she needed a babysitter.

"Why are you so happy?" Jen demanded. "Aren't you worried about Ryan?"

Annabelle lowered the volume. "Nope."

"Really?"

"Worrying doesn't achieve a thing. Ryan can take care of himself, and I trust that he'll do everything in his power to come home to me."

She envied the woman's confidence. She might feel more confident herself if she knew where Cash was or what he was even doing, but SEAL operations were kept under wraps, and she knew nothing except that this was a "minor" op, low-threat, and not likely to be lengthy. Knowing that didn't make her feel the slightest bit better, but this was their first separation in what would most likely be many, and she was determined to pass this first test with flying colors.

"Cash will be fine," Annabelle said as they drove through West Hollywood. "He and the others are trained for this."

"I know, but I'm still worried."

"You should worry about impressing that photo editor instead."

"Trust me, I'm doing that too." She bit her lip. "What if he hates my portfolio?"

"He won't. He's already seen all the photographs in it, remember? This interview is just a formality, Jen. You've got the job in the bag."

"I hope so."

The *Today's World* building came into view, and Annabelle drove into the underground parking lot.

"How do I look?" Jen asked after Annabelle parked in a space near the elevators.

"Gorgeous, as usual."

She smoothed out the front of her pale-blue silk blouse, tucked neatly into her knee-length black pencil skirt. She'd swept her hair up in a neat bun and opted for minimal makeup. She had no clue whether this was a formal interview or a laid-back meeting. She just hoped she looked professional enough.

She took a breath and looked at Annabelle. "Are you going to wait here?"

Nodding, the brunette fished her phone from the cup holder. "Yeah, I have some emails to send." Annabelle's smile was full of encouragement. "Kick some ass in there, okay?"

"I'll try."

An hour later, Jen slid back into the car and tossed the leather portfolio in the backseat.

"How did it go?" Annabelle demanded when she didn't utter a word.

Letting out a shaky breath, she met Annabelle's impatient gaze. "I got the job."

"You did?"

"I did."

The next thing she knew, Annabelle lunged across the center console and nearly suffocated her in a tight hug. "I knew you would! Congratulations!"

"Thanks," she said weakly.

Annabelle released her and started the car, still grinning like crazy. "So what's your first assignment?"

"They're starting me off with puff pieces. The magazine's running an interview with Senator Markowski for the next issue and they want me to take his picture. He wants it done at his house in Lake Tahoe, so I'm flying out there next week."

As they emerged from the parking garage, sunlight assaulted

Jen's eyes. She rummaged in her purse for her sunglasses and slipped them on. A part of her was still feeling dumbfounded. She'd gotten a job. A *photography* job. So why didn't it feel real to her?

Heading for the interstate, Annabelle glanced over with a deep frown. "Why don't you look happy? You just got the job of your dreams."

"I know. I guess it hasn't sunk in yet." She chewed on the inside of her cheek. "After Rick hired me, my first instinct was to call Cash, and then I got all bummed out when I remembered I couldn't."

Annabelle looked sympathetic. "Look, I know it sucks. The first time Ryan was gone, I was a nervous wreck too. But it gets easier."

She pictured Carson and Holly, and thought, *No, it doesn't*. But she bit back the words. Besides, maybe every couple was unique. Savannah and Matt, for example—Savannah was so independent she almost seemed to enjoy the time off from her boyfriend.

Maybe she and Cash wouldn't drift apart during his absences. Maybe the time apart would bring them even closer.

Either way, Annabelle was right. Worrying about things beyond her control was counterproductive.

"Did you still want to stop by your apartment before we head home?" Annabelle exited the off-ramp and sped toward San Diego's city center.

"If you don't mind. I really need that spare power adapter." Her charger had died on her last night, but she hadn't felt like driving all the way to her place to pick up the extra one she kept there.

"When are you moving out of Cash's?"

Jen shrugged. "A couple of days, probably."

"Why bother? I'm sure Hot Stuff will love it if you moved in with him." There was a playful twinkle in Annabelle's eyes.

"Yeah, but I doubt Matt will. Besides, I don't think I'm ready for that. We've only been together a month."

"And living together," Annabelle pointed out.

"Yeah, but that was out of necessity." And now that her crazy ex was out of the picture, it was time to return to her own place. She loved Cash, but it was too early for them to officially live together, especially since she had a brand-new career to focus on.

Annabelle parked the car in front of Jen's building. "Want me to come up with you?"

"Nah, I'll only be a minute."

Grabbing her purse, she dashed into the building. Her kitten heels clicked on the lobby floor as she walked to the elevator. She rode it up to the fifth floor, fishing her keys from her purse as she strode down the frayed carpet in the hallway.

The moment she entered her apartment, she experienced a sense of disorientation. Everything looked exactly the same—tiny living room, blue carpeting, mismatched furniture, sticky notes all over the place—yet it felt like a lifetime since she'd been here rather than a mere three weeks.

She went to the bedroom and got the laptop charger from the bottom drawer of her desk. She coiled the cord and tucked the adapter into her purse, then strode back to the living room just as a knock sounded on the door.

She frowned for a moment, before realizing Annabelle had probably come up to use the bathroom or something.

"Sorry, I locked the door," she called as she unlocked the deadbolt. "It's become a habit ever since—" Her breath caught in a startled gasp when she laid eyes on her ex. "Brendan?"

CHAPTER TWENTY-THREE

After one long moment of motionless shock, Jen snapped into action. She didn't give Brendan a chance to say a word. With a jolt of panic and a burst of energy, she slammed the door, only for him to stick his foot out and wedge it in the doorframe.

"Let me in, Jen," he begged.

What the hell was he even *doing* here?

A pair of brown eyes pierced into her, glittering with a mixture of anger and desperation. Brendan's face was as handsome as ever, except his nose had clearly been broken during that fight with Cash—bruised, swollen and slightly off-center.

"Go away," she snapped. "You're violating the restraining order."

She kicked his foot, then rammed her shoulder into the door to try to slam it. But he got both palms on it and pushed hard, sending Jen careening backward. She stumbled and lost her balance, and as her butt collided with the carpet, fear pounded into her.

Looming over her, her ex extended his hand. "Come on, let me help you up."

Fuck. She should've known the restraining order wouldn't do shit.

Scrambling to her feet, Jen held up her palms in a don't-come-any-closer pose. "You can't be here, Brendan," she said quietly. "If you don't leave right now, I'm calling the police."

His eyes flashed. "Stop being so melodramatic. I only came to talk."

"You're supposed to be in Oakland."

"I was." Desperation flooded his face. "But I had to come back. I couldn't just move to another city without talking to you first. Without convincing you to come with me."

He took a step toward her.

She took a step back.

"I'm not moving to Oakland with you," she retorted. "I want you to leave. Now."

Her gaze darted to the floor, where she'd dropped her purse when she'd fallen. If she bent to pick it up, she'd have to take her eyes off her ex, who didn't look very calm at the moment. Indignation had darkened his expression, and he was shifting on his feet, his body language agitated.

Fuck. Talk about falling into a false state of security. She'd foolishly assumed Brendan would leave her alone once he left town, but clearly she'd underestimated his level of craziness. Why had she come up here alone? She should have continued to take precautions and brought Annabelle.

"I can't go," he said, sounding miserable. "I can't leave until we work this out."

"There's nothing to work out. It's over."

"It doesn't have to be! Come to Oakland with me. Please, you know we can be happy together."

She glanced at her purse again. She could try taking her phone out—maybe he'd be too caught off guard to stop her.

"Jen. Look at me!"

She reluctantly moved her gaze back to him. "I want you to leave."

"Shit! I just keep doing everything wrong," he burst out. "But it's all because I love you. I *know* we can be good together. We had something amazing, and it hurts that you were so quick to throw it away."

He came at her again, and this time Jen didn't back up. Fueled by a wave of frustration, she brought her knee up and struck him in the groin, eliciting an outraged cry from his mouth.

"Stop it!" he yelled. "I just want to be with you!"

Her elbow shot up at the same time Brendan's fist came at her face, bringing a sting of pain and a rush of moisture to her left eye.

Blinking through the pain, Jen drove the heel of her hand into his nose and heard the bone crunch.

"You *bitch*!"

Blood erupted from his nostrils. As he cursed in pain, Jen ducked out of his grip and raced toward the kitchen with her purse, trying to run and get her phone at the same time. But she wasn't fast enough.

She heard footsteps, felt Brendan's hot breath on the nape of her neck, and then he fisted the back of her shirt and yanked her backward.

Jen struggled, using the fingers of one hand to try and gouge at his eyes. "Get off me," she grunted.

He got an arm around her from behind and dug his elbow into her windpipe. "How long were you sleeping with that muscle head?" he demanded. "Were you cheating on me the entire time we were together?"

She flung out her arm in search of something to grab onto. As Brendan pushed her against the stove, cursing and spitting out angry accusations, Jen fought to escape his grasp. When her hand collided with the metal handle of the cast-iron pan on the counter, triumph and relief exploded like fireworks in her gut. She gripped the handle, then swung the pan at Brendan's head. It collided into his skull with a loud thud, stunning him enough that his grip slackened.

With Brendan momentarily disoriented, Jen raised the pan high in the air and sent it crashing into the back of his head.

A second later, his unconscious body crumpled to the linoleum floor.

Gasping for air, she staggered backward, still clutching the pan.

Jesus. Oh sweet Jesus.

Had she killed him?

No. No, she could see his chest rising and falling. He was breathing, then.

"Jen! What the hell is taking so—*oh my God*." Annabelle came to a dead stop in the doorway.

"So much for sticking to me like glue," Jen said in a wry voice.

Annabelle glanced from Jen's face to Brendan's body slumped on the floor, then spoke in a brisk tone. "Did you call the police?"

"Not yet. I was too busy fighting him off."

"Well, you did a good fucking job. Carson would be proud."

Jen felt shell-shocked as she watched Annabelle call 911. When the cops showed up fifteen minutes later, she relayed the events that had transpired with a measure of calm she certainly did not feel. Her heart continued to pound. Her hands shook. Lingering adrenaline coursed through her veins, making it impossible to focus on her surroundings or the people around her.

Brendan regained consciousness while one of the uniformed officers handcuffed him, but he remained oddly subdued as he was being carted away. He'd been arrested for assault and violating the restraining order, and Jen supposed she'd have to see him in court at some point, but she couldn't think that far ahead at the moment.

What if she hadn't grabbed that pan in time? What if Brendan...had done what? She had no clue what he'd planned on doing. All she knew was she could have been seriously hurt. Or worse.

"You okay?" Annabelle asked after the cops left.

Jen gave a tired nod. "I'm fine."

"We should put some ice on that eye."

Eye? Oh, right. It took a second to remember that Brendan had struck her, and once she did, she registered the pain throbbing in her left eye. She reached up to touch it, and discovered that it was nearly swollen shut. Probably explained why half her vision was blurry.

Jen sank onto the couch and took an unsteady breath. She needed to call Cash and tell him what happened. Over voicemail, of course, because she knew his phone wouldn't be on. But she longed to hear his voice. She desperately wished he were here right now, holding her in his arms.

But he wasn't here. He was...well, she didn't know where he was.

God, she wanted him to come home. She didn't want to be alone. Didn't want to think about what just happened with Brendan, or how differently the situation could've turned out if she hadn't gained the upper hand.

Damn it, Cash. Come home.

ALMOST HOME.

Those two words had been buzzing in Cash's head for the

past seven hours, and he was so anxious for the chopper to land that he couldn't stop tapping his foot relentlessly and drumming his fingers on his thighs. He'd seen Carson displaying the same jittery eagerness countless times before. Come to think of it, Becker, Ryan and Matt did the whole foot-tap/finger-drum thing too.

Was it a relationship thing? Because their single counterparts, Dylan, Seth and Jackson, looked perfectly at ease as they chatted over the din of the rotors. Cash hid a surprisingly smug smile at the realization that he was officially part of the no-longer-single camp.

Shit, he couldn't wait to see Jen. He'd missed her something fierce.

He gazed out the window, his pulse racing as the San Diego skyline came into view. The sun hovered over the horizon line, filling the sky with brilliant shades of pink and orange. Made for a damn pretty sight. He wondered if Jen had ever seen the sunset from a helo. If not, he'd have to take her up sometime. After all, he did have that pilot's license he hardly ever put to use.

"I'm serious, this girl is a royal pain in the ass," Dylan was saying. "I don't know what my brother sees in her."

Cash shifted his gaze to the seat across from him. Dylan had been griping about his older brother's new girlfriend for the past ten minutes, and Seth, who was sitting next to the guy, finally rolled his eyes and said, "We get it. She's a bitch. For the love of God, can we talk about something else?"

"Fine. Let's talk about the chick you had over last week," Dylan said. He shot the other men in the chopper a grave look. "I slept with the door locked and a knife under my pillow. No joke—I was seriously worried she might murder me in my sleep."

Seth grinned. "Don't be an ass. Lisa's a cool girl."

"She had a *face* tattoo, man. And out of curiosity, is there any part of her body that *isn't* pierced?"

"Nope."

Cash chuckled. Seth had the most eclectic tastes when it came to women. Sometimes he went for the shy, fragile ones, other times it was the hardcore goths, then he'd switch it up and date a supermodel, followed by a plain Jane. The guy had no problem sampling every dish on the menu.

As Seth and Dylan's banter continued, Cash glanced at Carson, who'd been quiet for the entire flight. A helo ride without Carson's sarcastic remarks was weird, but Cash understood the lieutenant's somber mood. As far as he knew, Holly still hadn't moved back home, and Carson being gone for the past three days probably hadn't helped the situation.

After the chopper touched down on the base, Cash said goodbye to the others and practically sprinted to the parking lot, with Ryan hot on his heels. Since he'd left his car with Jen, he had to rely on Ryan to drop him at their building. Luckily, Evans seemed as eager to get going as Cash did. They were on the road in five minutes flat. While Ryan drove, Cash grabbed his phone from the glove compartment and turned it on. Probably made him a total sap, but when he saw the missed call and message from Jen, his heart did a dumb little flip.

He punched in the pass code for his inbox, desperate to hear Jen's voice, even if it was via voicemail. Two minutes later, his desperation transformed into a burst of rage.

"Goddamn it." He slammed his hand on the dash so hard he was surprised the airbag didn't deploy in his face.

Ryan looked over sharply. "What's wrong?"

"Fucking Psycho McGee attacked Jen."

"What? I thought he left town."

"Apparently he came back. The asshole showed up at Jen's apartment, muscled his way inside, and fucking attacked her."

His hands curled into fists. Jen had assured him in the message that she was okay and that Brendan had been arrested, but that didn't stop Cash from wanting to murder the son of a bitch.

"Is she all right?" Ryan asked.

"She claims she's fine." He clenched his teeth. "But who the fuck knows."

Ryan sped up without needing to be asked. With the Jeep's top down, the wind hissed in the front seat and slapped Cash's face as the scenery whizzed past his peripheral vision. The closer they got to their building, the angrier Cash felt. At Brendan. At himself.

Before he could stop it, a rush of guilt flooded his body and tightened his throat. Fuck. He should've been here to protect her. Jen hadn't said much in the message, and she certainly hadn't sounded accusatory or upset with him, but Cash was upset with himself. What kind of man couldn't protect the woman he loved?

"Get out here," Ryan said as he slowed down in front of the building. "I'll park the car."

Cash was out of the Jeep before it came to a complete stop. He still wore his dirty fatigues, his boots were caked with dirt and sand from their three-day stint in the desert, but he didn't give a shit about his appearance. He sprinted up to the second floor, his pulse drumming in tune to his hurried footsteps.

Worry and anger mingled in his blood to form a cocktail of nerves. Jen had said she was okay, but if so much as a hair on her head had been harmed, Cash was going to rip Psycho McGee's throat out, even if he had to break into the bastard's jail cell to do it.

"Jen!" he called when he dove through the front door. "Baby, you here?"

No answer.

His heart jammed in his throat. Had she left? She'd said she and Annabelle were heading back here, but granted, the message had been left hours ago.

What if she was gone?

What if she'd changed her mind about being with him?

Cold reality splashed him in the face as he realized he wouldn't blame her at all for that. He hadn't been there for her when she'd needed him. And wasn't that the crux of her no-military thing? That she wanted a man who'd fucking be there?

When he entered the living room and found it empty, his heart sank to the pit of his stomach. A quick peek into his bedroom revealed another empty room.

So that was it. She wasn't here.

"Cash?"

He spun around to find Jen by the bathroom doorway.

For a moment, he was frozen in place. He focused on her swollen left eye, already a ghastly shade of purple. Her lush mouth, pursed in a worried frown. Her long hair falling over one shoulder.

"You're here," he breathed in relief.

She cast him a strange look. "Of course I am."

Cash yanked her into his arms and held her so tight he heard her gasp for air. But he couldn't help himself. She felt so small and fragile in his arms. He breathed in the sweet feminine scent that was uniquely Jen, and his heart lurched.

He pulled back and gently stroked her cheek, right beneath her swollen eye. "Fuck," he mumbled. "Oh, fuck, Jen. Are you okay?"

"I'm fine. It looks worse than it feels."

The sight of her black eye sent a bolt of anger up his spine. "I'm going to drown the bastard," he hissed.

A faint smile played over her lips. "First of all, drowning is Carson's thing. Second, Brendan was arrested, so I suggest we let the cops deal with him. And third—what are you doing home? I figured you'd be gone for longer."

"I told you it was a minor op," he reminded her. Self-recrimination poured into him, and he swallowed hard. "I'm sorry."

Surprise flickered in her eyes. "Why are you sorry?"

The lump in his throat was so massive he could barely get a word out. "I'm sorry I wasn't here," he croaked. "I should've been here, but I wasn't and look what happened—that son of a bitch hurt you."

"Cash—"

His entire body burned with shame. "Go ahead and do it."

"What are you talking about?"

"Break up with me. I wouldn't blame you if you changed your mind about being with me." Misery hung on his every word. "You were right—you need a full-time partner. A man who's going to be there for you and protect you and—"

"Are you fucking kidding me?"

JEN GAPED AT CASH, WONDERING IF HE'D HIT HIS HEAD during his mission. Because he was talking like a crazy person. Kind of looked like a crazy person too, with that wild look in his eyes and the dark scruff covering his face. She'd been so happy to see him when she'd walked out of the bathroom and spotted him in the hall, but the more he babbled on about breaking up, the unhappier she became.

"No, I'm not kidding," he mumbled. "I wasn't here for you, and isn't that what you were afraid of? That you'd be forced to handle everything alone? And you had to fucking handle being *assaulted*! Holy hell, I should have—"

"Jeez, cowboy, would you shut up already? Nobody's breaking up with anybody."

He faltered, a flicker of confusion replacing the feral look in his eyes. "No?"

"*No.*" She reached up to cup his chin, the stubble there abrading her palms. "It's not your fault that Brendan showed up. If anyone's to blame for this, it's me, for not being more cautious when I went back to my apartment."

Cash still looked dubious. "You're not angry that I wasn't there to protect you?"

"I protected myself just fine. And you know what? As messed up as this sounds, I'm happy Brendan showed up this morning. Now the cops are involved and they can deal with him. Besides, the whole encounter was proof that I *can* take care of myself. The self-defense training my family shoved down my throat paid off, and I got out of the situation with nothing but a black eye when it could've been a lot worse." She smiled. "So no, I'm not angry with you. And hell no, I'm not dumping you. I was strong enough to deal with my psycho ex, and I'm definitely strong enough to be in this relationship with you."

Before she could blink, Cash tugged her into his arms again and kissed her. His lips were firm, his tongue insistent, his beard growth prickly as it scraped her chin. The kiss robbed her of breath and made her heart pound, and when they broke apart, the relief in his eyes was unmistakable.

"You mean it, right? You're okay that I wasn't here when you needed me? Because it could happen again. The military is my life. I *will* be gone at times."

She traced his lips with her fingers. "I know. And I can handle that. We can make this work." She paused. "And anyway, you won't be the only traveling partner in this relationship."

He cocked a brow. "Oh really?"

"Uh-huh. In fact, I'm flying to Lake Tahoe Wednesday morning. It's just a day trip, but it still counts as travel, right?"

"Is this your way of telling me you got the job?" he teased.

"Yep."

She yelped when he lifted her off her feet and hugged her. His happiness was contagious, making her forget about this morning's terrifying showdown with Brendan and reminding her of all the incredible things she had going in her life.

"I knew you'd get it," he said.

Her heart constricted as he bent down to capture her lips in another deep kiss that left her tingling in all the right places.

"I'm so damn proud of you," he went on, sweeping his thumb over her lower lip. "I believed in you from the start, and I'm glad you're finally believing in yourself."

"I am," she agreed. Emotion clogged her throat. "And even more than that, I believe in you, Cash. I believe in us."

CHAPTER TWENTY-FOUR

Carson paced Jen's living room carpet, distress creasing his forehead. "What if she doesn't come?" he said for the tenth time in the last five minutes.

"She just texted saying she's on her way," Jen reminded him.

He kept pacing. "What if she sees my car and realizes it's an ambush?"

"You parked at the grocery store around the corner," Cash spoke up. "She won't see your car."

"But what if she stops to buy groceries?" He sounded anguished. "Fuck. She's not going to come."

With a sigh, Jen rose from the couch and marched over to her brother. Cash stayed seated, watching her with an amused expression on his gorgeous face. For a second, she was tempted to go right back to the couch and kiss that sexy mouth of his, but she reined in the impulse. She and Cash had done plenty of kissing over the past two days—surely they could afford to take a short break to help her brother.

Clapping both hands on Carson's shoulders, she fixed him with a stern look. "Chill the fuck out. Holly is on her way here. Any second now, she'll knock on the door and—"

The knock came as if on cue.

Jen gave his broad shoulders a reassuring squeeze. "See?"

His Adam's apple bobbed. "How do I look?"

She swept her gaze over his perfectly starched dress whites, the blond hair he'd slicked back with care, the clean-shaven jaw, and his familiar blue eyes, the same shade as her own.

"You look as handsome as ever," she said softly.

Saying a silent prayer that Holly wouldn't bolt the second she saw Carson, Jen walked to the front hall and opened the door. "Hey. Thanks for coming," she told her sister-in-law.

Holly's low ponytail fell over one shoulder as she followed Jen inside. "It's no problem. You sounded so upset over the phone. I still can't believe you broke up with Cash! I thought you said the two of you were—*Carson*?"

The brunette stopped in her tracks when she spotted her husband. She immediately turned to Jen with a wary look. "What's going on?" She noticed Cash sitting on the sofa, and the wariness deepened. "You two didn't break up, did you?"

Jen smiled sheepishly. "No."

Carson took a step toward his wife, his nervousness clearly etched into his face. "Hey, Hol."

Holly frowned. "Why are you in uniform?"

"I figured it was appropriate." He shot her a faint smile. "I was wearing this uniform the night of Garrett and Shelby's wedding, remember? When we ran into each other again after you abandoned me in a supply closet."

After a beat, Holly smiled back. "I never thought I'd see you again after the club." Her face glimmered with humor before going dull again. "But what does that night have to do with right now?"

As the pair eyed each other, Jen edged away, wanting to give them privacy. Cash did the same—he'd already risen from the sofa and was creeping toward the bedroom.

But her brother stopped them before they could make their escape. "Stay," he said hoarsely. "I might as well grovel in front of an audience."

"Grovel?" Holly let out a breath. "Carson, I don't want to talk about—"

"I don't want you to talk," he said quietly. "I just want you to listen, okay?"

Holly hesitated, then nodded. She slid the strap of her leather purse off her shoulder and set it on the couch, but she didn't make a move to sit.

Carson shifted his feet, looking more nervous than Jen had ever seen him. Finally, he cleared his throat. "I fucked up, Hol. I know I fucked up and I've been trying to find a way to fix this for months now. I was seeing a therapist—"

"You were?" Holly gaped.

He nodded. "I thought she'd help me figure out how to make things right between us, but arrogant ass that I am, I kept ignoring her advice. She went on and on about communication, and I was all, less talk more action. Like my whole let's-have-a-baby idea." He gave a self-deprecating smile. "Because having a kid is really the way to solve a problem, huh?"

Holly laughed.

"I know it's hard for you when I'm gone," Carson mumbled. "It's hard for me, too. More than you'll ever know."

Something warm touched Jen's arm. She startled, then relaxed when she realized Cash had come up beside her. Without a word, he took her hand, the warmth of his touch seeping into her skin.

Across the room, Holly's eyes shone with unshed tears. "But I *don't* know, Carson. You don't give me any indication that you even miss me when you're away. You just try to pick up where we left off. You act like my entire purpose in life is to sit at home and wait for you to get back." She blinked rapidly. "But I can't do that. I have a life too. My job at the restaurant, my work with Annabelle. I can't just drop everything when you come home and make you the center of my existence. Especially when I'm not the center of *your* existence."

"I know. And I'm a jerk for suggesting you quit your job. I don't want you to do that. The only thing I want is for you to be happy." His voice cracked. "And I do miss you when I'm away, Hol. You're all I fucking think about."

Holly's tears spilled over, and damned if Jen didn't feel all teary herself. As much as she hated intruding on this personal moment, she was so very touched seeing her brother lay himself bare like that.

Carson cupped his wife's cheeks. "I want to make things better, but I need to know that you want the same thing. That you haven't completely given up on me."

"Of course I haven't given up. I love you, you idiot."

All the tension left Carson's body. "I love you too."

When Holly stood on her tiptoes to kiss him, Jen felt like a total voyeur. She squeezed Cash's hand, signaling that it was time to sneak away, but Carson foiled their next attempt too.

"Jen, where'd you put that printout?"

"Shit. I left it in the printer tray in my room. I'll get it."

She dashed into the bedroom and grabbed the sheet of paper, which she handed to Carson in the living room.

"What's that?" Holly asked.

"Our hotel confirmation," Carson replied with a grin. "We're going to Catalina."

His wife looked startled. "What? When?"

"Now."

"But I have to—"

"Work?" he finished. When she nodded, he shot her a guilty look. "Okay, don't be mad, but I called your boss at the restaurant and convinced him to give you a few days off. And before you freak out, I didn't do it because I don't respect or value your work."

Holly looked dumbfounded.

"I wish we could go away for longer, but I only managed to swing three days of leave. Still, I figured a three-day honeymoon is better than nothing." He looked ashamed. "We didn't make it on our Fiji honeymoon because the team got called away the day before we were supposed to leave." He cursed under his breath. "I kept assuring you we'd reschedule, but it never happened, huh?"

Holly sighed. "No, it didn't."

"I know Catalina Island isn't Fiji, but it'll do for now, right?" His boyishly hopeful expression made Jen grin.

"Yeah, it'll do."

"One more thing," Carson added. "No sex."

Holly's brows soared. "Pardon me?"

"Baby, as much as I'd like to fu—" Carson glanced at Jen and backpedaled, "—to do a lot of things to you, the next three days will be about my new favorite word: communication. I'm gonna talk so fucking much you're gonna wish I was a mute by the time I'm done."

Holly laughed. "Can't wait."

Jen was overcome with emotion as she watched them. She had to admit—her brother had done good. The mini-honeymoon had been her idea, but the heartfelt speech and uniform was all Carson. Apparently he wasn't a total lost cause.

Carson marched over to Jen and enveloped her in a bear hug that almost knocked the wind out of her. "Thanks," he murmured. "I owe you one."

"You know it." She stepped forward to give Holly a quick hug, then smiled at her sister-in-law. "Have fun in Catalina. But don't forget to make him grovel some more, okay?"

"Oh, I intend to," Holly assured her.

Holding hands, the couple headed for the door. At the last second, Carson halted and turned to look at Cash. "Take care of my sister, McCoy." He arched a brow. "You know what'll happen if you don't."

"Yeah, yeah," Cash said with a sigh.

As Holly and Carson practically floated out the door, Jen glanced over at Cash. "I think that went well."

The smile he shot her melted her heart. He was so devastatingly handsome, so sexy, so amazing, and she couldn't believe she'd ever had reservations about being with him.

Yes, their relationship would be hard. Yes, she might find herself waiting and worrying, the way her mother had done with the admiral, the way Holly did with Carson. But Jen now saw with perfect clarity why her mom and Holly had stuck it out for so long, why they continued to stick it out. Because when you found someone you loved with your entire being, you would do anything for them, suffer through anything, sacrifice and compromise and do whatever possible to make it work.

"I love you," she blurted out.

Cash flashed her a devilish grin. "Of course you do. I'm awesome." Then he offered a mock frown. "And you thought I was only good for a fling. Jeez."

Smiling, she stood on her tiptoes and looped her arms around his neck. "You're good for a lot of things, cowboy."

He lowered his mouth to hers, but stopped right before their lips could meet. "Hey, since we're in a relationship, can I refer to you as 'the old ball and chain' from now on?"

She let out a heavy sigh.

"What?" he demanded.

"No woman wants to be called old, cowboy. *Jeez*," she mimicked. "Maybe you do need to practice talking to women."

"Good idea."

In the blink of an eye, he scooped her into his powerful arms.

"What are you doing?" Jen squeaked, clinging to his broad shoulders.

"Taking you to your bedroom." He slanted his head, those blue eyes glimmering with heat. "You know, so I can practice talking. Then again, once I get you near a bed, I might have other plans for my mouth."

Her laughter followed them all the way to the bedroom.

The End

Keep reading for a preview of *Trouble Maker*, the next book in the *Out of Uniform* series.

Now available!

SNEAK PEEK

Miranda's shoulders stiffened. She slapped the intrusive hand off her arm and turned to scowl at the guy from the bar. "I told you, I'm not interested."

"But I am," he protested, the glazed look in his eyes leaving nothing ambiguous about his level of sobriety.

His gaze rested on the cleavage spilling from her low-cut red tank, then traveled down the length of her legs, bare beneath her black miniskirt. The tank-skirt combo was her "uniform," and as the guy leered at her, she mentally composed a letter to the club's owner stating all the reasons why female employees should not be asked to dress like ho-bags.

"C'mon, just gimme your digits," he pleaded.

Jeez, again with the digits? This kid was relentless. Might be time to dust off the old Erin Brockovich speech.

"Look," she said through clenched teeth, "I'm not—"

A raspy male voice cut in. "Beat it, buddy."

One second the flirty kid was in front of her, the next he was gone, scurrying away like he was being chased by the cops.

Miranda didn't need to turn around to know who was

standing behind her. While other women might have been overflowing with gratitude, she was just mildly irritated.

"I'm not going to say thank you," she grumbled. "I already told you I can take care of myself."

Seth Masterson stepped into view, his metallic gray eyes filled with the mocking glint she'd come to expect. "I know you can."

She arched her brows. "Yeah? So then why'd you interfere?"

He shrugged. "My way got rid of that moron quicker."

Despite herself, Miranda found it hard not to laugh. Yep, Seth's "way" was extremely efficient. All he had to do was level some poor dude with that lethal stare of his, and—*poof*—the unwanted admirer disappeared. Seth had been pulling this same magician's act for more than three months now, scaring off any man who dared to flirt with her. What started out as a quick stop-by a couple times a week, just to "check how she was doing," had become almost a nightly routine.

Now when she worked a shift, she was surprised if Seth *didn't* show up.

Any other woman might have swooned from all the attention, but Miranda wasn't one of them. Having her own personal bouncer was more aggravating than comforting. Nope, Seth Masterson didn't provide her with even an ounce of *comfort*. If anything, he achieved the opposite effect, unsettling her with his commanding presence. He had *bad boy* radiating from every sexy, muscular inch of him, from the perpetual beard growth on his face, to his scruffy dark hair, to the piercing gray eyes that were forever undressing her.

"Like I said, I could've handled it. Now if you'll excuse me, it's time for my dinner break." She brushed past him and strode into the break room.

Seth, of course, followed her right in. One thing she'd discovered about him? He didn't play by any rules, a trait she found ironic considering he was in the military, where rules were a way of life.

Sighing, she walked over to the small fridge across the room. She grabbed a bottle of water, uncapped it, and chugged half as she headed for the ratty plaid couch that had seen better days.

Seth lingered near the door, watching her with disapproval. "Dinner is a bottle of water?"

"Dinner was fish sticks and French fries three hours ago. I won't be hungry for a couple more hours." She stretched out her legs and stared up at the cracked plaster ceiling, letting out an aggravated breath. "Why do you keep coming by, Seth? You don't need to check up on me every frickin' night."

"I'm not here to check up on you."

"Oh really? So Missy called off her guard dog?"

"Nope. Mom's still insisting I keep an eye on you."

She held back a groan. She loved her former boss to death, but Missy Masterson, God bless her soul, had no idea what she'd unleashed when she'd asked her son to keep tabs on Miranda.

At first, she'd appreciated the gesture—the move from Vegas to San Diego had been jarring, and it was always difficult to adapt to a new city, especially when you didn't know a single person there. But now that she was more settled, she no longer needed Seth Masterson to hold her hand.

In fact, that was the last thing she wanted. Because another discovery she'd made about the man? When he touched her, she turned into a pile of hot, gooey mush.

"Well, tell Missy that while I appreciate everything she's done, I'm doing just fine."

Miranda took another sip of water, then set the bottle on the table by the couch and bent down to unlace her black sneakers. The club's owner might demand the female staff display whatever T&A they could, but he didn't begrudge them comfortable footwear. Still, she'd only been tending bar for three hours and already her feet were killing her.

As she kicked off her shoes and began to massage her right foot, she saw Seth's eyes following the movements of her hands. His expression took on that smoldering gleam, and then he left his perch by the door and approached the couch. His strides were long, predatory.

"Not doing as fine as you claim, huh?" he taunted.

She rolled her eyes. "My feet hurt. My life, on the other hand, is *just fine*."

The couch cushions bounced as he flopped down beside her. Instantly, the familiar scent of him wafted in her direction. Aftershave, a hint of pine, and the faint traces of smoke. Of course he was a smoker. A bad boy had to have his vices, after all.

She dug her thumbs into the arch of her foot, knowing the ache in her feet didn't bode well for the rest of the night. She had four hours left in her shift. Four hours of running up and down that bar catering to the Friday-night crowds. And tomorrow she'd be in the dance studio from morning until late afternoon. Her poor feet were definitely going to revolt if she kept this up.

"What's wrong?"

Seth's voice interrupted her thoughts. She glanced over, frowning. "Nothing's wrong."

"You just groaned. A weary, life-sucks-ass type of groan."

She blinked. "I did?" When he nodded in confirmation, she let out a sigh. "I was just thinking how I have to be at the studio at ten in the morning tomorrow and how much my feet are going to hate me for it. Tending bar all night and then standing en pointe all day is no piece of cake."

"No, I imagine it isn't."

He sounded sincere, not a hint of condescension in his

voice, and Miranda's eyebrows rose. "Really? You're not going to roll your eyes and tell me I know nothing about real pain? You know, 'cause I'm not a badass SEAL like you?"

"Trust me, babe, I've got nothing but the utmost admiration for dancers. Once, when I was a kid, I sat there watching my mom soak her feet after three back-to-back performances." Seth blanched. "The way her feet looked is comparable to any battle wound I've come across."

Miranda burst out laughing. She didn't doubt it. People often had an idealistic view of dancers as beautiful, magical creatures, but one look at a dancer's feet and that bubble of perfection was liable to burst. Calluses, blisters, cracked toenails, red, flaking skin...frankly, it was just plain gross.

For a moment it surprised her that Seth knew what actually lay behind the curtain, until she remembered he'd pretty much grown up backstage at the iconic Paradise Theater on the Vegas Strip. His mother had been the star of the show for twenty years before retiring, and now worked as the head choreographer. Missy also happened to be Miranda's mentor and staunchest supporter.

For a girl who'd grown up without a mom, Miranda had been utterly grateful to have someone like Missy in her life. After Miranda's grandmother died and left her a small inheritance, Missy was the one who encouraged her to buy the dance school in San Diego, and it was the best decision she'd ever made.

"I should get back to work." She leaned forward to slip into her sneakers, only to jump when she felt Seth's hand on her arm.

Her breath caught. She found herself going still. It had been so very easy to shrug out of that young guy's grip in the hall, but here, with Seth, she couldn't bring herself to push him away.

"How long are you going to fight it, Miranda?" His voice

was rough, his expression darkening with what she could only describe as sinful challenge.

She gulped. Ignored the flashes of heat rippling over her flesh. "Fight what?" she asked, feigning ignorance.

He laughed, slow and deep. "You're really gonna pretend it's not there? The chemistry between us?"

"We don't have chemistry."

She was a filthy liar. She and Seth had so much chemistry they could open their own laboratory. Or teach a college science seminar. Or—

He cut into her thoughts once more. "I've been very patient up until now. Pretending not to notice the way your nipples get hard whenever I'm around. How your cheeks get all flushed. And don't get me started on the way you look at me." His voice grew even raspier. "Those big hazel eyes of yours eat me up like I'm a big, juicy steak, baby."

Nipples hardening? Check.

Cheeks scorching? Check.

Eating Seth Masterson up with her eyes? Well, she couldn't tear her gaze from the sensual curve of his mouth or the strong line of his jaw, so yeah, might as well check that off too.

Even though Seth must have noticed all three responses, Miranda decided to keep playing dumb. It was the only way to maintain some semblance of control over a conversation that had swiftly and unexpectedly gotten out of hand.

"Big, juicy steak?" she echoed dryly. "Someone thinks highly of himself."

He just laughed again. "We both know you're attracted to me."

"Oh, we both know that, do we?"

"And I'm attracted to you," he said with a shrug. "But unlike you, I'm not gonna bat my eyelashes like a Disney princess and act like I don't want to get you naked."

She swallowed again. Harder this time. Her mouth was so dry she felt like she was swallowing sand, but she didn't dare reach for her water bottle because she knew Seth would comment and attribute her sudden thirst to the effect he had on her.

"I have to get back to work." Wiggling out of his grasp, she stumbled to her feet.

But he was equally quick. He stood up and caught her around the waist with one muscular arm. He didn't yank her against him, just rested one hand on the small of her back and used the other to tip her chin up so she had no choice but to look at him.

"Say the word, Miranda."

Her heart was beating so fast she could barely hear her own voice over the frantic hammering. "What word?"

"Yes."

"Yes what?" she stammered.

He gave that mocking chuckle of his. "That's the word—*yes*. And I want you to say it. I want you to give me the green light so I can finally put my hands all over you the way I've been fantasizing about for months now."

"Seth..." It was meant to be a warning, but his name slipped out on a breathy whisper, sounding very much like an invitation.

"Come on, baby, I've been such a good boy." His gray eyes gleamed with sex and danger. "Put us both out of our misery."

She stared into those stormy-silver depths, feeling her resolve crumbling. Losing herself in his seductive spell. God, it had been so long since she'd had sex.

So long.

He aimlessly stroked her lower back. "Miranda..." He trailed off, moistening his bottom lip with the sexy drag of his tongue. Then he leaned in close so that his lips hovered over her ear. "I want to fuck you."

A shiver ran through her. Oh crap. Oh no, no, no. She was *not* allowed to get turned on.

Too late.

Okay, she was beyond turned on. The pressure between her legs was unbearable, her nipples so hard they could cut glass, her breathing completely off-kilter.

Enough. She couldn't keep letting herself respond to this man. Seth was a bad boy to the core. He did what he wanted, when he wanted. He had no sense of decency, no filter that monitored the sarcastic or overtly sexual remarks that came out of his mouth. He wore all black and smoked cigarettes and never shaved. In other words—he was trouble.

And sure, that air of danger he radiated would have turned her on when she was a teenager, but guess what, it was the last thing she wanted nowadays. She'd already thrown her life away for one dangerous bad boy—and she'd gotten knocked up at eighteen as a reward.

The memory of Trent was all it took to banish her rising desire.

Squaring her shoulders, she pushed his hand off her waist and took a step backward. "What you want makes no difference," she said quietly. "I won't get involved with you."

Resignation fluttered across his face. "What's your reason this time?"

She set her jaw defiantly. "Same one it always is. I'm a mom."

When he blanched slightly at the M-word, she let out a wry laugh. Oh, for Pete's sake, why hadn't she just led with that instead of letting this conversation drag on for far longer than necessary?

In the four months she'd known Seth, he hadn't shown the

slightest interest in her kids. And if the subject did happen to come up, he usually donned a blank look and acted indifferent to everything she said. She didn't know why, but for Seth, children seemed to be on par with root canals and canine fashion shows, both of which he'd expressed extreme dislike for.

"I don't have time to fool around with you," she went on. "Or anyone, for that matter. Between raising two six-year-olds, working five days a week at the studio and part-time here at the bar, I barely have time to read the paper, let alone have sex."

To her aggravation, Seth grinned. "That just proves how much you need me."

"Oh really?"

"If reading a newspaper takes priority over having sex, then clearly you've never had your world rocked."

"I don't need any rocking in my world. I get motion sickness." She laced up her sneakers, then headed for the door.

He trailed after her. "Fine, I'll let this go. If that's what you want."

"It is." A rush of relief flooded her belly. Thank God. Fighting off Seth's advances the past few months had been much harder than she'd ever admit.

"Don't look so happy." He smirked. "I meant I'd let it go for *tonight*."

Crap. She should've known it wouldn't be that easy.

Seth blocked her path before she could open the door, running a hand through his messy hair. His hair was short, but definitely not the military cut every man in San Diego seemed to have. Black locks often fell onto his forehead and curled behind his ears, and she couldn't count the number of times her fingers had tingled with the urge to smooth back those unruly strands.

"When's your next shift?" he asked.

"Monday."

"Eight to close?"

It didn't surprise her that he knew the exact time of her shift. God knew he came to the club often enough.

"Hey, I have an idea," she said with a big fake smile. "Maybe you can go somewhere else on Monday. The Tavern or the Sand Bar, maybe Hot Zone—ooh, there's this new club on 4th that you might like. I heard it attracts a lot of young women looking for a good time..."

When she flashed him a *how-awesome-is-that* look, he simply laughed it off. "I'm not looking for a random lay. Trust me, if I wanted to get laid?" He lowered his voice to a smoky pitch and snapped his fingers. "I could get laid just like that. But see, that's not what I'm after."

A sigh lodged in her chest. "What are you after, Seth?"

"You."

Equal parts arousal and irritation pleaded for her attention. Ignoring both, she released her breath and crossed her arms over her chest. Seth's gaze immediately rested on her cleavage, more pronounced now that her pose was pushing her breasts up. She promptly let her arms dangle to her sides.

"I don't have time to play games with you," she muttered. "I have too much on my plate at the moment, and even if I wasn't busy, I still wouldn't say yes. I'm a mother, first and foremost. My kids are my life."

He rolled his eyes. "I'm not asking you to put the rugrats up for adoption."

"No, you're just asking me to pretend they don't exist and launch myself into some whirlwind sexual affair with you. How will that even work? You're going to sneak into my apartment after I tuck Sophie and Jason in and ravish me while they're sleeping next door? You'll pay for a babysitter while you and I go to some sleazy motel?" She shook her head. "For the millionth time, I'm not interested."

He rewarded her speech with his trademark smirk. "Has anyone ever told you that you look sexy when you lie?"

"What does that even mean?" she mumbled. "Whatever. Don't answer. In fact, don't say another word."

She brushed past him and yanked on the door handle. Out in the hall, the drum and bass bounced off the walls and vibrated beneath her feet. Perching her hands on her hips, she turned to scowl at Seth.

"I'm serious. Quit coming here every night. Quit hitting on me. Quit acting like being my former boss's son gives you some kind of say in my life."

As usual, he seemed unfazed by the rejection. Stepping closer, he brought those tempting lips to her ear again, his hot breath fanning over her skin. "See you Monday night, Miranda."

ABOUT THE AUTHOR

A *New York Times, USA Today* and *Wall Street Journal* bestselling author, Elle Kennedy grew up in the suburbs of Toronto, Ontario, and holds a BA in English from York University. From an early age, she knew she wanted to be a writer and actively began pursuing that dream when she was a teenager. She loves strong heroines and sexy alpha heroes, and just enough heat and danger to keep things interesting!

Elle loves to hear from her readers. Visit her website www.ellekennedy.com or sign up for her newsletter to receive updates about upcoming books and exclusive excerpts. You can also find her on:

Facebook (ElleKennedyAuthor)
Twitter (@ElleKennedy)
Instagram (@ElleKennedy33)
TikTok (@ElleKennedyAuthor).

Made in United States
Troutdale, OR
02/02/2024

17387954R00186